THIS IS A STORY OF WAR

Evolving in a hostile environment, the Tzen have fought and clawed their way to dominance in their own world. Now they and their planet lie in the path of a relentless, swarming foe. To survive the Tzen must attack, adapting to a new level of technology, fighting a new breed of winged warrior.

Defeat means certain extinction.

THE BUG WARS

New York Times bestselling author Robert Asprin presents his most exciting novel of alien worlds—and alien warfare.

DON'T MISS ROBERT ASPRIN'S ELECTRIFYING NOVEL . . .

THE COLD CASH WAR

The explosive story of a corporate future where hostile takeovers are the ultimate war game. The stakes are power and money. The weapons are real.

THE BUG WARS

ROBERT ASPRIN

ACE BOOKS, NEW YORK

THE BUG WARS

An Ace Book / published by arrangement with
the author

PRINTING HISTORY
St. Martin's Press hardcover edition published 1979
Ace paperback edition / April 1993

ISBN: 0-441-07373-5

Ace Books are published by The Berkley Publishing Group,
200 Madison Avenue, New York, New York 10016.
The name "ACE" and the "A" logo are trademarks
belonging to Charter Communications, Inc.

PRINTED IN THE UNITED STATES OF AMERICA

10 9 8 7 6 5 4 3 2

Dedicated to
Robert "Buck" Coulson,
whose song "Reminder" inspired
this book

BOOK ONE

BOOK ONE

CHAPTER
-1-

I became awake. Reflexively, with the return of consciousness, I looked to my weapons. I felt them there in the darkness, strapped to my body and attached to the panel close over my head. I felt them, and relaxed slightly, moving on to other levels of consciousness. I have my weapons, I am alive, I am a Tzen, I am duty-bound, I am Rahm.

Having recalled I am a Tzen, it did not surprise me that I thought of my duty before even thinking of my name. It is part of the character of the Tzen to always think of the species and the Empire before thinking of themselves, particularly the Warrior caste, of which I was one. It has occasionally been suggested, privately of course, that some of the other castes, particularly the Scientists, think of the individual before they think of the species, but I do not believe this. A Tzen is a Tzen.

I flexed my talons. Yes, my body was functioning efficiently. I was ready to venture forth. There had been no sound of alarm or noises of battle, but I still was cautious as I pressed the release lever of my shelf with my tail. The door slid down a fraction of an inch and stopped as I scanned the chamber through the slit.

The chamber was dimly lit, closely approximating moonlight. The air was warm—not hot, but warm and humid, the temperature of night in the Black Swamps. We were not being awakened for relaxation and food replenishment. We were being awakened to hunt. We were preparing for combat.

Without further meditation, I slid the door the rest of the way open and started to slide from my shelf, then paused. Another Tzen was moving along the walkway I was about to step out on. I waited for him to pass before standing forth and securing my weapons.

The fact that I outranked him, in fact was his immediate superior on this mission, was irrelevant. My waiting was not even a matter of courtesy, it was logical. The walkway was too narrow for two to pass, and he was moving on it first.

We exchanged neither salutes nor nods of recognition as he passed, his tail rasping briefly on the walkway. His ten-foot bulk, large even for a Tzen, was easy to recognize in the semidarkness. He was Zur, my second-in-command for this mission. I respected him for his abilities, as he respected me for mine. I felt no desire to wish him luck or a need to give him last-minute instructions. He was a Tzen.

He, like the rest of my flight team, had performed efficiently in practice, and I had no reason to expect they would perform otherwise in actual combat. If he or any of the others seemed lax or panicky in battle, and if that shortcoming endangered me or the mission, I would kill them.

The walkway was clear now, and I moved along it to the junction between the shelf-wall and the engineward flex-wall. For a moment, I was thankful for my rank. As flight team Commander, my flyer was positioned closest to the floor, which spared me climbing up the curved wall. Not that I would mind the climb, but since flyer training began, I had discovered I was mildly acrophobic. It didn't bother me once I was flying, but I disliked hanging suspended in midair.

I didn't spend a great deal of time checking over the flyer. That was the Technicians' job. I knew enough about the flyers to pilot them and effect minor repairs, but machines were the Technicians' field of expertise as weapons are mine, and anything they missed on their check would be too subtle for me to detect.

Instead, I occupied my time securing my personal weapons in the flyer, a job no Technician could do. I do not mean to imply by this that the Technicians are lacking in flight skill. They are Tzen, and I would willingly match any Tzen of any caste on a one-for-one basis against any other intelligent being in the universe. But I am of the Warrior caste, the fighting elite of a species of fighters, and I secure my own weapons.

In truth, it was doubtful they would be necessary on this

mission; still, it heartened me to have them close at hand. Like so many others, I had not yet completely acclimated myself to the new technology that had been so suddenly thrust upon us. The hand weapons were a link with the past, with our heritage, with the Black Swamps. Even the High Command did not object to the practice of carrying hand weapons on a mission. They merely limited the total weight of personal gear carried by a Warrior in his flyer. Nobody comes between a Tzen and his weapons, not even another Tzen.

Content with my inspection, I eased myself into the flyer and settled into the gel-cushion. With a sigh, the flyer sealed itself. I waited, knowing that as my flyer sealed, a ready light had appeared on the pilot's board; and that as soon as all the lights from this chamber were lit, we would be ready to proceed with the mission.

Unlike the colony ships, transports such as the one we were currently chambered in were stark and bare in their interiors, devoid of anything not absolutely vital to the mission. This left me with little to meditate on as I waited. Almost against my wishes, my thoughts turned toward the mission we were about to embark upon. My reluctance to think about the mission did not spring from a reluctance to fight or a fear for my personal safety. I am a Tzen. However, I personally find the concept of genocide distasteful.

Finally the flex-walls, both the one my flyer was affixed to and the one across the chamber, trembled and began to move. The mission was about to begin. Slowly they straightened, changing the parabola-cross-sectioned shape of the room into a high, narrow rectangle. The flyers on my wall were now neatly interspaced with those on the far wall. The net result was to stack us like bombs in a rack, poised and ready to drop.

As our flight team made their final preparations, we knew that the chambers on either side of us would be spreading their walls, taking advantage of the space vacated by our walls to ease the loading of its flyers. As I have said, there is no wasted space on a transport.

The floor of the chamber opened beneath me. As the bottom flyer in the stack, I had an unobstructed view of the depths below. I experienced a moment of vertigo as I looked down at the patch of darkness. We are not an aerial species.

Then I was in a free-fall. There was no jerk of release; I was just suddenly falling. Although I normally avoid stating opinions as fact, this is not a pleasant sensation.

As we had been warned during our briefings, the Battle Plan called for a night attack. This was tactically sound, since the Enemy are day-hunters, while we Tzen are accustomed to working at night. It gave us an immeasurable advantage in the impending fight. It also meant that the planet-face we were plummeting toward was dark, giving no clue of terrain features.

Crosswinds buffeted my flyer as I fell, but I was not concerned. Crosswinds, like atmospheric pressures and weather conditions, would have been taken into consideration by the pilot when he'd dropped us. In their own way, the pilots were specialists as highly trained as the Warriors.

The tingle in the footplate told me my flyer was in the outer fringe of one of the power sources dropped by scout ships. Still I fell. Now I could make out a few features of the terrain below. Far off to my left was a large body of water, below was some type of mountain range, while off to my right stretched an immense forest. Obviously it was a highly inhabitable planet. No wonder the Enemy had picked it as one of the spots to settle in. No wonder we had to take it away from them.

The tingle in the footplate was noticeably stronger now, but I continued to fall. I allowed myself to ponder the possibility of an auto-pilot malfunction, but dismissed the thought. The programs were so simple as to be essentially infallible, and thus far, I did not have sufficient cause to assume malfunction.

As if to confirm my conclusions, the auto-pilot chose that instant to react to the ground rushing towards us from below. With a soft pop, the mightly flex-steel bat wings that had been folded against the flyer's sides unfurled, catching the rushing air and slamming the craft from a dive into a soaring glide. The sudden deceleration forced me deep into the gel-cushion and narrowed my eyes.

A jab of pressure with both my heels on the footplate took the flyer out of auto-pilot and gave me full control. I allowed the flyer to glide forward for a few moments, then arrested its progress, hovering it in place with subtle play on the footplate. It was a moderately delicate process, but we had been trained by long hours of practice to be able to accomplish this almost without thinking, as we had trained in all facets of handling the flyers. The flyers were to be an extension of our bodies, requiring no more thought for operation than the operation of our legs. It was an advanced form of transport, nothing more. Our minds were to be focused on the mission, on the Enemy.

As I waited, I surveyed the immediate terrain, using both my normal vision and the flyer's sonic sensor screens. I was not overly fond of the latter, but their use was essential when operating a flyer. There would be times, particularly flying in the dark, when we would be traveling at speeds requiring warning of approaching obstacles well in advance of the range at which our normal night vision was effective.

I was hovering over a river valley, the rising thermals making the job of hovering an easy one. Ahead and to the right was the beginning of the vast forest range I had noted from the air. Obviously the pilot had been accurate in his drop calculations.

"Ready, Rahm."

It was Zur's voice telepathed into my mind. I did not look back. I didn't need to. His signal told me all I needed to know, that the team was in position behind me, each flyer in place in our tetrahedron formation, hovering and impatient to begin.

I telepathed my order to the formation.

"Power on one . . . Ready . . . Three . . . Two . . . One!"

As I sent the final signal, I trod down solidly on the footplate and felt the surge of power as the engine cut in. There was no roar, not even a whisper of sound. This was one of the advantageous features of this new propulsion system. The sparkling engines were noiseless, giving deadly support to our favored surprise attack tactics. The race that had developed the engine were fond of using it for noiseless factories and elevators. As a Warrior race, we had other uses for it.

Our formation darted forward through the dark on the first assault of the new war.

CHAPTER
-2-

Faintly in the darkness, we could see other formations paralleling our course. Somewhere behind us were four other waves, constituting the balance of our Division. One hundred formations, six hundred flyers pitted against an enemy numbering in the hundreds of thousands. Still, we were not overly concerned with the outcome. Our flyers gave us superior speed and maneuvering ability in the air. Our weapons were more than adequate to deal with the enemy. Given superior maneuverability and weapons, we would have an edge in any fight, regardless of the odds. Our military history had proven this to be true time and time again. Then there was the fact we were Tzen. I would trust in the fighting-born and -trained of the Tzen over any Insect's blind hive instinct. We would win this War. We would win it because we had to.

We had reached the trees now, our formation flying low and straight without seeking targets. The trees dwarfed our craft with their size. Their trunks were over thirty feet in diameter, and stretched up almost out of sight in the darkness. Our zone was some distance ahead. If the transport had timed its drops properly and if everyone maintained the planned courses and speeds, the attack should be launched in all zones simultaneously, just as our Division's attack was tuned to coincide with the attacks of the other divisions taking part in the assault on this planet. In theory this would keep the Enemy from massing against us.

I could see the dark masses of the nests high in the trees as we sped silently on. I strained my eyes trying to get a good look at the Enemy, but could make out nothing beyond general seething blobs. They were sleeping, gathered in great masses covering the nests, apparently unsuspecting of the shadows of death flitting through their stronghold. This was not surprising. They and their allies had ruled the stars virtually uncontested for over a million years. We Tzen had taken great pains to mask our existence, much less our development, until we were ready to enter into combat. Now we were ready for combat, and the Enemy would know us—if any survived, that is.

Still, I wished I could get a better look at them. It was difficult for me to accept the concept of a wasplike creature with a twenty to thirty foot wingspan. Studying drawings and tri-D projections was helpful, but nothing could serve as well as actually seeing a live enemy.

Though confident, I was uneasy. I would have preferred to have the first encounter with the Enemy on solid ground, or better still, on the semiaquatic terrain we were accustomed to battling on. I was uneasy about having our first encounter as an aerial flight against an aerial species. For all our practice with the new flyers, the air was not our element. I wished the initial battle did not hinge on our ability to outfly creatures born with wings. It made me uneasy. I did not contest the logic behind the decision. It would be disastrous to enter into ground maneuvers while the Enemy still retained air supremacy. But it did make me uneasy.

Suddenly something struck the side of my flyer too quickly to be avoided. It clung to the plexiglass, scrabbling and rasping, seeking entrance. It took a great deal of effort to keep my attention focused forward, to avoid flying into something, with the creature raging at the edge of my periperhal vision less than a foot from my head. I had a quick impression of multifaceted metallic eyes glaring at me and darting mandibles gnashing on the transparent bubble; then I rolled the flyer and it was gone. There was a quiet burst of sound behind me like a sudden release of compressed air, and I knew that Zur had finished off the interloper. I shot a sideways glance at the spot on the canopy where the creature had clung briefly before being shaken off. There were deep gouges in the bubble from the Enemy's efforts, and a few spots where the creature's saliva had begun to eat through.

I was pleased. The brief encounter had prepared me for battle far more than any mental exercise I could have devised. New energy coursed through my veins, adding that all-important extra split second of speed to my reflexes. Instead of developing it in the first pass, I would now be entering the conflict in a controlled battle frenzy.

For the first time I began to entertain hopes of emerging from the battle alive.

Then we were at our target zone. At my signal the formation expanded, each Tzen increasing the distance between his flyer and his teammate's. Then, as a unit, we climbed toward the treetops and the Bug War began.

The combat, like any combat, soon became too fast-paced for conscious thought. We had trained with our flyers and weapons until they were a part of us, and their use was as unthinking as flexing our talons. Our minds and senses were focused on the Enemy and the terrain.

Thoughts became a flashing kaleidoscope of quick impressions and hazily remembered instructions. Use the cold-burn rays as much as possible . . . less effective than the hot-beams, but they'll damaged the forest less . . . we'll want to settle here someday. . . . Swarm massing to block flight path . . . burn your way through . . . don't wander more than five degrees from your base course . . . sweep three nests simultaneously with a wide beam . . . if you wander you'll end up in a teammate's line of fire . . . turn 90 degrees . . . turn right, always right . . . Kor is on your right . . . don't trust her for a left turn . . . avoid the tree trunk and burn the nests as your weapon bears . . . Enemy on the wing tip . . . roll . . . burn the nests . . . don't wander from base course. . . .

We were working our zone in a broken sweep pattern. A straight geometric pattern would have been easier to remember and more certain for a complete sweep. It also would have been predictable. If we tried to use a geometric sweep, by the third pass the Enemy would be massed and waiting for us. So we continued our twisted, seemingly random pattern, crossing and recrossing our own path, frequently burning our way through swarms of the Enemy flying across our path in pursuit.

. . . Turn to the right . . . burn the nests . . . cold-beam rays only. . . .

We were constantly flirting with disaster. Our flyers could outdistance the lumbering Enemy; but if we used our speed, dodging trees required most of our attention, and we ran the risk of missing nests. If we slowed our speed to an easy pace for sweeping, the Enemy could either overtake us or move to intercept. So we flirted with death, sometimes plunging recklessly ahead, sometimes rolling as we turned to free our flyers of the Enemy clinging to the wings, threatening to drag us to the ground with the sheer mass of their numbers.

. . . Avoid the trees . . . burn through a swarm . . . turn to the right . . . burn the nests . . . roll. . . .

One thing bothered me. The mission was going too smoothly. I received no sign-off and visually confirmed on the passes when I was bringing up the rear. All our flyers were still with us. We had not lost any team members. If the other divisions were experiencing similar success, there could be difficulties when we headed back.

. . . Don't wander . . . roll . . . turn to the right . . . burn the nests. . . .

We were near completing the sweep of our zone. I was concerned about the north border, however. The team zones overlapped to ensure no ''live'' pockets were accidentally overlooked. This meant careful timing between the teams was necessary to be sure two teams didn't sweep the same region at the same time and accidentally fly into each other. It was a bothersome but effective system; however, something was wrong. We seemed to be the only ones working the region by the north border, and when we turned, we could see nests remaining beyond our zone.

Something was very wrong with the flight team to our north. The end of our sweep was upon us, and I had to make a decision fast. This was not particularly difficult, as there was really only one course of action to be followed. We could not risk leaving unburned nests behind. This was a genocide war. If we left any eggs behind, we would have to come back later and fight this action all over again, but this time against an Enemy that was prepared and waiting for us. We couldn't leave those nests behind.

As we completed our sweep, I signaled the formation to return to the north border. This undoubtedly caused some consternation in my team, but they were Tzen, and they followed without complaint as I led the formation in a turn to the left. In this situation, a turn to the left was safe. I didn't have to worry about Kor, as long as we were moving, to prolong contact with the Enemy.

The fighting became more difficult as we made our supplemental sweep. This was only to be expected. Not having had an opportunity to work out a coordinated random pattern, we were forced to work a simple back-and-forth geometric pattern. As it has been noted before, geometric patterns are suicidal.

We had reached a point where we were spending as much time burning swarms of the Enemy as we were burning nests when the long-awaited call was beamed into my mind. When we crossed into another flight team's zone we turned on the "trespass beacons" in our craft to alert the assigned team of our presence, and we were finally getting a response.

"I have a fix on your beacons," came the thought. "While I appreciate the assistance in covering this zone, I can now complete assignment without additional support. You may return to rendezvous point."

I noted her use of the word "I" instead of "we."

"What is your condition?" I queried.

"Five flyers lost. My own canopy is breached. It is therefore impossible for me to meet pickup ship. However, I can complete the mission. Feel free to return to rendezvous point."

What occurred to me was the difficulty our six flyers had had sweeping this zone, giving rise to the question of the lone flyer's ability to finish the job. I rejected the thought. She was a Tzen. If she said she could complete the mission, she could complete it.

"Return to rendezvous!" I beamed to my team and slammed my flyer into a steep climb out of the trees.

I experienced a moment of worry about Kor, but it appeared to be without basis. As we broke out into the predawn light, she was in her appointed position in the formation.

I did not ponder the nobility of the Tzen who sent us on, staying to fight alone. Among the Tzen, this was not exceptionally heroic. Rather, it was our expected performance of duty.

The sky was empty of other flight teams as we streaked toward the rendezvous point. This was not surprising, as our supplemental sweep had taken us extra time. The other units were probably already at the rendezvous point.

Far below I noticed a portion of the forest blazing. Apparently someone had been careless with the use of his hot-beam. I studied it as we flashed overhead. It was in a relatively small portion of the forest, set off from the main mass by a river. Hopefully the river would halt the fire's march. After all this trouble to keep the forest intact, it would be disappointing to see it all lost because of one flyer's carelessness.

We were almost at the pickup point, and our formation was climbing steadily to gain the necessary altitude. We could see the transport now, and as we drew closer, the small cloud of flyers waiting their turn in a holding pattern.

I tried to ignore the implications of this as our team joined the holding pattern. Either we weren't the only ones who had had our mission delayed, or . . .

I forced the thought from my mind. It was almost our turn for entry. I led my team away from the ship in a long circle, allowing maneuvering room for the members to rearrange the formation from a tetrahedron to a single file. Ready now, we turned our line toward the ship, setting a bearing for the open pickup port.

The port was closed. As we watched, the transport broke orbit and began to move away, gaining speed as it went.

CHAPTER
-3-

One of the most difficult phases in planning a military campaign is deciding an "Anticipated Casualty Rate." Interstellar combat has made this phase even more crucial. You estimate the number of warriors required to complete the mission after casualties. You then calculate your transportation and supply needs based on that number. If you underestimate your casualties, you run the risk of losing the battle. Overestimate and you are in danger of losing your entire force if your suppliers or fuel run out while you're still in space.

The High Command had arrived at a solution to this problem: they calculated the number of anticipated casualties and then stuck to it. They might suffer more casualties than planned, but never less. They planned for returning a specific number of troops to the colony ship, and when that number was on board the transport, they simply shut the doors. Anyone still outside was then considered a casualty.

Apparently this is what had happened to us.

As this was our first confrontation with the Insects, the High Command had had no data on which to base their casualty estimates, so they had estimated high. This ensured the mission would be completed. This also meant we were shut out.

This did not mean simply diverting to another transport. If there had been extra space available in another ship, we would have been directed to it. We hadn't. There was no more space. As far as the High Command was concerned, we were now officially dead.

I found my position curious, the live commander of a live "dead" flight team. What does one do after one is dead? I decided the crisis was of a magnitude to warrant getting the thoughts of the team.

"Confer!" I beamed to the formation at large. I expected a few moments silence while they collected their thoughts, but Kor's answer was almost immediate.

"If we're dead, the obvious course is to take additional legions of the Enemy to the Black Swamps with us. We may have gotten all the eggs and queens on the formal raid, but there are still a large number of workers we can destroy before the power sources burn out."

"Ahk here, Rahm. Should we accept so readily that we're dead? There is always a chance of a missed transmission from the transport. I would suggest we use whatever power remains to sweep for another transport. If we cannot find one, then we can decide a course of action."

"May I remind the team," came Ssah's voice, "that dead or not, Rahm is still in command. As Commander, it is his duty, difficult though it may be, to decide our course of action, not waste our time in idle debate."

"Mahz confirms Ssah's contention!"

I was about to reply to this implication of my shirking of duty, when Zur's quiet voice interrupted.

"If I may, Commander, there is no need for us to die. However, if the Black Swamp calls us home, there is much we can do for the Empire first."

His assertion intrigued me.

"Explain, Zur."

"There is another species of the Coalition of Insects present on this planet. This means the fleets will be back. If we can survive long enough, we can rejoin the Empire at that time. Even if we do not survive until rendezvous, we may be able to gather information on the Enemy to leave for the Empire's use."

His advice was timely and meritorious. If there was a chance we could still be of use to the Empire, there was nothing further to discuss.

"On my lead!" I beamed at the team and wheeled toward the planet surface. Behind me, the flyers broke from the circling holding pattern we had maintained for our conference to form the tetrahedron behind me. We were again Tzen with a purpose.

Time was of the essence now. The ground-based power sources for our flyers were not long-lived. They should have output beyond the forecast time of the mission to allow extra flyers to find secondary transports if available, but as we had cause to know, casualties had been light. That meant additional drain on the power sources. We had no way of knowing how much time was left before our engines would die.

"As we reach low altitude, scatter and search individually. We want a large, deep cave in the low mountain range, not more than five hundred meters from a water source, preferably with an overhanging ledge. Avoid the forests and high-altitude flying at all costs."

As Kor had pointed out, there were still worker Wasps about. It would not pay to have them discover the presence of lingering Tzen to vent their vengeance on.

"Commander, may I suggest—"

"You may not, Ssah! As you pointed out, this is my decision to make and I have made it. You have your orders."

The team scattered, each taking a sextant to canvas. Our flyers skimmed low over the rolling foothills, racing to find refuge before our time ran out. Each pass through my sextant took longer as the search pattern widened. I began to grow concerned. The pattern might spread too far without success, and then we would be in danger of being unable to regroup our flyers if the power source stopped.

I banked the flyer into another turn and started back through my sextant, alert for any sign of a cave such as we were seeking. In another few sweeps I would have to break off the search and try another plan. If we flew too far apart, we would be unable to contact each other telepathically.

"Commander! I have a cave."

"Message confirmed, Ssah. Is it large enough to get our flyers into?"

"I have already flown in and back out again successfully. It will suit our purposes."

Not for the first time I noted Ssah's tendency for unnecessarily reckless action. However, this was not the time to go into it at length.

"Team confirm and home on Ssah's beacon."

"Mahz confirms."

"Ahk confirms."

"Zur confirms."

I waited for a few moments. Kor did not confirm.

"Zur, Mahz, you are closest to Kor's sextant. Relay message or confirmation."

"I have her confirmation, Commander," came Mahz's reply.

With the order acknowledged throughout the team, I wheeled my flyer over and made for Ssah's beacon. Traveling at maxspeed, I soon had the cave in sight. The opening was low, with only a little over ten feet clearance, but more than wide enough to accommodate the flyer's wingspan. I saw two of the team, Ahk and Mahz, dart their flyers into the cave's mouth as I began my approach.

I cut power and leveled my glide two feet off the ground. I had to assume the cave was deep enough that I wouldn't have to worry about plowing into the flyers ahead of me. If it was not, the others would have warned me.

The entrance loomed before me; then I was through. The sudden change from early morning light to the utter blackness of the cave temporarily robbed me of vision. My sonic sensor screens, however, told me I had flown through an opening at the top of a wide cavern, about forty feet deep. I could make out the other flyers, four of them, grounded at the bottom of the cavern. I steered for them, wondering who the missing flyer was. I prepared for landing, taking a deep breath and exhaling it slowly. Even though my current glide speed felt slow compared to my earlier power-flight, the ground was coming up fast, and our flyers were not adapted for ground landings. My flyer touched down, jarring me with the impact, and slid along the cavern floor, the bubble making painful sounds against the rock. I ignored it.

"Who's missing?" I queried before my flyer had ground to a complete halt.

"Kor."

This could mean trouble.

"Mahz! Are you sure she confirmed . . . ?"

"Here she is now, Commander."

My eyes were becoming accustomed to the darkness now. I could make out the shape of Kor's flyer swooping silently down on us from the mouth of the cave.

I was burning with questions, but held them in check. You do not distract someone with questions while they're trying to crash-land a flyer.

Finally she touched it down, the flyer coming to a halt a few feet from the others. By this time we were all out of flyers and waiting for her.

"Kor! Explain your delay."

I was aware my head was sinking dangerously close to the flat position of extreme anger. Apparently she noticed it, for as she rose from her flyer, her head position denoted both anger and defense.

"I encountered the Enemy, Commander. There were three——"

"Did they see you?"

"Yes, but I destroyed all three of them and swept the immediate area for any others, that's why I was——"

"Zur!" I diverted my attention to my second-in-command, who had approached behind Kor as we spoke, his massive ten-foot height dwarfing her six-foot stature.

"Yes, Commander?"

"Is there any evidence known of telepathic powers in the Enemy?"

"None known, but it is not beyond speculation. Many of the lower orders of insects are known to communicate telepathically."

I turned from them abruptly.

"Ssah! Check your indicators. Is the power-source still broadcasting?"

"Yes, Commander."

"Then you and Mahz pivot your flyers around and use the hot-beams to seal the cave."

I turned back to Kor, my tail lashing angrily despite my efforts to control it.

"Kor, I have a direct order for you. Even though you are without question the most efficient fighter on the team, I will not have the unit's safety jeopardized by independent action. In the future, if you contact the Enemy, you are to so inform the team immediately. If you do not, it will be considered a direct breach of orders."

There was a rumbling crash, and the meager light in the cavern disappeared. The cave was sealed. I turned and raised my voice in the darkness.

"Now use your narrow beams to open a tunnel to the surface. I want it to be just large enough to allow us passage one at a time on all fours."

There was a moment of silence.

"That will be impossible, Commander."

"Explain."

"The power-source has just stopped broadcasting."

CHAPTER

-4-

We were effectively buried alive. I considered the problem carefully.

"Did anyone bring a glow-bulb in their personal gear?"

"I did, Commander." Ahk's voice came out of the blackness.

"I feel it would be in the team's best interests if you lit it now."

"Agreed. It is still in my flyer, so if I could get a sound fix from either of the two who were at the flyers when the cave was sealed——"

"Ssah here. Your flyer is about four feet to my left. Would you like me to keep talking to serve as a beacon, or do you have the location."

"I have it. I'll fetch the bulb now, Commander."

I heard a faint scratching as he moved past me. Even though nothing could be seen in this total absence of light, I knew clearly enough what he was doing to visualize it in my mind's eye. He was edging slowly sideways across the cavern, one hand sweeping the area in front of his head and shoulders, his tail probing for obstacles in the path of his feet and legs. It was not the first time Tzen had had to operate in a total absence of light. The probability of his stumbling was practically nonexistent.

"Ssah! When you scouted the cave, did you have an opportunity to give it a full scan with your sonic-screen?"

"I did, Commander."

"Are there any other openings to the outside of any size?"

19

''None.''

A pinpoint of light appeared, widening to disclose the entire small glowing ball as Ahk twisted the glow-bulb to its fullest setting. The light revealed the rest of the team standing around the cavern. They had remained motionless in the darkness to avoid blundering into Ahk's path, but now that a light source had been reestablished, they became animated again.

''Where would you like the light, Commander?''

''Just set it on top of your flyer for now.''

My eyes were rapidly adapting to the dim light. Features of the cavern were becoming visible again. I was impressed with the glow-bulbs and made a mental note to include one in my personal gear in the future. Though the visibility was improving, I was pleased that Ssah had used her sonics to check the chamber. It would have taken a great deal of time to perform a close visual check for other openings, whereas the sonics had provided us with the same data in a matter of seconds. It was an efficient use of available equipment.

''My preliminary scouting also showed no other life, plant or animal, in the cavern.''

This added bit of data from Ssah was needless. I had assumed that had there been other life, she would have told me in her initial report, particularly in Enemy-held terrain. I was not sure if this was another display of her tendency to overassert herself, or if it was a subtle implication that she felt my earlier question about the sonic scan was also needless. However, there were other, more pressing problems to be dealt with.

I surveyed the cavern again, gauging distances and performing a few mental calculations. No, oxygen supply should not be a problem. There would be no need to put the team in Deep Sleep while the work progressed.

I moved to my own flyer.

''Zur!''

He appeared at my side. I extracted a hand-burner from my personal weapon stock and handed it to him. He examined it swiftly. Not many Tzen used the hand-burners. They were still new and relatively untested in combat, so preference was usually given to the old hand weapons or their recent modified relatives. I had not really intended to use the burner when I chose my weapons, but brought it along to accustom myself to having it ready at hand. Our unexpected situation of being stranded had elevated its importance, and I had been mentally making plans as to how to best utilize its devastating capacities. The abrupt demise of the major power-source cut that planning short. The hand-burner's compact independent power-source now had an immediate demand to answer.

"Take this and get the tunnel established. Work by hand as much as possible, but feel free to use it as necessary."

Without further question he turned and strode across the cavern to begin the climb to the recent rubble of the cave-in. I considered the problem solved. Freed of that situation, I turned to the remaining team members.

"I will summarize our situation. We are stranded for an indefinite period on an Enemy-held planet with no support other than each other and whatever equipment and weapons we brought with us. There are two objectives which will guide our actions. First, we must attempt to gather whatever information we can on the Enemy to assist the Empire in its efforts to overthrow their influence. Second, we must survive in order to rejoin the Empire when the fleets return. These objectives are potentially contradictory. As such, when we finish speaking here I will meet with the team members individually to hear their opinions and advice as to how these goals can be best pursued. Questions?"

"Question, Commander."

"Yes, Ssah."

"Why is this to be handled in private conference rather than open discussion?"

I fixed her with my gaze.

"In a prolonged survival situation such as this, it will be necessary for me as Commander to have a knowledge of each team member's opinions, attitudes, and priorities beyond those required to lead a formation in a raid. Much of this information is of a highly personal nature, including what they think of me, what I think of them, and what they think of their fellow teammates. This is data which is not only unnecessary, it is undesirable for it to become general knowledge, therefore warranting private conferences. I trust you will remember that when and if you become a flight team Commander."

Her head flattened slightly at the rebuff, but she remained silent.

"Any other questions?"

There were none. I rose and started for the far end of the cavern.

"Ahk! I would speak with you first. The rest of the team is to secure their personal gear from the flyers."

Ahk was the only member of the team senior to me in both years and combat experience. Both his combat record and my personal impressions of him, however, could best be described as bland. I was anxious to obtain further data.

We sought and found comfortable places to squat and settled in before I began the conference.

"Ahk, even though I know little about you, your years of experience cannot be overlooked. I will doubtless be turning to you often for counsel and advice. I cannot help but wonder, however, with your record, why you are not of higher rank. Would you clarify this for me?"

"My slow advancement in rank is a direct result of my characteristic trait of habitual caution," he stated without hesitation. "This is born of seeing too many losses in combat from overzealous and reckless action. My conservatism excludes the type of noteworthy action which attracts promotion. What is more, my feelings are heightened with each battle I participate in, thus making the probability of promotion even more remote. I realize this, and accept it. However, do not mistake my caution for cowardice. Many have gone to the Black Swamps from the dueling ground who chose to label it thus. My abilities as a Warrior are well above average, and I can be relied upon to complete any assignment undertaken."

He shifted position, looking at me more directly.

"As for my opinion of you as a Commander, I find you more than acceptable. Even though you occasionally take risks I would avoid if left to my own devices, you carry them off with a firmness of resolve and a sense of control which eliminates needless danger. I will have no reservations in following your lead."

"What would be your recommendations for undertaking the task before us, Ahk?"

"I would recommend Deep Sleep for the majority of the team, Deep Sleep with varying wake times in event of something happening to the functioning team members. This would maximize our chances of having some of the team survive to rejoin the Empire. The fewer members left functioning, the less foraging for supplies will have to be done, and therefore the less chance of discovery by the Enemy. The functioning members could then guard those in Deep Sleep as well as scout the Enemy for additional information."

I inclined my head slightly toward the ceiling as I replied.

"Your recommendations will be taken under consideration. However, I will tell you I do not agree with your conclusions. Deep Sleep enabled our species to survive when times were lean, but I do not feel it should be resorted to here. The Longevity Serums developed by the Scientists caste virtually ensure that a Tzen will live until killed. With the overwhelming number of the Enemy present on this planet, I feel the best tactic to ensure against our being killed is to keep as many of the team conscious as possible and thereby maximize the fighting strength available at any given time."

He listened without rancor. He had his opinions, and I had mine. There was no question of who was right or wrong. I was the team Commander, and my orders would be followed.

"Also, would you provide a list of weapons in your personal arsenal at this time?"

"My weapons consist of a bandoleer of two dozen spring-javelins, a flexi-steel whip, an acid spray belt, a telescoping knife, and dueling sticks."

"What weapons, if any, would you be willing to make available for team use?"

He thought for a few moments.

"Any and all of them with the exception of the dueling sticks. This is, of course, assuming I would not be left weaponless, that something would either be left me or issued to replace the weapons taken."

This was acceptable to me.

"One more question, Ahk. What are your opinions of your individual teammates?"

His answer was brisk. Apparently he had given prior thought to this question.

"Zur is a highly efficient and terrifyingly fierce fighter. However, at times I fear he thinks too much. Sometimes I give pause to wonder if his heart is truely in the Warrior caste. While he performs his duties easily and well, they do not seem to give him any pleasure or pride of accomplishment."

He cocked his head in minor puzzlement.

"Kor is perhaps the finest fighter I have ever encountered. Of the entire team she is the one I would be least eager to face on the dueling-ground. Her reflexes and combat instincts are nearly beyond belief. I must admit to a certain unease around her, though. At first I thought it was envy of her talents, but it goes beyond that.

I think she takes more pleasure in killing than she should. That is, I feel more confident of victory with her on my side, but I would not wish to be the one to order her to stop.''

He paused thoughtfully for several moments, then bobbed his head in indecision.

"Mahz I have no opinion of. He seems capable enough, but is completely under the influence of Ssah. As things are now, he is an extension of her will. I would have to observe him in her absence before I could form an opinion.''

His head sank to a dangerously low position. I have seen Tzen issue challenges for personal duels with heads held higher.

"Ssah is dangerous. If you were to adopt my suggestion for Deep Sleep, I would propose her as one of the members to be rendered nonfunctional. Her presence is a threat to the survival of the entire team. Where you, Rahm, take calculated risks, she indulges in recklessness. Recklessness is dangerous in any combat situation, but in our current predicament it is disastrous. What is more, she has taken to habitually challenging your authority and decisions. It is my opinion that there will be trouble if she remains functional with the team.''

"Very well, Ahk. That answers my questions. If you have no further questions or opinions, pass the word for Kor. I would speak with her next.''

Kor was an enigma. She was small, a full foot below the six-foot minimum height requirement for the Warrior caste. As had been noted, however, her phenomenal aptitude for combat had earned her a waiver from the height requirement for entrance. She would doubtless be bred in an attempt to pass her traits on to the next batch of Warriors, providing . . . providing she proved to be reliable in actual combat. It was this question that was foremost in my mind as she appeared for her conference.

"Kor, I will not belabor my opinion of your abilities. They are superior and an asset to any fighting team. But aside from that, it cannot be ignored that this is your first combat mission for the Empire and your reliability under fire is therefore untested. As you, like Ssah, are part of a new wave of Warriors that received initial training under the new technology rather than being retrained from the old ways like the rest of the team, your performance is under constant scrutiny by me and by the High Command.''

I paused to allow her to react or reply. She didn't.

"It has been noted that you display an exceptional enthusiasm for battle. This has given rise to several questions, of which two require immediate consideration. First, is this enthusiasm an individual characteristic or is it a pattern of the entire new wave which the rest of us should grow accustomed to? Secondly, will this enthusiasm interfere with your ability to obey orders in a precise and efficient manner?"

She withdrew her head slightly, narrowing her eyes thoughtfully. I didn't rush her, as the questions required deep thought and judgmental weighings. There was a soft thumping as the tip of her tail twitched, impacting the floor of the cavern.

"Upon serious reflection, it is my belief that the enthusiasm with which I enter into combat is an individual rather than a new wave characteristic. To anticipate your next question or perhaps a question you would leave unasked, yes, I enjoy fighting. It is something I do well and efficiently. Most of my current status I owe to my fighting abilities, and my applying them is the only way I can serve the Empire. When I am not fighting I feel parasitic and useless. However, I am quick to acknowledge my lack of experience and not only will obey, but I actually appreciate the guidance I receive from seasoned officers."

She cocked her head quizzically at me.

"I have a question, Rahm. During our strafing run, I noticed a tendency on your part to pattern our sweep such that we would always turn to the right. Was this merely coincidental, or was it in fact a display of your concern for having me posted to your right?"

"It was not coincidental," I admitted. "I experienced some unease when speculating upon your willingness to break off an engagement on command. It occurred to me that if you did feel any resentment at being ordered to stop fighting, it could easily become focused on the Tzen issuing the order, in this case myself. If that occurred, I did not wish to perform a maneuver which would require your weapons to align, even briefly, with my flyer as you turned. As a Commander, I had to acknowledge the possibility, and lacking any basis to calculate probability, felt it necessary to take those preventive precautions. In part it was due to the realization that with your degree of skill, if you chose to attack me, I would probably be unable to defend myself."

She listened without any sign of irritation.

"Understood, Rahm. But I would assure you your apprehension

is needless. As I have said, I feel no resentment when receiving instruction from a veteran Warrior such as yourself. In addition, I have noted in myself a marked resistance to using my powers against other Tzen. I feel I have been trained to fight the Enemy, and that fighting each other is a misuse of that training. You may notice from my record that I have never fought a duel. My well-known abilities lessen the probability of being challenged, and my feelings about fighting another Tzen forbid me issuing a challenge regardless of provocation."

"What are your opinions of the others on the team?" I asked.

"I have none. They are Tzen and they do their share of the fighting. Beyond that I do not concern myself with their thoughts or motivations. As for yourself, my feelings are much the same. I am neither enthused nor disheartened by your performance as Commander. You perform your duties efficiently, and none can ask more of a Tzen than that."

"Do you have any suggestions for our plan of action on this planet?"

"As I have said, I readily acknowledge the superior experience in planning present on this team. However, as I am requested to express my opinions, I would recommend moving out into the open. We should seal the cave with the flyers inside and adopt a mobile format for our existence. A fixed location, particularly one with only one exit, is vulnerable. A wandering pattern in the open would allow us more flexibility for flight or counterattack, depending upon the specific situation."

"Would you list the weapons in your personal arsenal at this time?"

"I have a set of the weighted, spiked hand armor; a wedge-sword; an alter-mace; three steel balls, two and a half inches in diameter; two long knives and one short; and dueling sticks."

"What weapons, if any, would you be willing to make available for team use?"

She hesitated.

"I would be willing to surrender any of them, but would prefer not to. As you have noted, I am exceptionally effective in combat. This is because I have spent much time practicing with these specific weapons in a particular array. I can switch weapons in midcombat without motion loss because I do not have to pause to think. I fear that would be lost if I had to readjust my style. The only weapons I would release without hesitation would be the alter-mace and the dueling sticks. The alter-mace is my newest addition, and I am not yet at home with its use. The dueling sticks . . . well . . . I've already explained my willingness to part with them.''

"That answers all my questions, Kor. Unless you have any additional questions, pass the word for Mahz.''

She rose to leave, then hesitated.

"No further questions, Commander, but I do have an amendment to an earlier statement.''

"What is it?''

"I said I had no opinions on my teammates. Upon reflection I must change that. When you mentioned that Ssah and I were of the same new wave of Warriors, I experienced a rush of irritation and suppressed an impulse to request that you not classify her and me together. I realize now that is to some degree an attitude or opinion on my part. I cannot define it clearly or give adequate reasons, but I would rather not associate with her if given a choice.''

She left them to fetch Mahz. I was looking forward to my conference with Mahz. Like Ahk, I was having difficulty forming an opinion of Mahz when he was so much in Ssah's shadow.

"Make yourself comfortable, Mahz. There is much I would—''

"I'd rather stand, Commander, and if you'll allow me to express myself first, I feel we can keep this conference brief and to the point.''

"Proceed.''

"Before we occupy considerable time discussing my opinion of you and the rest of the team, I would state that I do not feel those opinions matter.''

He hastened on before I could interrupt.

"Not that I am suggesting you would not give proper consideration to my thoughts; rather that I do not. You see, early in my career, I constantly monitored and assessed my abilities, far closer than my trainers did. In doing so, I was forced to admit I had no exceptional qualities. Not that I am incompetent or incapable, just not exceptional. I do not possess the phenomenal fighting ability that Kor does, nor the flair for leadership and tactics that you and Ssah have. As such, I decided that if I was to rise in rank and power, the best asset I could offer would be service, to pick a rising Tzen and serve him or her faithfully as an aide, helping them to advance and advancing with them.''

He paused to look at me directly.

"The Tzen I have chosen to support is Ssah. In that choice, my own opinions pale to insignificance. What she supports, I support. What she opposes, I oppose."

"Why have you chosen Ssah?"

"And not yourself? I have no objections to you, Rahm. That is not what swayed my choice. Several factors came into account in making my decision. She is new, while you are an acknowledged veteran. While you have already established working relationships with several Tzen such as Zur and Ahk, she has none. This makes it easier for me to establish myself at her sword hand. If I were to be offered a second-in-command position with an established officer, it would have happened by now, and it hasn't. Consequently I choose to focus my efforts with a younger, newer Tzen. She has a tendency toward reckless, independent action. If she learns caution, these exploits are apt to attract the attention of the High Council, and she, and therefore I, will rise in rank. If she does not learn caution and is killed, then perhaps my loyal service will have been noted, and I will be requested to attach my services to another ambitious Tzen, and the process will start anew."

I considered this for a few moments.

"Have you considered the dangers inherent in submerging your will completely in favor of another's?"

"I have not completely submerged my will, Rahm. If Ssah should undertake a course which in my opinion is not in the best interests of the Empire, I will speak up or move to block her. I am an ambitious Tzen, but am still a Tzen."

"What weapons do you have in your personal arsenal at this time?"

"A wedge-sword, a whip sword, a telescoping thrusting spear, long knife, and dueling sticks."

"What weapons, if any, are you willing to place at the disposal of the team?"

He didn't hesitate.

"I will have to think that over and consult with Ssah before giving you my reply."

"That answers my questions. Unless you have any further questions, pass the word for . . . ."

I hesitated in midsentence. Zur's massive bulk had just appeared in the gloom of the cavern. I waved Mahz away and beckoned Zur to report to me.

"Is the tunnel complete?"

"Yes. I left Ahk posted at the mouth as lookout and came back to report to you."

He handed me back my hand-burner. I glanced at the charge indicator: less than a quarter-charge remaining! That wasn't good.

"Shall we have our conference now, Rahm?"

I considered it. I knew my second-in-command better than I knew any of the other team members. However, when we talked, there would be much to plan and discuss.

"Not yet, Zur. For now, pass the word for Ssah."

CHAPTER
- **5** -

Flattened against the tree trunk some ten meters in the air, I slowly surveyed the terrain. The trunk swayed gently in a gust of wind, and I swayed with it. This did not worry me. Swaying trees are a natural movement and do not attract even a watchful eye. However, my turning my head to look about would not be a natural movement, so I did it extremely cautiously. Even if I could be detected through the foliage, my silhouette was altered enough by the tree trunk so as not to arouse suspicion. As such, only my head movement would betray my position. Due to our eyes being mounted on the sides of our heads, the peripheral vision of a Tzen is extremely wide, requiring less than a six-inch movement to scan a full 360-degree field. I took almost a quarter hour to move my head the necessary six inches.

Still nothing.

Aside from random movement of lesser life forms in the meadow ahead of us and at the edge of the river behind us, there was no activity. Still our ambush waited.

Zur, Ahk, and Kor were with me in the ambush. They were well hidden on the ground. I did not worry about their being discovered. They were Tzen, and Tzen don't move when waiting in ambush.

I knew our techniques of concealment were effective against the Leapers. We had been observing them for over a month now without being discovered. A few hours ago a Leaper came down to the river to drink. It came to the far side of the river, exempting it from our ambush, but had not detected us, though it was within a dozen meters of our position. I was not worried about our ambush being discovered.

Nor was I worried about finding a victim. Our site had not been chosen at random. The tree trunk I clung to overhung the only major break in the strand of trees that lined the river for several miles. We had observed that the Leapers tended to avoid entering tree cover, possibly due to a habitual adherence to a coexistence pact with the now nearly defunct Wasps. Whatever the reason, this opening was the main thoroughfare between the hunting ground of the meadow and the water source of the river. A victim would be along eventually.

I was in an exposed position serving as spotter and ready to provide cover fire if needed. Even partially charged, my hand-burner would give us a definite edge if plans went awry.

Thinking of my hand-burner turned my thoughts once more toward my conference with Ssah. For the hundredth time I went over the details in my mind.

The conference had not gone well. Ssah was one of my offspring. She was probably unaware of this. I had not mentioned it to her; it would have made no difference to her thinking as it had made no difference to mine. I had simply noted it as a point of interest in her genetic record when going over her personnel file prior to the mission.

The mating with her Mother had been an experiment by the High Command. Her Mother was a bit of a misfit, a Scientist who was more imaginative than inquisitive. At the time of our mating, my leadership potential was already being rated as well above average, but it was noted that my methods were strongly influenced by earlier precedence, that I lacked inventiveness . . . imagination if you will. It is my guess that with this crossbreeding between Warrior and Scientist, particularly considering the individuals concerned, was an effort to produce a more imaginative leader for the Warrior caste.

Some experiments are more successful than others. In Ssah, they had produced a Warrior leader who was unrestrained by the traditions and concerns of the caste. She was the only result of that mating I had encountered to date, but if she was anything like the others, the entire hatching should have been destroyed after the first round of tests.

"Ssah, I disapprove strongly of many of your methods and

attitudes. Tactics such as flying into the cavern before reporting its location to the rest of the team jeopardized our survival. Had you crashed your flyer or been attacked in the interior, we would have been left unaware of the situation, and an entire sextant would have gone unscanned.''

She met my gaze with indifferent neutrality as I continued.

"Then there is your habit of questioning my orders. It is every Warrior's right to question the orders of a superior, but I feel that many of the objects you raise are pointless. They frequently either repeat questions covered in earlier discussions or briefings, or are of a rhetorical nature seeming to be designed with no other intent than to goad me. Before I can work with you comfortably I will require further clarification on your logic and motivations.''

She faced me levelly as she replied.

"My actions are easily understood if you understand my one basic premise. I feel that I should be leading this team instead of you.''

I felt my head lowering against my will as I answered.

"The High Command commissioned me and appointed me as Commander of——''

"I know," she interrupted. "I do not expect you to relinquish command, as I would not were I in your position. I recognize this logically. However, I also recognize my own feelings on the matter. I do not attempt to justify them, but merely state them as a cause for my behavior.''

I had regained control of myself, and my reply was level.

"Do you also acknowledge the danger to the team potential in your attitude?''

"Of course, that is why I would strongly urge that you follow my proposed plan of action in this minicampaign.''

Though still affected by her audacity, I was nonetheless curious to hear her plan and settled back to listen.

"Realizing the friction that would doubtless result from having a running power struggle within the team, I would propose that we scatter the team, divide it into three two-Tzen teams. In addition to relieving the pressures of our current situation, there are several other advantages inherent in this plan. First, it would lessen the chances of the entire team's being wiped out in one chance encounter with the Enemy. Thus, there would be a higher probability of at least some of us surviving to pass the gathered information on to the Empire. Second, with three teams working independently, we could gather more information than any single unit. Third . . .''

She hesitated and glanced back toward the cavern, then continued in a conspiratorial voice.

"Third, it would allow us to rid ourselves of some of the less desirable elements on the team.

My head wanted to lower again, but I kept it level.

"Explain your last comment."

"The composition of the teams should be clear, even to you. Mahz is a good Warrior, and his loyalty to me is undeniable. He and I would form one team. You are a capable Commander. Understand my earlier comments were not meant to deride your abilities, but rather to say I felt mine were better. Zur is slow, but his strength makes up for any lack of speed. The two of you would make a team with a better-than-average chance of survival."

She hesitated again.

"And Kor and Ahk? What about them?"

"Kor is bloodthirsty, and Ahk is a coward. If they don't kill each other off, the Enemy will."

I abandoned any hope of control.

"You claim you want to lead the team, yet at the same time you tell me you would willingly try to kill off one-third of the members?"

"Rahm, you and I both know a good small team has as much or better chance of survival as a large sloppy team."

"Do you have the vaguest conception of what we are facing on this planet, Ssah? The Enemy doesn't count its strength in troops, they count it in swarms. Swarms! Against that we have six Tzen. Six! And you want to divide our strength? Divide it and cut our numbers to four!"

I caught myself and forced my head and voice level, though both had a dangerous tilt.

"I reject your proposal, Ssah. It is my opinion that the six of us should remain together as a single unit to maximize our strength and firepower. As an example of how desperate I feel the situation is, at this time I even consider your presence an asset!"

"If those are your opinions——"

"Those are my orders!"

She rose to leave.

"If there are no further questions——"

"There are! Would you list your weapons in your personal possession at this time?"

"Certainly, I have a half dozen spring-javelins, an acid spray belt, two wedge-swords, a long knife, and, of course, dueling sticks."

"What, if any, weapons are you willing to place at the disposal of the team?"

"Neither Mahz's nor my weapons are to be used by another team member. We selected our weapons for ourselves. I trust the other team members had the sense to do the same. We withhold our weapons for personal use."

"That is your prerogative if you choose to exercise it. That answers all my questions. If you have no additional questions. pass the word for Zur. I would speak with him next."

She started to turn away, then turned once again to face me.

"Commander, there is one weapon I neglected to list with my arsenal."

She met my eyes coldly and levelly.

"I also have a fully charged hand-burner, identical to the one you loaned Zur to burn a tunnel with."

So here we were. Ssah with her fully charged hand-burner, backed by Mahz, was guarding the cave and the flyers, while I clung to a tree trunk covering the balance of the team with my meager quarter charge.

Suddenly there was a flicker of movement a hundred meters into the meadow. A Leaper! It moved out of the bush into the open, hesitated for a few moments, then made a twelve-foot leap in our direction and hesitated again.

I studied it narrowly. It was relatively small, scarcely six feet long. This probably meant it was still young. Good. If our guesses were correct, its exoskeleton would be softer than that of a full adult.

I watched it as it leaped in our direction again and paused once more. Either it was hunting or it was being exceptionally wary.

Even though we had been observing them for over a month, I still had a horrified fascination with the nightmarish lethalness of its appearance. Its hindlegs were twice the size of the other four, giving it incredible power on its leaps. The middle legs were primarily for walking and balance, but the forelegs . . . the forelegs were awesome. They had developed into slender pincers, saw-toothed on the inside and lightning fast. We weren't sure if they were poisoned or not; that was part of our mission today. More likely they were designed to grasp and hold a victim for the terrible mandibles. The Leaper's jaws were also enlarged pincers, razor-edged and saw-toothed and three times the size of the pincer forelegs. I had once seen a Leaper tear a four-footed warmblooded creature in half with its jaws, which was one reason we didn't know if the forelegs were poisonous. Once a victim was dragged within reach of those jaws it didn't survive long enough for us to tell if it died of poison or not. Hopefully we would have the answer to that and other questions soon. Zur wanted a specimen to dissect, and we were here to get one for him.

The Leaper moved toward us again. It was definitely coming to the river and would pass through our ambush. I ignored it and began scanning the meadow behind it. There was no sign of other Leapers about.

I beamed a warning to the waiting ambushers.

"Get ready."

Although there was no betraying movement, I knew the teammates were readying themselves. Prolonged stillness tends to lock and cramp the joints. They would be alernately tensing and relaxing their muscles, restoring circulation so that they could spring to the attack without loss of time or motion.

There was still no sign of other Leapers on the meadow. This would tend to confirm our observations and disprove the current Empire theory. According to Zur's briefing, the Empire was aware of the occasional solitary Leaper, but chose to interpret it as an outlying scout for one of the major packs. It was our conclusion from prolonged firsthand observation that in actuality most of the loners were just that—loners, unattached to any pack.

The Leaper was almost on our position now, and it switched to its short-distance crawling walk, a curious waddling procedure.

"Get ready," I beamed for a second time and scanned the meadow again. Still nothing. The Leaper passed under my tree trunk and approached the river bank.

"Now!"

Ahk seemed to rise up out of the ground to the Leaper's right. He drew back his arm and the spring-javelin snapped open, the two halves telescoping out from the center hand-grip and locking in place.

The Leaper saw him instantly and froze. It seemed both startled at his sudden appearance and torn by indecision as to whether to attack or flee. Then it saw Zur and Kor leaping from cover on its left, and its decision was made. It gathered its mighty hindlegs for a desperate leap, but it was too late.

Ahk's arm flashed forward, and the spring-javelin darted out. It pierced the Leaper's thorax and passed through into the ground, effectively pinning it in place.

A high-pitched squeal rent the air, like a prolonged shriek. I quickly scanned the meadow again. Still no other Leapers in sight.

I started to call down to silence the beast, but saw my advice was unnecessary.

Zur stepped up to the pinned Leaper, hesitated for a moment to gauge its wild thrashing, then raised his wedge-sword. He darted forward with an agility surprising in one of his bulk, swayed past the snapping mandibles, and struck with all the power in his massive arm. In the same movement he ducked under one of the groping pincered forelegs and rolled clear, coming to his feet with his sword raised again in the ready position.

His guard was reflexive, but unnecessary. The sword stroke had split the creature's head open, killing it even though its limbs continued to thrash and grope with stubborn life. Without guidance, though, its death throes were blind and easily avoided. Most important, the creature's alarm signal had been silenced by the blow.

I scanned the meadow once more. There was no sign of Leapers moving to support their fallen member. We had guessed correctly! Our victim was a loner. We had gambled and won. As a prize, we had a specimen for dissection.

Then we saw the Wasps.

CHAPTER
-6-

When we made our initial strafing run on the Wasps, our targets were the queens and the nests. The battle plan had not included eliminating the workers. As it was our first attack of the Bug Wars, High Command had deemed such an action a pointless risk of Warriors and equipment. Without eggs hatching or new eggs being laid, there would be no replenishment of the worker population as the existing workers reached the end of their life span. Thus, by the time the fleets returned to attack the Leapers, there would be no opposition from the Wasps.

This philosophy was fine for the fleets, but we were still on the planet, and so were the worker Wasps. Even though the initial attack had made a sizable dent in their numbers and still more had perished in the month we had been there, there were still an overwhelming number left.

They were constantly patrolling the airways, singly or in small groups, though we weren't sure why. They were there and that was all that really mattered. We had experienced no difficulty in avoiding them . . . until now.

There were three of them, apparently alerted by the death shrieks of the ambushed Leaper. The first warning we had of their presence was when they dropped from the treetops some seventy-five meters distant in the tree line. They approached us in a slow, heavy drone not more than a dozen feet off the ground. Caught in the open, Ahk, Zur, and Kor had no hope of escaping detection.

With cold calculation they shifted weapons in preparation for battle. I was uncertain if I had been detected in my lofty perch. I remained motionless, and the other team members did nothing to betray my presence.

The Wasps seemed to be in no hurry to press the attack. As they neared our position, instead of swooping to the attack, they rose lazily to the treetops once more. They touched down in the higher branches and rested there, staring down at us and fidgeting nervously among each other.

I might have been able to burn the three of them where they were, but I was loath to further deplete the energy source if the situation could be handled with the hand weapons. Then, too, the day would come when the hand-burners would be fully discharged and we would have to rely upon the hand weapons entirely. It would be best to begin practicing for that day now, when the cover fire of the hand-blasters was still available.

"Confirm count of three Enemy, Commander," came Zur's telepathed message.

"Confirmed. No indication of additional Wasps or Leapers in the immediate area."

The two forces considered each other warily. This would be the first actual confrontation between the Coalition of Insects and the Tzen Empire. Surprise attacks such as the original strafing mission or our ambushing the solitary Leaper were deliberately planned to favor the attacker and play into the defenders' weakness. Now, for the first time, individuals of a roughly even number were squaring off for head-on combat, each side with an equal degree of preparedness or nonpreparedness, as the case may be.

Although we had seen hundreds, even thousands of Wasps when we were strafing the nests, it was quite a different thing to face the Enemy from a short distance when they were awake, alert, and ready to fight instead of viewing them from inside a flyer's canopy as they buzzed around groggy and confused.

They continued to stare down at us with those dead metallic eyes, occasionally shifting position and touching antennae as if in conference. Their bodies were a glossy ten feet in length, and in flight their wings spanned over twenty feet, presenting a formidable and not particularly vulnerable target.

My teammates were not idle. With a cold calmness, they warily made their preparations for battle. Ahk had opened half a dozen of his spring-javelins after first retreating to a position near the base of one of the towering trees. Grasping his flexisteel whip in one hand, he began sticking the javelins in the ground around him, forcing one end deep into the soil. At first I thought he was attempting to prepare by having a ready supply of missiles close at hand, a tactic that seemed unwise to me considering the extremely tough exoskeleton of the Wasps. Then he turned and drove two of the javelins into the tree trunk behind him, leaving them to jut into the air at an unlikely angle, and I saw his plan. He was erecting a maze of sharp spikes between himself and the Enemy—negating any chance of being taken by a sudden rush. It seemed there was still much I could learn from this campaign-scarred veteran.

Zur stood alone in the open about a dozen meters from Ahk. In his hands he held the long-shafted alter-mace that had originally been part of Kor's arsenal. He stood in almost lazy stillness, the rigid shaft gripped in his hands; but his eyes never left the Wasps. They would find him no easy target. A ten-foot Tzen with an alter-mace is an opponent to be reckoned with.

Another dozen meters from Zur, completing the triangle, was Kor. She was waiting near, but not taking cover from, a slightly sloping tree trunk. The heavy, spiked hand-armor glittered at the end of her arms, but she didn't seem to notice the weight, tossing one of her steel balls back and forth from hand to hand as she watched the Wasps.

"Commander!"

It was Kor's voice that was beamed into my mind.

"Yes, Kor?"

"Request permission to commence combat."

"Granted."

I gave permission not so much out of impatience as curiosity to see what action she had planned. I didn't have long to wait.

Slowly at first, then smoothly accelerating, she began to turn and rotate like a warmblood chasing its tail. Her own tail, however, rose slowly until it was pointed straight up; then with a sudden whiplike action she bent double and hurtled the steel ball at the Wasps, levering her tail down as she did for added power and balance.

I would have thought the distance too great to throw one of the steel balls with any accuracy, much less with any power, and apparently so had the Wasps. As if to prove my assumptions wrong, the ball flashed past me as if fired from a power sling and smashed into one Wasp's thorax with an audible 'crack!'

The impact knocked the Wasp from its perch, but it caught itself in midair, apparently unhurt, and hovered there, soon to be joined by the other two. They hung in the air for several long moments, and I thought they were going to alight again. Then, without warning, they attacked.

To be accurate, two of them attacked, descending unhurriedly toward my teammates on the ground. The third rose and began to fly away, assumably to bring others. I tracked the messenger with my hand-burner, not daring to fire until battle had been joined. The two attackers passed by my lofty perch, and I decided I could wait no longer. I triggered the burner and watched the messenger flame and fall. Then I turned my attention to the scene below.

The two attacking Wasps were centering on one target—Kor. For a moment I lost sight of her as my line of vision was obscured by the descending attackers, though I could see Zur and Ahk leaving their chosen positions and moving to assist their team-mate. Then Kor was in sight again, moving fast, rolling sideways along the ground. Apparently she had waited until the last possible instant, waited until the Wasps' trailing forelegs were about to close on her, then evaded by dive rolling under them, passing dangerously close to their acid poisoned stings.

The Wasps hesitated, seemingly confused by the sudden move-ment of their target. Intelligent beings shouldn't hesitate when fighting Tzen. The split-second stabilization of his target was all the opening Ahk needed. The flexi-steel whip lashed out, striking the Wasp nearest him just behind the head, severing it from the body.

Still functioning, but without guidance, the headless body veered sideways, crashing into its partner. The second Wasp wobbled in midair from the impact and tried to steer away. Again, the maneuver came too late.

Zur was behind it, swinging the alter-mace. He had changed its setting at some point, and the once rigid shaft was now as limp and flexible as a rope, adding incredible whipping velocity to the already awesome power of his arms.

The blow struck the Wasp in the abdomen, spinning it around and bringing it crashing to the ground. The beast apparently realized its vulnerable position immediately and again tried to take to the air, again in vain.

Kor's dive roll had taken her to the base of the sloping tree trunk. As she regained her feet, she sprang onto the trunk, clawed her way several yards up it, and launched herself at the rising insect.

She landed on its back, her weight and impact driving it back to the ground, and she clung there, one arm wrapped around the beast's neck; her free hand, weighted with armor and clutching another steel ball, rose and fell repeatedly as she smashed at the Wasp's head. The insect thrashed and writhed on the ground, dragging Kor back and forth as she clung stubbornly to her precarious hand hold. The beast was bent almost double now, desperately probing with its sting to find its tormentor.

That I could do something about. Ahk wasn't the only one with spring-javelins. I clung to the tree trunk with one hand, my feet, and my tail, as I leaned out, opened the javelin, and hurtled it downward. My aim was true. The javelin struck the Wasp's abdomen, pinning it to the ground and ending the threat of the sting.

"Kor!" I called. "Break off the attack. It's dead!"

And it was. Reflex was keeping its limbs moving, but Kor's pummeling had caved in the beast's head.

"Acknowledged, Commander."

She sprang clear of the Wasp's death throes and stood waiting.

I scanned the meadow once more, but there was still no activity. I began to descend the tree trunk, cautiously. Leaping wildly into thin air was fine for hatchlings like Kor, but I had too much respect for my own vulnerability to risk injury needlessly. Besides, as I have said, I'm slightly acrophobic.

I will admit to a certain feeling of contentment as I descended, however. We had our specimen Leaper for Zur to dissect, and I was no longer as worried about the team's ability under fire.

CHAPTER
-7-

The team was enjoying a brief period of rest. We were secure in our cavern with Mahz guarding the entrance, and, more importantly, we had eaten.

We had made several adaptations to the cavern in the month since our arrival. One of these was the addition of a series of crude pits, pens, and cages in which we kept small warmbloods as a ready food source. While we can consume dead meat, we prefer it live. What is more, it proved to be easier to maintain livestock than devise a means of keeping the meat from spoiling if we killed them upon capture.

However, the situation posed more problems than simply maintaining a ready food source. Like other reptiles, Tzen tend to be sleepy and sluggish immediately after a heavy meal, a condition we could not afford now. We were not on a secure colony ship or transport where we could sharpen ourselves for combat by long periods without food, then glut ourselves after the battle and sleep it off while others took our place on the battle line. We were in a situation where we needed each Warrior at peak efficiency all the time. As such, instead of following our usual feeding pattern, we were forced to eat often and lightly, therefore obtaining minimal recovery time. This was particularly hard on Kor. Her small frame and high energy output left her constantly hungry. She would always have to cut short her feeding before her hunger was completely satisfied. As a result, she was beginning to grow irritable, a condition I would have to find a solution for if the team was to continue to function smoothly.

Unlike the rest of us, Zur had chosen not to eat following our battle with the Wasps. Instead, he busied himself at the rear of the cavern, working by torchlight to dissect the body of the Leaper we had killed.

As I rested, I watched his deft motions as he cut and probed at the corpse, pausing occasionally to murmur notes into his wrist recorder. It was good to see him in his element once more.

Zur was a misfit on the team, indeed in the Warrior caste. Unlike the rest of us, he was not raised and trained as a Warrior. His background was as a Scientist, and it was only after failure to meet the standards of the Scientist's caste that he had become a Warrior, largely owing to his imposing stature.

This constantly set him apart from the rest of the team, even though they knew nothing of his background. He fought well and efficiently, and they were glad to have him as a teammate, but there were periodic occurrences and utterances that clearly marked him as non-Warrior-raised.

One example of this was my conference with him immediately following our arrival on this planet. Even aware of his background, I was shocked to discover he was without a personal arsenal. Well, to be accurate he was not completely unarmed. He was still a Tzen. But his armament consisted of only a long knife and a wrist dart-thrower and a supply of acid and tranquilizer darts. For a Warrior he was naked! Instead of weapons he had used his weight allotment to bring along an assortment of information discs and blank discs for recording.

"Knowledge is my weapon, Commander," he had informed me.

I will not argue the relative value of knowledge, particularly with a Scientist. Further, I will acknowledge the discs he brought both increased our odds of survival and gave us a means of ensuring whatever data we gathered would be passed on to the Empire. However, I will also state as a Tzen and a member of the Warrior caste that I felt much more optimistic about our odds of survival after I issued him a wedge-sword and an altermace!

Watching him work and recalling our conference, I found my thoughts wandering back to when Zur and I first met. Normally, I would not waste time in idle reminiscence, but I had recently eaten and I let my mind wander back—back to the conference when I first met Zur, and, for me, the Bug Wars began.

I was awakened prematurely from Deep Sleep, a sign in itself that something was amiss. There were other Warriors moving about, but too few for it to be an attack or even preparation for a campaign. However, I was a Warrior, not a Scientist, and curiosity was not one of my major motivating drives. As such, I simply followed my orders and reported to the designated conference room.

The Tzen waiting for me was of gigantic proportions. I recall wondering at the time why he was a Scientist rather than a Warrior. We could put that Strength to good use. He motioned for me to join him at the viewing table in the middle of the room.

"Rahm, the Scientists' caste has received authorization to waken you as one of several experts to aid us in seeking a solution to a puzzle confronting us. First, will you confirm the service record—that you have fought in several campaigns against other intelligent life forms, and in at least one case, a culture whose technology was more advanced than our own?"

"Confirmed."

"Realizing this, we would like your military analysis and opinion on a recent discovery."

Reaching down, he pressed the levers to activate the viewing table. The picture of a city sprung into view. A magnificent city, far advanced of anything I had ever seen before. It was in a state of total ruin.

"An exploratory expedition discovered this city in the northern reaches of the Black Swamps. Its builders obviously possessed a technology far superior to anything we have ever imagined, much less hoped to achieve. Could you give us your opinion on it?"

As he spoke, the scene was slowly changing, now playing across the faces of the structures, now moving into the interiors. I watched the table for several moments before speaking.

"While these scenes are interesting and from a technical viewpoint, if I am to give a military analysis of the ruin, I must view those aspects of the city I am most familiar with. Could I see the defense installations, the armories, and the barracks?"

"There are none."

I considered this answer. Then I reviewed my question. Occasionally there are communication difficulties encountered in cross-caste conversation. In this case, however, the question was too simple to have been misunderstood, yet the answer was incredible.

"None at all?"

"It has been checked and rechecked. There is absolutely no evidence anywhere in the city of anything which was designed for violence. While there are items which could be used in a crude, makeshift manner, there is no trace of any weapons or armed force commensurate with the level of technology shown throughout the city."

I continued to study the ruin. After several thoughtful moments, I was ready.

"It is obvious that the city and probably its inhabitants were destroyed in an attack. There is evidence in the ruins of attack from above and below as well as at a ground level. This indicates an organized, concerted attack controlled by intelligence. If there is no local weapons technology, it was not the result of a civil war, but rather the attack of an outside force."

I paused and watched the table for a few more moments.

"The extent of the damage would indicate a mechanized attack; however, there are signs that this assumption would not explain. Here is a building with the front partially ripped off. I say specifically ripped off rather than blown off. Notice the machinery in the interior of this room remains undisturbed, which would indicate the absence of an explosion. The portion of machinery toward the front, apparently of similar design and material as that in the rear, has been sheared off even with the breach in the wall. From this I would conclude that the limited extent of the damage is due not to the nature of the machinery, but rather the limited, nonexplosive, nonchemical nature of the attack."

I took over control of the table to enlarge a specific portion of the view.

"The key thing to note is the nature of the breach. As I said, the fact that this portion of the wall was ripped out would indicate a mechanical attack, yet the scars on the wall resemble those marks left by the jaws of a beast rather than a machine."

I raised my head to address him directly.

"My conclusions from what I have observed would then be that a city built and operated by beings of advanced technological knowledge but no concept of violence was attacked and destroyed by a group of intelligent beings who were either in the form of, or built their war machines in the form of, giant, powerful beasts. To extrapolate on that conclusion, such an attacking force is, first, extremely powerful, and second, willing and able to use that power ruthlessly against a culture which was not threatening them. Such a force could constitute a serious threat to the existence of our Empire. It would therefore be my military recommendation that Top Priority be given to averting any possibility of attack by such a force, specifically by hunting it down and destroying it completely."

My analysis and recommendation did not seem to surprise him.

"Your opinions are noted and logged, Rahm. Your analysis coincides with the preliminary analysis submitted to the High Command. The probability of a Major War is high enough that you are asked to stop at the breeding chambers before returning to your sleep. As always, time is the key factor. Let us hope the Enemy grants us enough time to gather and analyze information and to prepare our Armies before battle is joined."

I turned to go, as the business at hand seemed to have been completed, but he raised a restraining hand.

"Before you go, Rahm, there is one additional point I would like to discuss with you. As it is of a personal nature, quite apart from the official orders bringing you here, you're not required to remain."

I was in no hurry; besides which, this massive scientist had piqued even my lax curiosity. Personal conversations were rare between Tzen; between castes, practically unheard of. I gestured for him to continue.

"As my part in this current survey of analyses and opinions, I have interviewed many of the Warrior caste. Curiosity has prompted me to look into their military records in an effort to determine why these specific Warriors were chosen to be polled. From what I have found in your and other records, confirmed by having met you personally, I have extrapolated that you will soon be advanced in rank. Should that come to pass, I would request that I be allowed to serve under you in the upcoming war."

His position took me aback, though I tried not to show it. Intercaste pride is such that one makes an extra effort to not be unsettled by a member of another caste.

"As your request hinges on the accuracy of your extrapolation, I would inquire as to the progression of your logic before replying."

"In any war, additional officers are needed. The High Command invariably reviews the records of combat veterans before considering any new Warriors for appointment. Not only is your service record exemplary, it displays many of the specific traits the High Command looks for in its officers. Realizing this, it is only logical that the probability is high that you will receive your appointment prior to the impending war.''

"And what do you envision these 'officers' traits' to be?''

"The major one is careful attention to those around them, a conscious plotting of attitudes and behavior patterns and the extrapolation of future behavior. In this regard, they are not unlike the Scientists' caste, which is why I am able to note the process so accurately.''

"However, I fear you are drawing the wrong conclusions,'' I corrected him. "That particular trait is common among the officers because it is common among all veteran Warriors. It is contributory to our survival to be aware of our teammates.''

He rose and began to pace as he replied.

"But all Warriors do not measure each other on the same scale. This is because they are putting the resulting data to different uses. It is difficult for me to explain to you, Rahm, because it is such a fine line you have crossed that you assume that others have done the same. Consider it in this way: others view each other with a positive-negative judgment. That is, as they look at another Warrior, they ask themselves, Is this Warrior efficient or not? Will he be dangerous to me if I accept a post next to him on the battle line? You and others like you who are either officers or officer material do not make positive-negative judgments. You observe another's strengths and weaknesses and adjust your actions accordingly. If you were currently in an officer position, it would mean that rather than rejecting a Warrior from service under you, that you would simply place him in a position on the team which would utilize his strengths and guard his weaknesses. That is what the High Command is looking for, officers who take what's given them for personnel and make it work, not Warriors who would waste everyone's time picking and choosing looking for a perfect team.''

I needed time to think that premise through, for both its accuracy and its applicability to me, so I changed to another line of questioning.

"Returning to your own situation, why would a Scientist want to go along to the Wars, or more specifically, why would an officer want to take the burden of accepting a Scientist on his team?''

"I did not express myself clearly. I do not wish to serve under you as a Scientist, but as a Warrior. My progress in the Scientist caste has slowed to immobility, and my superiors have suggested to me with increasing frequency that I could perhaps better serve the Empire in another caste. If this is to be the case, my personal choice for an alternate career is the Warrior caste."

Though I tried to suppress my outrage at the implications in his statement, my next question came out more tense than I would have liked.

"Then you feel that the Warrior's path is easier to follow than the Scientist's?"

"For me it is. Do not misunderstand me. I am not attempting to depreciate the difficulty of the Warrior's caste. However, for me fighting has always been easy, too easy. That's why I entered the Scientists' caste. With my build, it was no great achievement to run faster or hit harder than the others in training. It required no effort, so I had no feeling of serving the Empire. Having failed as a Scientist, however, it is time for me to swallow my personal feelings and preferences and serve the Empire in the capacity I am most suited for, specifically as a Warrior."

"So you turn to me with my lack of positive-negative judgment, expecting me to somehow make special allowances for you?"

"Not at all. I expect to carry my full weight as a team member. However, I would hope to find a commander who did not hold my non-Warrior background against me, but rather would use my supplemental knowledge and abilities to best advantage. I ask no more than any Tzen, and that is the chance to be efficient, to make maximum use of all my abilities."

I was finding his logic difficult to grasp.

"But by your definition any officer would do this. Why make this request specifically to me?" I asked.

"In theory that is the case. In actuality the lack of positive-negative judgment frequently only applies within the Warrior caste. Many of your fellow Warriors, while cognizant of the value of the other castes and therefore rendering proper respect, maintain an aloof, patronizing, almost disdainful air when dealing with those outside their own caste. Not that this trait is exclusive to the Warriors; the other castes also display it, including the Scientists. I find it particularly distressing in Warriors because that is the caste I wish to enter. I have not sensed that disdain in my talk with you and as such have requested service under you. Not because I expect special consideration, but because I expect you would use me fully as you would use any of your caste-raised Warriors."

I thought about his proposal for several moments, then turned to go.

"Your proposal is not disagreeable to me. If the predicted promotion indeed comes to pass, I will accept your service."

I paused in the doorway.

"What is your name, Scientist?"

"Zur," he replied.

Zur it was, and his service has proved to be as true as his prediction of my promotion. Not only had he not given me any cause to regret my choice, his abilities had prompted me to name him my second-in-command, a move none of the other teammates seemed displeased with, even Ssah.

"Commander!" Zur's voice interrupted my reverie.

"What is it, Zur?"

"Could you come here for a moment? I have discovered something in my dissection you should be made aware of."

So much of after-eating relaxation. I rose and moved to join him.

CHAPTER
-8-

The onslaught of cold weather brought a period of inactivity to the team. I ordered the majority of them to go into Deep Sleep until the advent of spring. Even though our standard survival kits contained drugs by which we could counteract our bodies' natural reactions to extreme temperatures, I saw no need to use them. Activity among the Leapers had ceased as they either moved to hibernate or expired in the encroaching cold. As there was no data to be gathered in their absence, and as we lacked both the personnel and the equipment to exterminate them as they slept, it was only logical that we take advantage of the slack time for some much-needed rest.

Zur and I remained awake longer than the others. Kor also maintained consciousness, but that was as first watch on the tunnel entrance. Zur and I were conferring, both to organize and analyze the data we had accumulated so far on the Leapers, and to increase my own knowledge of the data already accumulated by the Empire.

I make no apologies for the limited information I possessed when originally undertaking this mission. There had been much to learn and relatively little time to learn it in. Following the discovery of the ruined city and the subsequent inference of the existence of the Coalition of Insects, the full might of the Empire's Scientist and Technician castes had swung into action as the Warriors slept. Every effort had been expended to decipher the language of Builders—or the First Ones, as they came to be referred to—and in turn, in using that language as a key to unlock the secrets of their history and technology. This process was not new to us. As has been noted, it was not the first time the Tzen had encountered an intelligent, technically advanced race.

Investigating the First Ones brought an incredible wealth of new information into the coffers of the Tzen. It is difficult to determine which was more fantastic to us—their technology, which allowed them to travel and colonize the Star-lanes, or the fact that they had no concept of War or violence. Realizing the latter, however, we found it easy to see how they came to the abrupt end that they did.

Even before pushing out into the reaches of space, simply from our race's history in the Black Swamp of our home Planet, the Tzen have learned a basic principle of survival: not to take anything, not to build anything, unless you can defend it. Whatever you have, whether it be a source for water or the blood in your veins, there is bound to be someone or something else that wants it, and the only thing stopping the Enemy from taking it is you.

The First Ones apparently never learned this lesson. Whether they thought that nothing wanted what they had, or that others would be content with sharing, was never determined. However, when they first encountered the Insects and detected intelligence, the First Ones attempted to share their knowledge with them. They taught the Insects about the Star-lanes and the vast number of inhabitable worlds in the universe to demonstrate that there was no need for territorial-food wars. They even showed the Insects how to operate some of the cruder interstellar transports to make these new worlds available to them.

The Insects worked on a much simpler logic process. Being a population-sensitive culture, they felt there would never be enough worlds for everyone. Realizing this, they could only view the First Ones as potential competitors for the inhabitable worlds. Following this logic, they used the ships the First Ones gave them along with the knowledge of the locations of the other colonies and launched an attack, an attack that brought the First Ones and their culture to an abrupt end. Then, having eliminated the known competition, the Insects pulled back to their home system, expanding out slowly as the population pressures dictated. This process had continued uninterrupted until the rise of the Tzen.

The First Ones were the Technicians, and the Insects the first Conquerors, but the Tzen were the first Warriors. Our victories had never hinged on the helplessness of our opponents. Therefore, unlike the Insects, we did not shun the technology left behind by the First Ones. Although they had not developed any instruments of War, many of their inventions and discoveries were readily adaptable to that purpose.

Having long since realized that any discovery has the double capacity of creation or destruction, our Scientists and Technicians applied themselves to finding combative uses for the First Ones' technology until we were ready to do battle with the Insects—their vast numbers versus our weapons and military experience.

The period of preparation, once the Warriors were awakened, was both rushed and crowded. Like most of the Warriors, I had realized the urgency of our training and had focused most of my concentration on the specific tools of our caste, such as the flyers and the new weapons, covering the balance of the vast storehouses of knowledge suddenly at our disposal with a minimal skim and a glance.

In our current predicament, however, I found increasing need for the information I had so lightly passed over, and was immensely grateful for the presence of Zur and his library of information discs. I occasionally encountered difficulty keeping him from digressing into more detail than I deemed necessary; but even restricting the scope of our studies, I was astounded at the length of time required to cover the necessary material. As the days and weeks marched on, my respect for Zur grew. While I had always regarded him highly as a Warrior, this increased awareness of these seldom-glimpsed depths of his talents surpassed even my stringent requirements of effectiveness.

I commented on this to him once as we paused in our studies to eat and rest, reclining on the ground. Even in his after-feeding lethargy, his thoughts were quick and concise as he replied.

"There is a balance at work here, Commander, which at times I think you overlook. Knowledge is a powerful weapon, but only if it is used. Had the Coalition of Insects utilized the knowledge of the First Ones as we have, it is doubtful we would be here today. The Tzen are effective not because we have knowledge, but because we use it. The Scientists seek and organize the knowledge, the Technicians render it usable, and the Warriors apply it. On a smaller scale, my information would be of little value if you as the Commander were unwilling to benefit from it. As I pointed out when we first met, I feel there are many officers who would be reluctant to take advantage of my assistance."

"I must disagree with you, Zur. I do not feel I am that unusual as an officer. In all phases of our training we rely heavily on the Scientists and Technicians. Why should it be any different in the field?"

"Why indeed? Perhaps some notion that once in the field, none know combat as well as a Warrior and information is something best left for the classrooms. I do not say that no other Commander would listen, but how many would listen as readily or for that matter seek out my advice?"

"I would like to believe the majority of officers would," I insisted. "If not, we are being less than efficient in our ways of waging war."

"Perhaps you are right, Commander," he conceded. "I will readily admit that like your appreciation of the Scientists' caste, my own appreciation of the Warrior caste, particularly their officers, has grown significantly on this mission. There have been many small things I was previously unaware of, Kor's development as an example."

"What about Kor's development?"

"I assume you are aware that she now has definite opinions about each of her teammates. I assume this knowledge on your part because even if she has not reported her opinions to you, you were instrumental in her forming them."

I raised my head to look at him severely.

"It is a characteristic that any veteran Warrior has definite opinions about his or her teammates. Many consider it vital to their own survival," I said carefully.

"I am aware of that, Commander. That is why I specifically refer to it as development on Kor's part. I merely suggest that she may have had outside assistance in this phase of her development which enabled her to progress much more rapidly than might normally be expected."

"If you are observant enough to have noted that, then you have also noted that it is Akh that she spends most of her off-duty time with," I pointed out. "Realizing that he has more combat experience than anyone on the team including myself, I should think it obvious that if anyone is advising her in her development, it is he."

"Agreed, Commander. However, I have also noted that you were the one who encouraged him to take an interest in Kor's development."

"Surely you are aware, Zur, that no Tzen Commander can order a Warrior to share his knowledge and experience with another."

"Indeed I am, Commander. What I had not been aware of prior to this mission was the possibility of informally convincing a veteran Warrior that it is in his own best survival interest to advise another less-experienced Tzen in the finer points of field survival."

I was silent for a few moments, then reclined again, lowering my head to the ground.

"I would be inefficient as a Commander if I did not strive to obtain maximum effectiveness from each Warrior in my command regardless of methods."

"That is what I am learning, Rahm. This is also why I do not regret having aligned myself with your command."

CHAPTER
-9-

I have never felt as helpless as a Warrior, much less as a Commander, as when I was forced to idly watch while Ahk died.

It was early spring, and the activity level of the Leapers was unknown. That lack of knowledge was what prompted me to wake Ssah and Ahk from Deep Sleep. We needed to send out scouts to determine if the Leapers were active in sufficient quantities to justify waking the rest of the team.

The two of them had gone out with the usual strict orders to avoid contact with the Enemy, while I remained behind as entrance guard. They headed out shortly after dawn to minimize the possibility of chance encounter, as the Leapers seldom moved about until several hours into daylight.

While remaining motionless as entrance guard for long hours, there is little to do except think. Ironically, my thoughts that day were on how well our team had survived under adverse conditions. We had survived the shutout and ensuing crash landing, and although only six in number, had held out for almost a year in Enemy-infested terrain. Not only had held out, but had gathered valuable information for the Empire, and had done it without losing a team member.

It occurred to me to ask Zur to set aside one of his blank information discs for me to record my notes as Commander. In addition to information on the Enemy, there were valuable lessons to be learned here about survival tactics. To that end, I set about mentally organizing my thoughts on how I had led the team in the period since our landing, the methods of utilizing the strengths of each individual on the team, the points I would change, the items I would leave intact . . .

My thoughts were interrupted by the death cry of a Leaper. I snapped my senses back into focus and listened intently, but heard nothing more.

I was surprised to note it was nearly sundown. While I had been watching the terrain unblinkingly the entire day, my thoughts had been so intense I had failed to notice the passage of time. It was time for the scouts to return.

Another shriek sounded. I was fully alert now. The source of the sound was out of my line of vision, somewhere beyond the hills that hid our cavern, somewhere in the vicinity of the forest line where Ssah and Ahk were. The Leaper activities corresponding with the time of the scouts' return could not be coincidental. We had trouble.

"Zur . . . Zur . . . Zur . . . Zur . . ." I beamed desperately into the cavern behind me.

It took a distressingly long time to arouse him.

"Zur here!" came the weak response finally.

"Trouble on the forest line . . . Possibly our scouts . . . Going to check it . . . Rouse the others and stand by . . ."

As I beamed the last part of my orders, I was on my feet and running. As I plunged down the slope of the first hill, another scream split the air. I redoubled my speed, laboring uphill, then plunging into the next valley.

Suddenly my training returned to me. This wouldn't do. Dashing around blindly and recklessly in a crisis situation is the action of a panicky, soon-to-be extinct, nonintelligent species, not a Tzen Warrior. I forced myself to a halt, clenching my fists as another shriek sounded. I needed information—information to relay back to the rest of the team and to govern my own actions.

I turned and hurled myself back up the slope I had so recently descended. A rock formation jutted up into the sky on this ridge, one we had occasionally used as a lookout post. It would serve me now.

I clawed my way up onto one of the ledges and flattened, scanning the distant forest line. I caught a faint movement and forced focus, accepting the inevitable headache for the advantage of temporary telescopic vision.

It was Ahk. I glimpsed him briefly as he crouched breathless at the foot of a tree, spring-javelin in one hand, flexi-steel whip in the other. Then he disappeared, darting around the tree trunk as a Leaper struck the spot he had so recently vacated. The insect backed up, momentarily stunned by the impact. Before it could recover, Ahk was back in sight. His whip flashed twice in the setting sun, and the Insect heeled over, two of its legs missing. Ahk was running again, along the tree line. Knowing the Leapers would outdistance him in open terrain, he was using his maneuverability to best advantage. There were several twitching carcasses in view giving mute testimony to the effectiveness of his tactic. It must have been their death throes that had alerted me to the situation.

I wondered why he did not simply duck into the forest to elude his pursuers. There were eight of them that I could see, a small pack, maneuvering to cut him off. Suddenly he dove flat as another Leaper bounded over his prostrate body from the shadows of the forest. That's why he was working the tree line! The Leapers were entering the forest now!

He rose to one knee and hurled his spring-javelin at the Leaper that had just threatened him, pinning it to the ground.

Suddenly he was down, another Leaper landing on him from behind as he threw.

I tensed, sending a sudden stab of pain through my straining eyes. Then the Insect was flipped backward, and Ahk was on his feet again. For a moment I was at a loss; then I realized what he had done. He had triggered another spring-javelin while under the creature, using the force of the ends telescoping out to push the Leaper up and off him.

He was running again, stumbling now, as two more Leapers crawled into view from the forest's depths. How many were there?

Where was Ssah?

I started to look for her, but had my attention wrenched back to the action. A Leaper caught Ahk as he turned to change directions, closing its mighty jaws around his waist and lifting him into the air. He dropped the javelin and his hand went to the small of his back, and the Insect fell away, rolling in agony. The acid belt!

He was moving again, but now was in visible pain. There were terrible wounds in his sides from the Leaper's attack, and they slowed his movement. The other Leapers also saw it, and redoubled their efforts to catch him.

Casting about desperately, Ahk tried one last desperate move. The whip darted out again, but this time not at the Insects. His target was a low-hanging tree limb jutting above him. The whip wrapped around the limb and held. In a flash he was up, pulling his weight upwards with the strength of his arms.

Too late! One of the Leapers caught his legs, tugging mightily to pull him back to the ground. He tried to raise the additional weight, then let go with one hand, groping for another weapon. Another Leaper clambered up its comrade's body and fastened its jaws around the Warrior's neck. Ahk jerked once, then his head toppled off, severed completely from the body. The body clung to the whip for a moment, then fell heavily into the gathered pack below.

I did not watch the pack devouring its victim. I was looking beyond them. As I followed Ahk's upward progress, I had seen something else.

I saw Ssah crouched in a tree some ten meters beyond the action. More importantly, I saw the unfired hand-burner in her hand.

CHAPTER
- 10 -

There were three of us moving through the predawn gloom. Kor, Zur, and myself were undertaking this assignment, leaving Ssah and Mahz behind on entrance guard.

This allotment of duty stations was not random. Combat was a certainty on this mission, and that would require cooperation and confidence in the unit to engage with the enemy. Both Zur and Kor had separately requested that I not assign them to a mission with Ssah, and I will admit to a certain reluctance on my part to rely on her. In fact, of the entire team, only Mahz maintained any contact with her beyond what was required for assigned duties. Unfortunately, this resulted in Mahz's being avoided as much as Ssah was.

The team members' opinions of Ssah, while never high, had degenerated to an all-time low after Ahk's death. In fact, things had reached a point where I had to overstep my authority as Commander and outlaw dueling for the duration of our stay on the planet. This order understandably caused a great uproar of protest among the team members, including Ssah and Mahz, but I stood firm on my decision. A duel now, regardless of who was involved or what the outcome was, would weaken the team, and we couldn't afford to lose another member. Instead, I reminded them that although they had a Warrior's right to protest my order, it was still a direct order in a Combat Zone. As such, while they could press charges with my Superior once the mission was over and we had rejoined the Empire, for the time being they were to follow my orders to the letter. If any member chose to defy a direct order under these conditions, I could level whatever punishment I felt necessary, up to and including death, without benefit of a trial and call on any other team members to assist me in enforcing that sentence. There is no known case of this regulation's being enforced in the entire history of the Warrior caste, but the rule was still on record should I need it.

It was perhaps a misapplication of regulations, which if challenged, would give rise to a debate on interpretation of authority and other priority versus personal judgment. However, I felt that this in itself was just. A personal interpretation of regulations had gotten me into this situation; so, by the Black Swamps, a personal interpretation of regulations would get me out of it.

My interrogation of Ssah following Ahk's death had been one of the most frustrating and unsatisfying conversations of my career. I had not returned to the cavern after witnessing the incident, but instead waited in the foothills for her to appear. The first loss of a Tzen under my command and the physical strain of prolonged close-focus had combined to erode my mental state so that by the time she arrived, my mood was not good.

"Explain!" I demanded as levelly as I was able.

"Explain, Commander?"

"We have just lost a team member, Ssah. As Commander, I wish to know why, so that we might avoid similar occurrences in the future. You were on assignment with Ahk at the time of his death and are therefore the logical source of information regarding the 'incident.' Now explain!"

She still seemed puzzled, but launched into her story.

"Ahk and I moved out this morning specifically assigned to scout Leaper activity. We roamed several sectors, but by the close of the day had detected no activity, either individual or group. We were returning to the cavern when we heard the sounds of a pack of Leapers approaching rapidly from behind. As we were under strict orders to avoid contact with the Enemy, we attempted to escape notice by seeking refuge in some over-hanging branches. Whether his foot slipped in the soft soil as he leaped or he simply misjudged the distance, I don't know; but Ahk missed his first jump. Before he could jump again, the first of the Leapers burst into view and spotted him. Rather than betray my position, he chose to attempt to elude his pursuers in a running flight. His efforts failed, and after the Leapers left the area, I climbed down and proceeded back to the cavern. Before I could reach the cavern, you approached and engaged me in this rather unconventional debriefing.''

I stared at her in silence until she began to cock her head quizzically.

''Is your hand-burner functional?''

''Yes.''

''Then why didn't you provide cover fire for Ahk when he was caught by the Leapers?''

''It would have been against direct orders.''

''What orders?''

She cocked her head in question again.

''Your orders, Commander. Before we left you gave us specific orders to avoid contact with the Enemy and to enter into combat only in self-defense. I was not threatened in that situation, so to open fire would have been in direct disobedience of your orders.''

I considered this for several moments before continuing with my questioning.

''Are you then claiming that had I not issued orders against contact with the Enemy that you would have given Ahk supporting fire?''

She paused for thought before answering.

''No. I still would have withheld fire.''

''Explain.''

''It has become quite apparent since our landing that the hand-burners could be a decisive factor in any battle with the Leapers. Realizing this, I could not justify depleting the power of my burner to benefit any single individual. Rather, I would feel obligation to preserve its power in lieu of a situation critical to the entire team. Secondly, priority had to be given to getting the report of our scouting mission back to the team. Entering into needless combat could have jeopardized the delivery of that report.''

''But your report was of no activity, a fact which was proven invalid by the Leapers' attack.''

''On the contrary, Commander. The attack gave us something to report. By my inaction, I have survived to report definite Leaper activity in the area.''

The debriefing was getting circular, but I pressed on.

''To clarify something you said earlier, you claim you withheld fire to conserve the power charge. Isn't it true, however, that the Leaper pack was small enough in number that you could have eliminated them with minimal drain to your burner?''

''True, Commander, but they were so scattered during the battle that it was impossible to estimate their number until they closed in to feed on Ahk's body. At that time, with Ahk already dead and my presence undetected, it would have been foolish to waste power by entering into combat.''

I sank into silence once again, but she continued.

''If I might add some unsolicited comments to the debriefing, Commander, your attitude on this matter puzzles me. You have constantly criticized me for taking reckless and independent action. Your only advice to me has been to try to become more team-oriented and less indulgent of my own desires and motivations. In this situation, however, when I have acted strictly by your orders and in the best interests of the team, you act more as if you were interrogating a criminal than like a Commander debriefing a Warrior. I cannot help but question whether you are asking pertinent questions seeking information, or if you are groping about for someone else on whom to blame your own incompetence as a Commander.''

It was at this point that I decided we could not afford a duel, though the frequency with which I review my decision leads me to believe I am not particularly pleased with the conclusions.

However, now it was time to turn my thoughts to the mission at hand. Even though I acknowledged its necessity, I did not relish the thought of what it entailed. We had accumulated an impressive bulk of data on the Leapers. We were now familiar with their anatomy, breeding habits, life cycle, and diet. There was still one bit of information missing that would be invaluable to the Empire, and that was what we were seeking today. This mission was to appraise the Leapers' military ability.

To date, we had witnessed only one tactic employed by the Insects in hunting or fighting. So far, all they had done was rush their victim, relying on their mobility, power, and strength of numbers to overwhelm any opposition. What we wanted to test was whether they could devise and execute an alternate plan given proper conditions.

Even though the sun still had not risen, I decided there was ample light for our final briefing. I signaled a halt, and the other two gathered about me. I squatted, cleared a space on the ground in front of me, and started scratching diagrams with my claw as I spoke.

''I want to take this opportunity to review our plan once more to be sure there is no confusion. The plan as stated involves danger enough without running the added risk of uncoordinated execution.''

They studied the diagram intently.

"Some distance ahead is the river. The key point is, of course, the shallows."

I tapped the indicated position.

"Zur and I will wait there while Kor proceeds upstream a minimum of one thousand meters. At that point she will attempt to attract the attention of a pack of Leapers. Once she is spotted, she will evade them by retreating into the river and moving downstream."

I again indicated the point on my ground sketch.

"We know that the river between there and the shallows is both too deep to afford the Leapers footing and too wide for them to attempt attacking from the bank. The critical question is, will the Leapers simply follow along the bank, or will they actually divide their forces and send a portion of their numbers ahead to the shallows. If they——"

"Commander!"

I was interrupted by a telepathed thought from Kor. I looked at her questioningly.

"Continue gesturing at the ground sketch," she continued to beam, "but unobtrusively scan the terrain around us."

I did, and saw the cause of her concern. In an unusual display of predawn activity, there were Leapers quietly creeping into view out of the shadows around us. Both from their stealth and from the focus of their motion, it was apparent that not only had we been spotted, but we were the object of their ambush.

CHAPTER
-11-

With the suddenness of a serpent's strike the situation had changed. We were the hunted, not the hunters.

Later I would look back on the reactions of my teammates with admiration and appreciation. They did not panic either physically or mentally. Not so much as an angry lash of a tail marred their performance as they waited. They didn't rail or beleaguer me with questions, but instead gave me several much-needed moments of silence in which to formulate our plans. Later I would remember, but now my mind was preoccupied, appraising our situation.

What at first glance seemed like more than a hundred Leapers, on closer scrutiny proved to be fewer than fifty, still more than enough to make the situation desperate, but perhaps one not quite as hopeless as the first appraisal had indicated.

In many ways it was fortunate that the Leapers had chosen this expedition to ambush. As I noted earlier, we were expecting combat on this mission. As such, we were prepared both in armor, and more importantly, in frame of mind, for a fight. Therefore, the only real change necessary would be to adapt our tactics to the terrain chosen by the Enemy for the battle. It had been stressed frequently in our training as Warriors that the day that Tzen couldn't adapt to the Enemy's terrain would be the day the Empire crumbled. It seemed we were to have the opportunity to test that axiom. I studied the terrain carefully.

We were on the downslope of the last foothill of our range,

crouched in an area of open grassland dotted by large clumps of brush. About one hundred meters to our left the brush gave out, yielding to an open grassland. Two hundred meters ahead was the tree line that lined the river below the shallows, which was our original destination. To our right, the brush-dotted grassland continued, marred by only one notable geographic feature. The crest of the hill we were descending rose sharply to our right, almost trebling in height; and instead of a gentle slope, slide activity had exposed a steep sand-and-gravel cliff face.

The trees by the river would be our best chance for safety, so of course there is where the Enemy had allotted their greatest strength, fully half their force. The balance of the force was divided roughly equally, with half forming a line in the grasslands to our right, and the other half silently creeping down the slope behind us.

Any questions we had about their military aptitude were answered by that formation. We could read their plan in the patterns. They definitely did not want us to reach the river, and assuming we survived the initial clash, had aligned their troops to drive us to our right, out onto the open grassland. Once there, their superior mobility on open terrain would bring the affair to a rapid close. It was slightly ironic that we had walked into this ambush while on a mission to test if they had the intelligence to head off an escaping fugitive.

I reached my decision.

"Follow my lead," I beamed to my teammates. "Move as if we hadn't seen them, but ready your weapons."

With that, I rose and began walking to the right, paralleling the tree line. Zur and Kor followed, ambling along with such exaggerated laxness that I feared it would betray our plan. Although Tzen favor a surprise attack, we are not a deceitful race. As such, I was afraid our clumsy theatrical efforts would be immediately transparent.

It seemed my fears were groundless. The Leapers did not immediately charge or in any other way indicate they suspected their prey had been alerted. Perhaps they are even less deceitful than we are.

However, our feint was not having the desired effect. I had hoped that as we moved deeper into their trap they would shift some of their force from blocking the river to seal the trap, encircling us completely. If enough moved, it might weaken the wing at the tree line sufficiently for us to suddenly punch through their line to the river. Unfortunately the force by the river didn't budge.

My teammates were as ready as they would ever be. Zur had unlimbered the alter-mace and was idly snapping the heads off flowers as we passed. Kor was rolling one of her steel balls up and down on the blade of a wedge-sword as she walked and making it look easy.

It would be foolhardy to try for the trees with the Leapers in their current arrangement. The blocking force would simply move forward and engage us in the open, allowing the other two wings to close on us in an area with no cover. We would have to do this the hard way.

I leisurely removed the coiled flexi-whip from my shoulder. Actually, I shouldn't call it a flexi-whip, since it had been modified. I had affixed one of Kor's steel balls to its tip, the weight of which, combined with the whip's lashing action, could pulverize rock. It wasn't a flexi-whip anymore, it was a Bug-killer.

"Subtlety does not seem to be working," I beamed at the team. "Break for the cliff on my count . . . ready . . . three . . . two . . ."

As a unit we wheeled and began jogging for the cliff. As we ran, we spread the formation slightly until there was space of about two and a half meters between us to ensure weapons room, and we held at that distance. It is neither a fast-moving nor an impressive formation, but once set in motion it doesn't stop for anything. Though it is not a particularly terrifying sight, few have stood in the path of a jogging formation of armed Tzen and survived.

For a few precious moments there was no activity in the Enemy ranks. Apparently they were having difficulty comprehending that we had seen them and were charging them head-on. Then a series of chirps and squeals went up behind us, and the Leapers moved into action.

There were roughly a dozen of the Enemy between us and the cliff. Normally we could have dealt with them with ease, but by turning our heads slightly as we ran, we could see the bulk of the pack closing rapidly on us from behind. The Leapers in our path would have to be dealt with swiftly if we were to survive.

I drew my hand-burner. The charge remaining had been too weak to assist Ahk, but at short range it might save us today. A Leaper bounded over a bush at Zur, who smashed its head with the alter-mace. It died with a shriek and battle was joined.

Three Leapers appeared in my path. I burned the second, caught the leader with the Bug-killer, and burned the third in mid-air. A spring-javelin flashed past me and out of sight behind a bush. As I passed it, I saw a Leaper that had been waiting in hiding pinned and writhing.

One appeared a scant two meters in front of me, seeming to pop out of the ground. I burned it and leaped over the body. My leap carried me into an unseen dip, and into the midst of three more. I burned one and clubbed another out of the air in front of me with the butt of the whip, but the third sank its jaws into my blaster arm and clung there. I tried to keep running and pull my arm free, but was slowly being dragged to a halt when Kor appeared, smashing the Leaper's head from behind with her armored fist while severing its jaws with her wedge-sword. It was painful, but I managed to twist the burner around and catch another that was crawling over the edge of the dip.

Then we were free and running again. The cliff face was only a few more meters ahead, but we could see a group of two Leapers waiting there for us. The pack was almost upon us now.

"Kor! Clear the cliff, Zur, with me . . . turn!"

My second-in-command and I whirled and faced the charging pack as Kor continued on. We backed slowly toward the cliff as we fought, confident that Kor would have disposed of the last two by the time we got there.

"Clear, Commander!"

We dashed the last two meters and turned. With Zur on my left, Kor on my right, and a cliff at my back, I lowered my head and hissed in the face of the Enemy.

For a moment they hesitated, then surged forward in a wave. We weren't running now, and the bodies began to stack around us.

I draped the Bug-killer over my shoulder as I burned a Leaper, opened a spring-javelin and pinned a second, then caught a third as I snatched the Bug-killer from my shoulder again. I saw one go down to one of Zur's acid darts and another to one of Kor's thrown steel balls as I took two more with the Bug-killer.

"Caught! came Zur's calm voice from my left.

I turned and saw him struggling in a tug of war with a Leaper for his alter-mace as he tried to keep two others at bay with his dart-thrower.

"Covered!" I called as I burned the Leaper that was clinging to his mace.

Suddenly I felt jaws clamp on my calf. A Leaper I thought dead had inched forward and attached itself to my leg. I started to burn it, but had to avert my shot to pick another target out of mid-air. Before I could recover, the Leaper that had my leg rolled, causing me to fall and lose my balance.

"Caught!" I said.

"Covered!" came a voice, and Kor was there. She chopped at the Leaper with her wedge-sword. Straightening quickly, she backhanded another out of the air as I shot between her legs to burn a third, which was creeping into her vacated position.

I forced myself to my feet as the battle continued. The hand-burner finally gave out, leaving me barely enough time to snatch and open a spring-javelin and bat a leaping Enemy to one side. A throw to pin it, and I was ready again, Bug-killer in one hand and wedge-sword in the other.

There was a lull in the action as the Enemy fell back. I was both tired and puzzled. Either I had completely lost my feel for combat, or there were more Leapers than I had originally counted. I scanned the terrain.

There was another small pack of Leapers emerging from the tree line and still another pack visible in the distant grassland. All were heading in our direction. Apparently either Leaper communication or the sound of our battle was drawing reinforcements into the area.

"Weapons status check," I beamed.

"Eight . . . no . . . seven acid darts left," Zur corrected himself as he picked off another Leaper that was starting to creep close.

I noticed he was bleeding steadily from an ugly gash on his upper arm, and suddenly realized all three of us were suffering wounds. My calf wound began to throb, but I ignored it, opening a spring-javelin to meet a Leaper who was crouching to attack.

Before I could throw, the beam of a hand-burner darted from the crest of the cliff behind us, finishing the Leaper and in rapid succession several others. The ranks of Enemy surrounding us gave ground as the beam lanced out again and again.

I didn't have to look. It was Ssah.

CHAPTER
- 12 -

The reappearance of the Empire fleets did not come as a surprise. We had spotted their scout flyers with increasing regularity and realized invasion was imminent. Accordingly, we began to make our preparations.

Our flyers were light enough to be carried easily by two, but that was on level ground. Unfortunately, they were not designed for a takeoff, but rather required a drop or launch to become airborne. As such, it was necessary to carry or hoist them to a higher level of the cavern. By the time our task was complete and five flyers were balanced precariously on the lip of a ledge near the ceiling of the cavern, I had had more than one occasion to question the wisdom of my decision to use the flyers again.

It was our speculation that all or part of the force would be surface troops, roaming the grasslands on foot hunting the Leaper packs. It would be an easy matter to join up with these forces without freeing our flyers. Still I reasoned that we could be of greater service acting as air cover for the troops. The Wasps had long since died out, and I wanted to take advantage of the air supremacy that we had fought so hard for. Then again, there was always the chance our speculations would turn out to be wrong. I had no desire to be stranded here again because we had been too lazy to arrange our own transport.

Another major portion of our time was occupied in releasing the warmbloods we had kept penned for food. This turned out to be a greater task than we had originally planned. We had known it would be necessary to take them some distance from the cavern before releasing them to avoid luring Leapers into the area with a sudden abundance of game. What we had not counted on was the warmbloods' reluctance to depart. Apparently they preferred to be penned and fed to having to wander and forage, and resented our attempts to return them to their natural situation. They persisted in attempting to follow us back to the cavern, even when pelted with rocks. In fact, some of them were so stubborn that they would hide themselves and attempt to follow at a distance unnoticed. They were quite crafty at this tactic, and it was not uncommon for a Tzen on a release assignment to arrive back at the cavern with more warmbloods than he had left with.

They became such a nuisance that we seriously discussed the possibility of killing them, a rare solution for a race such as ourselves, which only kills for food or defense and occasionally for honor. We considered the possibility and discarded it. We were Tzen. We did not kill simply because something annoyed us. Another solution would have to be found.

Before the elusive solution was discovered, the fleet arrived.

I was guarding the entrance at the time of their arrival. I had never viewed one of our attacks from the defender's viewpoint before and was impressed by its suddenness. One moment the view was clear and serene, and the next the air was filled with flyers. There was no warning, no opportunity to watch the formations approach; they were suddenly there, crowding the sky with their numbers.

There were swarms of the single flyers such as we used, but my attention was held by the huge flyers of a design unfamiliar to me. As I viewed them, I noticed streams of what looked like clear balls being dropped as they swooped low over the grasslands. Curiosity made me force-focus my eyes on these balls as they fell. The increased magnification of force-focus revealed a Tzen Warrior encased in each ball as it plunged downward. Apparently the ball was composed of a substance not unlike the gel-cushion of our fliers, and this was a new method of dropping surface teams.

I scanned the immediate vicinity one last time and retreated into the cavern again.

"Load your flyers," I announced to the team.

They needed no further explanation. As I said, we had been expecting the fleet's arrival. I joined them as they quietly gathered their personal gear and began their climb to the flyers.

Before entering my flyer, I paused to scan the cavern a final time. The last of the warmbloods had long since been released and the pens dismantled. There was no trace remaining of our garrison.

I suddenly realized the others were already sealed in their flyers and waiting for me.

"Open fire!" I beamed to them and entered my flyer.

Four hot-beams darted out simultaneously, and before their assault the wall of the cavern began to melt away. By the time I had sealed my flyer an opening had appeared, and sunlight began to stream into the cavern again. I added my weapon to the group effort. I deliberately allowed the firing to continue overlong, burning an exceptionally large opening. It had been a long time since any of us had flown, and it was doubtful we were up to precision maneuvers.

"Cease fire!"

We sat motionless for several long moments waiting for the rock to cool and until we were sure that any rockslides caused by our burning had run their course.

"One at a time. . . . Wait until the flyer ahead of you has cleared the entrance before following!"

With that, I set the foot disc and trod down on it to start the engine. As I felt it begin to convert its power, I rocked my body forward in the flyer. It slid off the edge of the ledge and plunged toward the floor of the cavern. Immediately I began working the controls, and the wings spread, catching the air and changing my fall into a swooping climb. A few adjustments, and I was out in the sunlight.

I quickly took the flyer into a slow spiral climb and hovered over the entrance waiting for the rest of the team to emerge. As they appeared one by one and climbed to join me, I felt a certain sense of accomplishment. Over a year on Enemy-held terrain and we survived with all equipment intact and only one member lost. Then I thought about Ahk and the feeling faded.

I was about to signal for a formation movement, then noticed there was another formation of flyers working in the near vicinity. I activated my flyer's intrusion beacon to advise them of our presence.

"Identify!" came the beamed thought from the other formation's Commander.

"Commander Rahm and survivors of the last attack on this planet. We request permission to join your command for the duration of this mission."

There was pause.

"Survivors from the last attack?"

"Confirmed."

"Then you have not been informed . . ."

There was another long pause.

"Clarify," I prompted.

"The Black Swamps have been destroyed!"

My mind reeled under the impact of the news. Shocked disbelief swept over me, followed closely by a dark rage. The Black Swamps!

We had all known that this might happen. It was for that reason we had relocated the Empire into the colony ships before entering into the War. Still, the reality was a crushing blow. The Black Swamps! The Swamps were the point of origin of our race as well as our traditional burial grounds. We came from the Black Swamps and would return to the Black Swamps. It was part of our heritage, part of the Empire. Particularly with the new technology, it was one of the few stable elements of our culture. The Black Swamps! Destroyed!

A cold resolve settled over me. Before, we fought the Insects because we had to. Now it was a Blood Feud. We would do whatever we had to to destroy them. Completely.

I suddenly realized how long we had been hovering there inactive. The other Commander had maintained a respectful silence while we absorbed the shock of the news.

"Commander!" I beamed quietly.

"Yes?"

"We have gathered much data on the Enemy vital to the Empire and to this attack. Request permission for my second-in-command to rendezvous with the flagship as soon as possible to pass this information on for the Planetary Commander's consideration."

"Rahm," Zur's voice came to me. "I——"

"You'll follow the orders given you!" I snapped back, interrupting his protest. "Well, Commander?"

"Permission granted. I will relay the request and obtain data on an accelerated rendezvous point."

"I would further request permission to lead the balance of my force in attacking the Leapers."

"Also granted. Proceed at your own discretion."

"On my lead. . . . Ready . . . three . . . two . . ."

We wheeled our flyers and dove on the grasslands. I took them in low, dangerously low. We had to swerve around bushes as we ranged back and forth, pursuing and burning Leapers as we found them.

The Black Swamps destroyed! I signaled the team for another run. There was a frenzy to our attack above and beyond that displayed by the other teams. Unlike them, we knew we were working against a time limit. We wanted to kill as many of the hated Bugs as we could before Zur reached the flagship. We knew once our information reached the Planetary Commander, the mission would be aborted. By our analysis of the data we had gathered during our stay on the Planet, there was no chance that this type of attack would succeed against the Leapers.

CHAPTER
- 13 -

". . . having a highly developed telescoping oviposition situated at the indicated point on the diagram."

The Planetary Commander paused as lights flashed on the Leaper anatomy diagram on the wall-sized View Screen behind him.

We were in the main briefing room of the fleet's flagship. I and my teammates were arrayed along the walls at the front of the room on either side of the View Screen, heroes on display. The Planetary Commander was completing an unenviable task, that of explaining to the Commanders of the fleet why the mission had been aborted so soon after its onset.

"In the absence of any evidence of egg beds or central nests, we had assumed that either the Leapers bore their offspring live, or that the eggs were carried internally until mature, so that they hatched soon after being laid. If this had been true, our plan of a surface attack to wipe out all existing Leapers would have been a viable tactic."

He paused to look at my team.

"The firsthand experience of Commander Rahm and his team has proved this assumption is incorrect. The Leapers lay their eggs singly and buried deep in the earth. The exact time required for an egg to mature and hatch is currently unknown, but it is far in excess of a year. There is even a possibility that they lay dormant until triggered by a specific telepathed command from an adult."

He looked directly at the assembled Commanders.

"This means that if we succeeded in eliminating every living Enemy, that the eggs would remain, hatching at unknown intervals over an indefinite period. The only current possibility for combating this would be to establish a large standing garrison to constantly hunt the new hatchlings before they could lay more eggs. Even if this tactic could succeed, we are not equipped on this mission to establish such a garrison. As such, it is my decision as Planetary Commander to suspend action until such time as an effective plan can be formulated. This decision has been supported by the High Command, and orders to that effect are currently being relayed to the other fleets engaged in similar attacks.

"Finally, we are fortunate that our casualty estimates were for very light losses on this mission. Consequently, relatively few Tzen will have to be stranded on this planet. We will be able to leave them ample supplies and weapons to ensure their survival until our return. We have been assured by the High Command that space for them on the next return flight will be planned for, giving them a very high probability for rejoining the Empire."

He scanned the room slowly.

"Any questions?"

There were none. He turned to me.

"Are there any comments you would wish to add, Commander?"

I moved to take his place in front of the assembly.

"I would call the assembled Commanders' attention to the great assistance my second-in-command, Zur, rendered in the gathering of the data you have been given as well as in the overall survival of the team. This was to a large part due to his earlier training in the Scientists' caste. I would suggest to the Commanders that they recall this in the future if their Warrior's pride prompts them to refuse the service of a Warrior who was not raised in the Warriors' caste. I will further be submitting a recommendation to High Command that the Warrior caste's training program be expanded to include rudimentary Scientist training, and that information discs containing data about the Enemy and the target planet be made a mandatory part of each Warrior's equipment when undertaking a mission."

I turned and looked at Ssah before continuing.

"Further, I would publicly commend the action of Ssah. Her rapid analysis and reaction to a specific situation saved the lives of half the team and ensured our survival to deliver our report to the Empire."

With that I turned to the Planetary Commander.

"I feel that with our participation in this meeting, our part of this mission is completed. At this point I wish to formally and publicly decry one of my team, specifically Ssah. Her lack of action, her failure to save a teammate in a fatal situation, her constant endangering of the team with her self-centered drive for power—all contribute to my thoughts when I state that I find her conduct intolerable and unworthy of a Tzen, much less a Warrior. I call upon the assembled Commanders to witness my formal accusation of ineffectiveness of my teammate Ssah."

The Planetary Commander looked at Ssah.

"Ssah, do you wish to reply at this time?"

"I deny the charges leveled at me by Commander Rahm. Further, I would lodge countercharge that the Commander himself created the situations he described by his failure to provide firm leadership and his inability to issue clear and definitive orders."

The Planetary Commander turned to me once more.

"Rahm, do you wish this matter settled in a Court of Warriors or by personal combat?"

"Personal combat."

"Choice of weapons?"

"Dueling sticks."

"Will you represent yourself or appoint a champion?"

I had given long thought to this question, knowing it would be asked. While I was sure either Zur or Kor would be willing to serve as my champion and would doubtless have a better chance of victory, this duel I wanted to fight myself.

"I will represent myself."

He turned to Ssah.

"Ssah?"

"The conditions set forth by Rahm are satisfactory to me. I will also represent myself."

"Very well. You will meet in precisely one hour. A proper site will be arranged, and the information will be passed to you. I will officiate at the duel myself.

Thus it was that an hour later I was standing in one of the flight team bays waiting to face Ssah. I stood with dueling stick in hand, facing the wall with my head down and my back to the room as is prescribed by Tzen dueling etiquette.

A Tzen dueling stick is a deceptively simple weapon. Assembled, it is merely a metal rod one and a half inches in diameter and roughly four feet long, with a tapered point on one end. It was composed of several sections that fitted into each other, allowing it to be dismantled and carried in a pouch. It was in this ability to dismantle the weapon that its subtlety began to be hinted at.

Although it was primarily a thrusting weapon, there were many ways it could be used. It could be held one-handed like a sword, held two-handed like a short staff, or thrown like a javelin. By removing several sections and holding them in the other hand, it could actually be handled as two weapons. Although the possible combinations were finite, the arguments between Tzen as to what was the most effective manner of using it were not.

We waited with backs to each other and heads lowered to reduce the temptation of sneaking a look at our opponent's preparations. You were not to know what tactic you faced until you actually faced it.

"Ready!" As challenger, I replied first.

"Ready!" came Ssah's voice from the far end of the room.

"Turn and face your opponent!"

We did, and the Planetary Commander left, shutting the door behind him. His job was done. He had ensured that neither of us had brought extra weapons or assistants to the duel or had taken advantage of our opponent's exposed back during the waiting period. From here on it was up to us.

Ssah had retained the pointed section of her stick and assembled the other sections into one long rod, thus giving herself a staff and dagger combination.

I had correctly anticipated both her double weapon move and her implied intent for a close battle. I had divided my own stick into two equal lengths, giving myself two short sticks, one with a point.

I began to move toward her warily. Instead of advancing to meet me, she moved sideways to a wall. I hesitated, puzzling over her tactic, and in that moment of hesitation she sprang up onto one of the wall walkways and stood looking at me expectantly.

I considered her position. Obviously she wished to fight in an area where the footing would be restricted, as well as the space in which to swing a weapon. She stood facing along the walkway, her dagger between her and the wall, her staff free to swing.

I accepted the challenge and moved to the other end of the walkway. As I approached her, I switched hands with my weapons so that the pointed stick would be between me and the wall and the blunt stick would be on the outside.

We eyed each other, neither willing to make the first move. I was counting on her youth and recklessness to goad her into action, and I was right.

She sprang forward, aiming an overhead blow at my head with her staff. I blocked it with my blunt stick, bringing my arm across my body for a backhand block, at the same time thrusting for her chest with my pointed stick. A split second behind the thrust, I snapped a backhand blow at her head with my blunt stick. She parried the lunge with her staff while ducking under the blow at her head, then jabbed at my knee with her staff.

The move caught me off guard. I had not expected her to thrust with the blunt staff. The attack landed, and even though there was no point, there was sufficient power behind the jab to cause my knee to explode in pain.

I backpedaled, clumsily, striking at her extended arm with my blunt stick. She avoided it easily, but it achieved the results I desired. It kept her from immediately following up on her advantage.

I was in trouble. My injured knee would seriously impair my footwork in a terrain where footwork was already restricted.

I braced myself for her next attack, then realized she was waiting patiently at a distance for me to make my next move. She was going to make me carry the battle to her, forcing me into additional movement on my already injured knee.

I considered retreating back to the floor of the bay, but realized that if I attempted it she would worry me with small attacks every step of the way, wearing me down and perhaps finishing the fight before I reached solid footing.

I debated jumping for the floor, but decided against it. The heavy impact of landing might injure my leg further. I would simply have to fight this her way.

I moved forward slowly and was surprised to see she stood her ground. I had been expecting her to retreat before my advance, forcing me into additional movement. I decided on a desperate tactic to settle the fight before it occurred to her to turn it into a foot race. I deliberately advanced within range of her staff, hoping to bait her into trying a long attack where I could attempt to wrest the staff from her grip.

She didn't take the bait. Instead, she gave a small hop and jumped off the walkway. The move surprised me so that I didn't see her twirling until it was too late. She twisted her body around in a neat circle and used the centrifugal force to make a whip-strike at my leg with her staff as she fell.

Because it came from a very low angle, I had no opportunity to block it. The staff smashed into my injured knee, and I felt my leg buckle. I fought for balance, lost it, and started to fall. At the last instant I glimpsed Ssah waiting below with her dagger upraised, and used my good leg to propel myself out off the walkway, turning my fall into a headlong dive.

I didn't have time to roll, and crashed into the floor with stunning force, taking the full impact on my head and arms. I was in pain, but didn't have time to recover. I knew Ssah was rushing on my fallen body, dagger ready to finish me before I could regain my feet.

I didn't try to regain my feet. Instead I rolled and thrust blindly up and backward with my pointed stick, aiming at a point between where I had landed and where I had last seen Ssah.

She was there, in mid-air, dagger poised. My weapon took her in the throat, and I felt the shock of the impact all the way to my shoulder. I released my hold on the weapon and rolled away as she crashed to the floor.

She tried to rise, my stick protruding from both sides of her throat. She turned hate-filled eyes in my direction, but I remained passively at a distance. Finally, the eyes glazed and she sank forward.

I waited for several minutes before moving. Then, satisfied that she was indeed dead, I limped painfully to the door and let myself out into the corridor.

The Planetary Commander was waiting there.

"It is finished," I told him.

He nodded and began sealing the door. When he was finished, he pressed a button on the wall, and we both listened as the bay floor opened, dropping Ssah's body to the planet below.

In this, at least, she and I had agreed before the duel began. Whichever of us emerged triumphant would dispose of the other's body in this manner. Normally, when possible, Tzen preferred to be buried in the slime of the Black Swamps, where their decomposing bodies would remingle with the mud and water from which our species first evolved.

The Insects had ended that. Their ships had dropped swarms of the Aquatics on the swamps. The Aquatics were the only omnivorous members of the Coalition, and they bred abnormally fast, even for insects.

The Black Swamps were gone now, denuded and lifeless after the devastating assault. As such, we simply disposed of Ssah's body in the most convenient manner. With the Black Swamps gone, it really didn't matter where our corpses went.

BOOK TWO

BOOK TWO

CHAPTER
-1-

I waited.

Perhaps for the first time I began to appreciate the difficulties of command. Unlike a soldier of the ranks or a flight commander, the problem is not how to perform the tasks ordered by your superiors. Rather, it is how to occupy periods of inactivity while waiting for your subordinate to carry out your orders. As a Tzen, this is particularly difficult for me. Prior to accepting this assignment, I had never experienced the phenomenon of leisure time. I was either fighting, training, or sleeping. I was not accustomed to doing nothing. It was not a manner of passing time I found favorable. It was not efficient.

Logically, however, I had no choice. I had been awake for several days finalizing plans with Krah, the ship's commander. Now that that planning was complete, I had given orders to awaken the section leaders of the expeditionary force for their final briefing. This had been done, but I found I had underestimated the time necessary for them to become coherent after prolonged deep sleep. This was clearly an oversight on my part. I should have recalled my own recovery period and planned accordingly. I hadn't, but I would not waste energy berating myself for the error. I would simply note it to ensure against its reoccurrence.

I waited.

I could have spent the time with Krah, but had decided against it. She was, of course, a Technician. I have found that Technicians as a caste are far more talkative than the Warriors. Since my awakening, she had been trying to draw me into conversation about the mission, and my failure to respond had only caused her to redouble her efforts.

As an effort to avoid potential friction with her, therefore, I elected to wait alone. In my opinion, Krah had as much information on the mission as was necessary to perform her duties. Explanation or discussion beyond that would be inefficient.

Horc entered the conference room and seated himself without a word or salutation. Perhaps I was judging the Technicians harshly in using Krah as an example. As head of the Technicians' portion of the expeditionary force, Horc would probably be a more accurate model to draw conclusions from. The smallest of the force, he was a foot shorter than Krah's six feet, and displayed none of Krah's tendency toward long-windedness. Then again, he himself might be considered atypical. He had left a position coordinating and directing the work of fifty Technicians to accept this assignment as head of a three-Tzen field team. I would have to inquire into this inconsistency in logic when opportunity presented itself.

We both looked up as Tzu, head of the Scientists' team, entered. It suddenly occurred to me that recovery time might be directly proportional to size of the individual involved. Horc, who had recovered first, was only five feet high; whereas Tzu, who was seven feet high, had recovered ahead of the Warrior leaders. I made a mental note to broach the theorum to the Scientists. If it proved true, then staggering the arousal times could eliminate the unpleasant periods of inactivity waiting for individual recovery periods.

As head of the three-Tzen Scientist team, Tzu's job was perhaps the most difficult on the force, next to my own; yet she seemed to bear the burden surprisingly well. This would be the first attempt to her or any of her team—actually, for any of the Scientist caste—to perform their duties in a combat area. I wondered whether her composure indicated control, or simply a lack of comprehension of what they were undertaking.

Zur entered the room last, closely flanked by Mahz. The team he was heading consisted of a full count of six Warriors, allowing him to bring his second-in-command to the briefing. Had I been asked, I would have questioned Zur's choice of Mahz over Kor as his second-in-command. Zur had not asked my opinion, however, and as always, a team leader is allowed autonomy in matters concerning his team. As might have been expected, his choice, whatever logic had prompted it, proved a wise one. Mahz was performing far better in his new role than I would have expected.

I paused for a final check of the attending staff's condition. All eyes were clear, none seemed sluggish of action or otherwise indicated any lingering effects of recovery. We were ready to begin.

"Let me open by putting your minds at ease. There have been no changes to the plans I have previously discussed with you individually, nor is the situation any different than anticipated. This meeting is to serve as a final review of plans with all staff members present, that each will be aware of the others' duties and restrictions."

I paused for reactions. There were none. Again, I felt the uncomfortable weight of leadership. Apparently none had considered the possibility that anything would occur in any way other than the one I had planned.

"We are currently in orbit over what is believed to be the home Planet of the Coalition of Insects. Our mission is to investigate the existence of a natural enemy of the Leapers, and to seek a means by which said enemy can be transported to Leaper-occupied planets in sufficient quantity to curb or eradicate the Leaper population."

I considered yielding the floor to Tzu for the next portion of the briefing, but decided against it. I was in command of the mission, and would have to accustom myself to exerting authority over others, even those of other castes. I continued.

"The records of the First Ones in our possession regarding this planet are incomplete. The Coalition launched their attack before the reports were complete, and the very fact that the First Ones were overrun by that attack would cause us to question the validity of the observations that were made.

"What we do know is what we have observed on our own and other planets, that there exists a natural balance of population among living organisms. Every living thing has a natural enemy in its own environment. The High Command is therefore confident that somewhere on the planet below there exists a natural enemy to the Leapers which held their population in check prior to the First Ones' giving the Insects a means for spreading to other worlds. We must find it, devise a means to transport it, and above all, ensure that it is not more harmful to the Empire than the Leapers we seek to destroy.''

I realized I was becoming long-winded. Apparently my exposure to Krah had affected me more than I realized. I forced myself to continue with the agenda.

''To accomplish this mission, we have assembled a force consisting of members from all three castes in order to bring the full resources of the Empire to bear on the problem. We will work from a fortified base on the planet surface. While the ship will remain in orbit during the mission, the majority of the ship's crew will go into Deep Sleep shortly after our departure, leaving only a skeleton crew on watch. This means that while pickup is assured, we should not count on support from the ship once the mission is in progress.''

The next part of the briefing I did not look forward to. If I encountered any difficulties with the team, it would be here.

''The team of Scientists under Tzu will carry the bulk of the mission, investigating, analyzing, and submitting recommendations on the target organism. Horc, you and your team of Technicians are to maintain the base, as well as design and build any devices as may prove necessary for the success of the mission. The Warrior team under Zur, with Mahz as his subordinate, will be responsible for security throughout the mission, as well as providing firepower to implement whatever plan is ultimately settled on.''

''Question, Commander?''

''Yes, Tzu?'' It had been too much to hope the deliniation of authorities would go unchallenged.

''Under the current plan, the Warriors have responsibility for security, particularly in clearing the landing site. I would request that a Scientist be included in that landing party.''

''Explain?''

''The Warriors are well trained for dealing with immediate and obvious dangers. I feel, however, it would be in the best interests of the mission to have a Tzen trained in scientific observation to detect potential dangers in the landing site.''

''Zur will be leading the landing party and has been trained in scientific observation.''

''I would prefer a Tzen who had been successfully trained as a Scientist.''

I glanced at Zur, who remained impassive.

''Your point is well taken. We will include such a member.''

"Commander?"

"Yes, Horc." The Technicians were not going to go unheard either.

"I would request permission to awaken the technician team prior to the arousal of either the Scientists or the Warriors. This will enable them to complete our final check of the fortification unit prior to the dropping of the advance landing party, ensuring uninterrupted flow of the mission once it is set in motion."

I deliberately lowered my head a fraction as I replied. I wanted to stop this bickering in its early stages before it got out of hand.

"You have already submitted to me your time requirements for final equipment check. Simple comparison of those requirements with the time estimates of the Warriors for clearing the landing site shows you will have ample time to perform your duties after the landing party's descent."

"But what if our check discovers an equipment flaw?"

"Then I suggest you fix it. I trust your team's ability to effect repairs will remain consistent whether the other teams are awake or not."

"What I meant, Commander, is that if our check discloses equipment flaws requiring lengthy repairs, it could strand the landing party on the planet surface without support for a longer period of time than anticipated in the plan."

"I have been led to believe in my earlier discussions with the technicians' team that the probability of such an equipment flaw is so small as to be almost nonexistent. Has your estimation of that probability changed, Horc?"

"No, Commander."

"Then might I further remind you that half of the Warriors in the advance party were able to survive for over a year on an enemy-held planet without support—in fact, without power sources. I therefore maintain that if the unanticipated equipment failure occurs, they should be able to hold position for a few extra days."

"Very well."

"However, that does raise a question of my own. Tzu, does your request to send a Scientist with the advance landing party change your time requirements for final checks on your laboratory equipment?"

"No, Commander, that factor was included in our original calculation.

"However, while I have the floor," she continued, "might I reemphasize the standing order that no team members other than the Scientists should enter the laboratory area unless accompanied by a member of the Scientists' team. The equipment and chemicals there could prove dangerous to any unfamiliar with them.''

"The same order, of course, holds true for the Technicians' workshop," interjected Horc.

"Your comments are noted."

"Question, Commander," Zur interrupted.

"Yes, Zur?"

"You have said that the Warriors are to have supreme authority in matters regarding security. Does that authority extend to team members not of the Warriors' caste?"

What Zur was asking was if he had the right to kill a Scientist or Technician. I considered my reply for several moments before speaking.

"As in any mission, the first duty of each Tzen is to the Empire. Every Tzen, Warrior or not, has the right to move against another Tzen if in his or her opinion the actions of the other are jeopardizing the success of the mission. However, it should always be remembered that if such action is taken, the instigator should stand ready to justify that action before a Board of Inquiry."

I moved my head slightly to include all the staff members in my gaze.

"If reckless, careless, or independent action on the part of any member jeopardizes the mission, the offending Tzen should expect to suffer the consequences. I would not, however, want to see such action taken merely because a Tzen is from a different caste and therefore annoying. The possession of an extra sense is also not to be considered a capital offense.

"This is an experimental mission on several levels. First, it is the first joint field mission involving all three castes. Second, we have several team members from the new hatching who possess what is referred to as color-sight, an ability to see things the rest of us cannot. Finally, it is the first prolonged mission on the enemy's home planet.

"I will not attempt to minimize the difficulties inherent in the first two points. We are all painfully aware of the tensions involved in working with teammates whose logic priorities differ from our own. I freely admit I cannot comprehend the new color-sight and am therefore unaware of its potential advantages or difficulties. However, as a Warrior, I know we cannot fight a two-front war. We cannot fight the Insects and each other simultaneously. If we allow our personal differences to grow out of proportion, then the mission is doomed."

I looked around the assemblage once more.

"Are there any further questions?"

"I have one, Commander."

"Yes, Mahz?"

"If the Scientists are to carry the main brunt of the mission, why do we have a Warrior as mission commander?"

I was both annoyed and glad that the question had been asked.

"For lack of a better explanation, I would say that it's because that's how the orders were issued by the High Command."

"Commander," interrupted Tzu, "with your permission I might have a more solid explanation."

"Permission granted."

"The Commander is being generous in his analysis of the structure. The keyword of the Warrior caste is *efficiency*. When you appraise a problem or set priorities, you ask 'Is it efficient?' In the Scientists, our key word is *interesting*. Frequently our priorities are determined by what is the most interesting subject at hand to study. While this attitude is beneficial in the laboratory, it is not conducive to a specific field problem. It would be my contention that a Warrior was placed in command of this mission to ensure our efforts would be directed to the subject at hand. If not, we would be in danger of being distracted by a new rock formation or plant, whether or not it was pertinent to the immediate problem."

"While we are on the subject of avoiding distractions," interrupted Horc, "the Technicians also have a key word. That keyword is *workable*. It occurs to me that whatever fine points remain can be settled in the field. For the time being, we have a workable team and a workable plan. Shall we set it in motion?"

As none disagreed, we adjourned the meeting and began the mission.

CHAPTER
-2-

We waited in the fortification.

Waiting seemed to be a major portion of my new position. If I had been aware of this beforehand, I might not have accepted the promotion, not that I had really been given a choice. I was the only Commander who had successfully led a force for an extended period of time on an Insect-held planet, so I was the logical choice to head this mission. Still, I did not appreciate inactivity.

The fact that both the Scientists' and Technicians' teams were also sharing my inactivity did nothing to ease my discomfort. It was taking longer than anticipated to secure the landing area, but not enough time had elapsed to justify calling for a report. Final equipment checks were completed, and like myself, the other teams were impatient for action. However, impatient or not, Warriors or not, they were still Tzen, and they didn't complain.

We all lay on gel-cushions waiting for the "clear" signal from the landing party. I was using the cushion originally intended for the third Scientist, the one who had dropped with the landing party. I must admit I found this a marked improvement over the original plan.

By that plan, I had a choice of using the turret gunner's scantily padded seat or one of the vats of gel set aside for keeping specimens. Of the choices, I preferred the third. Any one of the three, however, was better than dropping with the advance team. The acrophobia I felt when being dropped in a flyer paled to insignificance when compared to what I experienced when forced to take part in a bubble drop. Even though it was proven bubble drops were currently the most efficient means to dispatch troops from orbit, my reactions to them were so strong that I would actually be incapacitated for several precious minutes upon landing. As such, our plans included my riding down with the fortification.

"Landing area secure, Commander." Zur's voice was beamed into my mind.

Involuntarily, I touched the booster headband as I replied.

"You exceeded your time estimates, Zur. Explain."

"We had to clear a nest of Wasps from the area."

"Wasps?"

"A different species than the Coalition Wasps we exterminated, but the Scientist, Zome, felt they constituted a potential threat."

"Understood. Anything else to report?"

"No, Commander. The homing beacon is in place and activated. We're ready to cover your descent."

"Very well. Stand by."

I shifted my focus to the Technicians.

"Horc!" I beamed.

"Yes, Commander," Horc's voice answered in my mind.

"The Advance Party has cleared the landing area and set the beacon. Take command of the launch land proceedings. Krah should be standing by for your orders."

"Acknowledged, Commander."

As the final step, I raised my voice to the Scientists in the immediate area.

"Stand by to descend. The advance party has confirmed a clear landing area."

"How long before departure, Commander?" asked Tzu.

"I would estimate—"

The fortification detached itself from the bottom of the transport and began its plunge to the planet's surface.

"I withdraw the question, Commander."

It was just as well. I was unsure of my ability to complete my answer. When I stated my preferences for mode of descent, it was not meant to imply that I enjoyed the prospect of being dropped in the fortification. Rather, I found it at best a meager improvement over being dropped in a bubble. Free-fall in any vehicle is not a pleasant sensation to me. I made a mental note to inquire into the possibility of having ships land to dispatch troops instead of dropping them from orbit.

I had been told the fortification was a masterpiece of design, and that if its performance on this mission was satisfactory, it would be used as a prototype for similar installations in the future. The main body of the installation is a half-globe, ten meters in diameter, surmounted by a turret gun bay. The half-globe was hollow, and bisected by a wall, dividing the Scientists' lab from the Technicians' workshop. This entire structure was in turn mounted on a disc twenty meters in diameter and three meters thick. This disc contained the Warriors' quarters and armory as well as providing cover for the immediate perimeter of the installation. I was also told it was aerodynamically unstable and had the glide pattern of a rock.

Our descent was described to me by Horc as "not quite a glide . . . more like a controlled fall." This afforded me little reassurance as we waited for impact. The only comforting fact I had to cling to was that the Technicians were also on board, which meant they at least had confidence in its design.

I felt the gel-cushion surge up against me, a pause, then another surge. I deduced from this that Horc was using exterior engines, probably similar to those that powered our flyers, to slow our descent. Its surges became more frequent and longer in duration until it became one uninterrupted pressure, almost as if we were in a one and a half gravity field.

I began to relax. I should have realized that the Scientists and Technicians were less accustomed to physical hardship than the Warriors. As such, the landing would be understandably softer than those I had experienced before. This illusion was shattered as we impacted with a bone-jarring, eye-flattening crash.

There was a moment of silence as we collected our shattered minds and bodies.

Tzu broke the silence.

"Commander," she began hesitantly.

"We've crashed!" interrupted Rahk. The second of the two Scientists on board, he was of the new Hatching, color-sighted, and outspoken. "Trust the Technicians to——"

"That will be enough, Rahk," Tzu said to stop her subordinate's tirade. "Your comments, Commander?"

Before I had time to answer, the hatch to the adjoining compartment opened and Ihr lurched into view. She was the junior member of the Technicians' team, also of the new Hatching, also outspoken.

"You might be interested to know," she informed us, "that according to the instruments, that was the softest landing this vehicle has achieved. If we had been allowed a bit more practice with the controls and time for a few polish modifications in design, we might have been able to set it down gently enough to conform to the delicate standards the other castes seem to require."

"Actually," I said before Rahk had a chance to respond, "the landing was well within our tolerance levels. Do not worry yourself about the Warriors' ability to withstand hardship, or the Scientists' either."

"Worrying about the comfort of the other castes is not one of my duties, Commander."

"Ihr!"

Even from the next compartment there was no mistaking the rebuff in Horc's voice.

"Horc asks," Ihr continued hastily, "that you remain stationary while we settle the fortification."

She disappeared before I could respond. Ihr was going to be a problem. Horc had warned me that his junior member did not like the other castes, and Warriors in particular, but I had not expected her feelings to be so obvious.

I stole a glance at the two Scientists to try to interpret their reactions. They were silent, but from the focus of their eyes I suspected they were communicating telepathically. Observing their respective postures, I surmised that Tzu was reprimanding Rahk for his earlier outburst. I hastily averted my eyes so as not to betray my awareness of the situation. Tzu was a Tzen. She could and would handle her own team.

We could hear the cold-beams mounted in the base of the fortification working as we began to settle. I directed my attention to the scene outside the dome, eager for my first glimpse of this new planet.

Even though I had not been enthusiastic over landing in this or any other free-fall vehicle, now that I was down, I could admit a certain admiration of its design. The dome afforded one-way visibility of the surrounding terrain. That is, we could see out, but nothing could see in. This could be a definite advantage in a hostile environment.

The fortification was sinking steadily. I could now see some of the area around us as well as view the activities of the advance party. Neither the Scientist Zome nor Zur were to be seen, but the bulk of the Warriors' team was in full sight, stationed at scattered intervals around the fortification. Weapons at the ready, they barely glanced at us. Instead, they scanned the sky and brush for any danger while we were in this vulnerable phase of our mission. Even though their deployment appeared random and haphazard, I saw Zur's handiwork in their arrangement. Zur did not approve of stationing guards at static, regular intervals. Rather, he positioned them as necessary to cover each other's blind spots, to leave no brush tangle or erosion gully uncovered. When Zur planned a defense, I knew I could relax . . . that is, as much as a Warrior ever relaxes.

I was mildly surprised to see Eehm, the third Technician, at work outside the fortification. She must have left the fortification as soon as it had touched down. Apparently Horc shared Zur's near fanatical obsession with effective deployment of troops. Eehm was busy unrolling the wires that were to be our outer perimeter alarm system. She was intent in her work, ignoring everything but the job at hand. This could be both good and bad. It was good because she was not allowing herself to be distracted, she wasn't worrying about doing the Warriors' job for them. It was bad because in Enemy terrain, no one can afford to completely ignore one's surroundings.

The sound of the cold-beams ceased. The upper surface of the disc was now level with the ground. The fortification was secure.

"We're not level!" Rahk was looking at a small instrument balanced on the floor next to his gel-cushion.

I didn't bother wondering what it was or where it came from. Scientists carry instruments the way Warriors carry weapons.

"I trust it will not seriously impair the performance of your duties?" I asked.

"We are used to working around the shortcomings of the Technicians," Tzu assured me.

"Commander!" Horc's head appeared in the hatch. "Could I see you a moment?"

He swept the Scientists with his eyes. If he noticed the instrument on the floor, he gave no indication.

"If you'll retain your places, we should be done in another few minutes."

He disappeared before they could respond. Technicians seem particularly skillful at timely retreats. I rose and followed him.

"Down here, Commander!" His voice came up to me from the armory.

I descended the ramp and found him bent over, unbolting a hatch in the floor.

"I see the Scientists didn't waste any time discovering we were out of level," he said, not looking up from his work.

"You heard?"

"It wasn't necessary to hear them. I saw the Q-Box on the floor."

"The what?"

"The Q-Box. The instrument they were using to check level. The Technicians built it for them, so of course they use it to criticize our work."

"Do you find the Scientists difficult to work with?"

"No worse than the Warriors." He paused in his labors to look at me directly. "You see, Commander, as a Warrior, you've been relatively isolated from the other castes. The Technicians, on the other hand, have to deal with both Scientists and Warriors as part of their normal work. Had I been asked, I would have said a Technician should head this mission if for no other reason than his ability to deal with the other castes."

He abruptly returned to his work. I was beginning to find the Technicians' habit of ending conversations before rebuttal vaguely annoying.

He lifted the hatch and set it aside. He stuck his head into the inky hole as his hand went to a mechanical box attached to his belt at the small of his back. The hiss and blinding light of a cold-beam filled the armory, startling me with its suddenness.

Horc grunted and pulled his head out of the hatch as the beam died.

"I was afraid of that. The number six beam is malfunctioning."

As he spoke, he detached the box from his belt and began adjusting dials and setting slides.

"Here, Commander," he said, handing me the box.

"When I give you the word, trip the far left switch."

"Me? What about Ihr?"

"She's busy dismantling the control panel. That's why we're using the remote unit. It's not difficult, Commander. Just trip the switch when I signal you."

With that he slid through the hatch and disappeared.

I felt immensely uncomfortable waiting there with the strange device in my hands. The myriad of dials and levers on its surface were completely foreign to me.

Taking care not to change my grip or touch any of the controls, I turned the unit over to examine it more closely.

My action was answered by a flash and hiss from below as the cold-beams activated.

For the first time in my career, I froze. Horc was still under the beams! My curiosity had triggered the box! I had killed one of my teammates!

As abruptly as they had started, the beams stopped. A heartbeat later, Horc slid out of the hole and began replacing the hatch lid.

"We are now level, Commander, and any Tzen that wishes to dispute it should—"

He broke off, looking at me for the first time.

"Is something wrong, Commander?"

I forced my voice to remain level.

"You didn't signal."

"Oh, that! No insubordination intended. The problem was not as difficult as I anticipated, so I flattened into a dead zone and triggered the beams manually. I was under the impression you were reluctant to handle the controls, so I did it myself."

"In the future, Horc," I intoned, "if you or any of your team set a plan of action, you would be well advised to follow it. We are in a Combat Zone, and failure to communicate could be disastrous."

"I'll remember that, Commander." He bent to finish his task.

I decided to let the matter drop. If I pursued it further, Horc might realize my anger was more from relief than from concern for proper procedure.

"If my usefulness here is over, I'll give the 'all clear' to the Scientists. They are probably most eager to begin their work."

"Of course, Commander."

I started for the ramp, only to be met halfway by Ihr.

"Commander, the advance party is trying to get your attention."

I hurried past her up the ramp. Now that I was not concentrating on Horc's work, I could detect Zur's signal.

"Rahm here, Zur," I beamed.

"Commander, we have a problem here which requires your attention."

I was about to tell him to wait while I passed the movement

permission on to the Scientists, then observed they were already moving about readying their lab for operation.

"Explain the nature of the problem."

I had visual contact with Zur even if he couldn't see me through the dome. He was standing in a small conference group that included him, Mahz, and the Scientist Zome.

"We have lost one of the Technicians."

CHAPTER
-3-

"How did the Technician die, Commander?"

"That is not necessary information for you to perform your duties, Commander." My head hurt from the prolonged use of the booster band. "Simply drop a replacement as soon as it is possible."

"I will have to deny your request, Commander," came Krah's voice in reply. "I do not have the personnel to spare."

"Perhaps you are right, Krah. Perhaps you should be more closely appraised of the situation." I realized I was starting to flatten my head in annoyance, which was a pointless gesture, as Krah was still in orbit above us and therefore unable to observe the gesture.

"The situation is this. I am in command of this mission, including the ship's personnel. In that capacity, I am not requesting, I am ordering you to drop a replacement for the dead Technician. Further, I happen to know you're overstaffed by two members. This was specifically planned by myself and the High Command. Do you know why?"

Krah did not answer, but I knew she was still listening, so I continued.

"It was planned this way so that if this very situation should arise, that I would be free to kill you in a duel and there would still be an extra Technician available. Realizing this, I would suggest you arrange to have the extra Technician dropped immediately.

Yielding to the logic of the situation will allow you to operate with one extra member in your crew. Failing to do so will not only mean the ship has to function at normal staffing, it will have to function without you. Do you agree? Or do you honestly feel you can beat a veteran Warrior Commander in a duel?''

There was a long silence before the reply came.

"I will select and drop a replacement immediately, Commander.''

"Very well. And Krah . . .''

"Yes, Commander.''

"I would suggest you choose the replacement carefully. If we are given a Technician who is either incompetent or overly difficult to work with, I would be forced to consider it an attempt on your part to sabotage the mission.''

"Understood, Commander. Krah out.''

I removed the booster band and surveyed the immediate terrain coldly. For all my officious arrogance in speaking with Krah, I was not pleased with the mission's progress. In my last assignment, I had lost only one Tzen in a year's time, even though we had crashed on a hostile planet. Now, despite our planning and equipment, we had lost a Tzen before we had even finished establishing the base camp.

I reviewed the incident for a trace of overconfidence.

The Technician, Eehm, had been laying the wires for the defense network. She had been so engrossed with her work, she had backed through a calf-high, meter-diameter patch of vegetation flagged by the Scientists as "unknown.''

Well, we knew about it now . . . or at least some things about it. The Scientists insisted it not be destroyed until they had an opportunity to examine and test it fully. What we did know about it was that when heavy contact was made with the stems, they shot out thorns that served as a fast-acting nerve poison, not unlike the wrist needle guns used by some of the Warriors.

Eehm had died with alarming speed, but not painlessly. She had not made a sound, however. Technician or not, careless or not, she was still a Tzen, and we were in Enemy-held territory.

I reviewed the situation once more. No, there was not overconfidence there, just carelessness. I considered telling Horc to warn the Technicians to be more careful, but decided against it. He had already been told, in far more convincing terms than I could ever achieve.

"Horc!" I beamed toward the fortification.

"Yes, Commander?"

"A replacement Technician will be dropped shortly. I want you to report to me immediately if he proves incapable."

"Very well, Commander. The defense wires are in place now, would you care to join me in inspecting them?"

I considered delegating the task to Zur. It would be a boring chore; and technically, as part of the defenses, it fell under his jurisdiction.

"Certainly. Do you have visual contact on my position?"

"I do. I'll join you shortly, Commander."

I had decided against delegation. Horc had specifically requested my participation in the inspection. It occurred to me this could be for one of two reasons. Horc was a Technician, and as such he might be sensitive to intercaste rivalries. If there were to be any criticism of the Technicians' work, he would prefer it come from me. This was a tacit acknowledgment of the impartiality of my position as Commander. He felt I would not find fault simply to make his team look bad, or at least that I would be less inclined to do so than the head of the Warriors' team. Then again, perhaps he simply wanted a conference.

He appeared, seeming to spring out of the ground by the now camouflaged fortification. Even though I knew its precise location, I was only barely able to detect it visually. I made a mental note to comment on it to Horc before our tour of the defenses was over.

"This way, Commander," he beamed.

I moved to his side and squatted. By looking closely, I could just make out the ultrafine wire running along the ground.

Without comment, he rose and began walking along the near invisible line. I followed, not even pretending to watch the wire. Erect, I couldn't see it, so contented myself with checking the pattern of its layout as we looped and twisted across the terrain.

The defense wires were still a marvel to me. They could be set to detect an object as small as a sand flea crossing their scanfield. Not only would they report the breach, they could feed back to the fortification the size, mass, and body temperature of the object, as well as the speed and direction of movement. Normally, this information would appear on a View Screen for a guard to analyze. If we came under attack, however, the flip of a lever would feed the data directly into the turret gun mounted atop the fortification. It, in turn, could automatically direct fire against the intruder, escalating as necessary until the danger was eliminated. In short, with the system in full operation, anything that moved within three hundred meters of the fortification would be eliminated.

This was a vast improvement over our last stay on an occupied planet.

"Commander!"

"Yes, Horc?" I beamed back.

"Would you have been offended if I had asked Zur to conduct this inspection?"

"No. I would have delegated it to him except for the fact that you made your request to me."

"I would have approached him directly, but I felt you might interpret it as bypassing your authority."

So much for my theories.

"Might I suggest that we return to the fortification and let you and Zur conduct the inspection, as we both agree it is more logical?"

"Agreed, Commander."

"One question, Horc. Is the system operational?"

"It is."

"In that case," I spoke aloud for the first time, "I feel the area is secure enough for open communication."

He cocked his head at me quizzically.

"Do you not require approval from the Warriors before accepting the system?"

"Horc, you are as much a Tzen as any Warrior. Your life depends on the reliability of this system as much as ours does, perhaps more. If you feel the system is adequate, it is all the assurance I need. The inspection by the Warriors is more a token courtesy between castes than a required clearance."

He was silent for a few moments.

"I am finally beginning to realize, Commander," he said at last, "why you were chosen to lead this expedition."

I did not know what reply to make to this statement, so I changed the subject.

"I have been meaning to comment on the camouflaged design of the fortification, Horc. Could you explain to me, in terms a Warrior can understand, how you achieved the effect?"

"It is simply another application of flexi-steel, the same material we use on the wings of your flyer. All surfaces of the fortification which are exposed when it is entrenched are actually double-layered. The outer layer is flexi-steel, which we allow to contract, forming the buckles, ridges, and uneven surfaces which blend with the surrounding terrain; add a mock-up of a tree stump with exposed roots to hide the turret gun, and you have your camouflage."

''And we can still see out from inside?''

''Yes.''

''How do you keep the uneven outer surface from distorting the view?''

He thought for a few moments.

''I could try to explain, but I'm afraid I would have to use some rather specialized technical terms.''

''In that case, I withdraw the question. As long as it works, you'll have no complaints from me. Overall, it is the most undetectable job of camouflaging I have ever seen, or *not* seen, to be accurate.''

''Perhaps.''

Something in his voice caught my attention.

''You sound dissatisfied. Is there some flaw I am unaware of?''

''I'm not sure,'' he replied. ''I wanted more information before I brought it to your attention, but perhaps it is better you were appraised of the situation immediately. It has to do with a comment made by one of our color-sighted team members.

''Would that be Hif, or Sirk?'' I interrupted.

''Hif; but I checked her observations with Sirk, who concurred. It seems he had also noticed the problem, but was reluctant to infringe on the Technicians' domain.''

''What was their observation?''

''According to them, the fortification does not match the surrounding terrain.''

I studied the fortification before replying.

''Normally, I would say they were incorrect based on my own observations. I must admit, however, I do not fully comprehend this 'color-sight' the new Hatching has.''

''Neither does anyone else, as far as I can discover. It's a genetic experiment the Scientists are trying, based on some of the notes found from the First Ones. We're supposed to find out in the field if it has any practical value to the Empire.''

''But what is it?''

''It lets them see things we can't. . . . Well, to be accurate, it lets them see the same things we see, but in a different way.''

''That's what I have difficulty understanding.''

''Perhaps I can clarify it a bit by describing a demonstration I once witnessed,'' suggested Horc.

''Three blocks were placed on a table; one dark, the other two noticeably lighter. We were asked if we could distinguish between the three blocks. To a Tzen, all the witnesses replied that while one block was dark, the other two were identical. Then a color-sighted Tzen was brought into the room and asked the same question. He replied that each block was a different color, the dark one was what he called 'dirt', and the other two were 'sky' and 'leaf' respectively.''

"I fail to see what that proves," I interrupted.

"There's more," he continued. "The demonstrator then picked up the light block which had been designated 'sky' and marked its bottom with an 'x.' The color-sighted Tzen was then told to shut his eyes, and the blocks rearranged. Time and time again, he was able to identify the marked block, even though the 'x' side was down.''

"Did he truly shut his eyes?"

"Sometimes he was asked to leave the room while the witnesses rearranged the blocks. Still he was able to find the 'sky' block unerringly. He could see something about that block that we could not.''

I thought about this.

"What good is such an ability to the Empire?"

"That is one of the things we are supposed to be testing on this mission, and we may have found our first example. The two color-sighted members claim our fortification is a different color than the terrain, that the fortification is 'steel' while the rocks around it are 'sand.' According to them, it will be immediately obvious to any color-sighted creature that comes across it.''

Again I lapsed into thoughtful silence.

"Does anyone know," I asked finally, "if the Insects are color-sighted?''

"Not that I know of. You might ask the Scientists, but I don't think they even know what to look for.''

"In that case, I feel the matter should take top priority. Pass the word to Hif and Sirk to report to me immediately. Also ask Tzu to join us. Finally, inform Zur to place his Warriors on full alert until I've had an opportunity to consult with him.''

"Yes, Commander, but . . .''

"What?''

"Do you feel it wise to act with so little information?''

"Horc, there are thirteen of us outnumbered by a factor of several million to one by the Enemy. We lack information and we must act immediately, not in spite of that, but because of that. We need some answers and we need them fast. If we don't get them, we may well have to abandon the fortification.''

CHAPTER
-4-

The resolution of the matter of whether or not the Leapers were color-sighted was so quick and simple it was almost anti-climactic. We could take no credit for the discovery. As some-times happens in a combat area, the solution presented itself, and we merely capitalized on it.

We had not yet convened our meeting, when the defense web reported a small pack of twenty Leapers entering the area. Orders were immediately beamed to the team members outside the fortification, appraising them of the situation and instructing them to take cover. The rest of us gathered in the Technicians' side of the dome and watched, with Zur personally handling the turret guns.

The pack passed within ten meters, moving slowly, trying to flush game. There was a bad moment when we realized two of our teammates were directly in their path, but beamed warnings enabled them to shift position long before they were detected.

We tracked the pack as long as we could visually, then by the Defense Net when they had passed out of our field of vision. At no time did they give any indication of having noticed our fortification.

There was some debate as to whether their passing through the area was happenstance, or if our drop had been observed and they were actually searching for us. One point we were all in agreement on, however—the Leapers, at least, were not color-sighted. Hif and Sirk assured us that our position would be glaringly apparent to any color-sighted beast, yet we had gone undetected.

The subject of color would still have to be looked into, but for the time being it was removed from top priority status.

This, however, triggered another debate as to what was to take top priority instead. The Scientists, having now had their first view of Leapers in their native habitat, were eager to begin work.

"We should have a team trailing that pack," insisted Tzu. "The more firsthand information we can accumulate, the faster we can complete the mission."

"Not until we have completed our surveys of the immediate area. It was explained to you in our briefings, Tzu, that we will not engage in Scientific expeditions until our mapping scouts have completed their work."

"Come now, Commander, this is not the Empire's first contact with this planet. We have undertaken three major campaigns: against the Wasps, against the Aquatics, and the aborted campaign against the Leapers. Surely we have sufficient geographic notations in our data files to proceed."

"It is true we have information in our files, Tzu," I stated. "Outdated information. As Commander I will not risk the mission or the lives of the individuals on the team needlessly, and that includes relying on outdated information when current data is readily attainable."

"But my team is impatient to get to work. We do not feel inactivity is a means of serving the Empire."

"Nor does anyone else, yet it seems inactivity is something we must all learn to deal with on this mission. As a possible relief, I would suggest you put your team to work checking the unidentified flora within the established defense net. We have already lost one team member to a plant your team did not have time to check."

It was admittedly unfair criticism, but Tzu seemed insensitive to it.

"Very well, Commander. But I will again stress the importance of field expeditions at the earliest possible time. Firsthand observation will enable us to direct our research to the most promising candidates, rather than attempting to study everything and hope to find our target by random chance."

I left her then, as there was nothing else to say on the subject. I sought out Horc, at work in the Technicians' lab. I could have beamed contact with him; but for this discussion, I wanted personal interface.

"Is the View Screen ready yet, Horc?" I queried.

"Shortly, Commander," he replied, not looking up from his labors. "The arm-units are complete, if you wish to distribute them."

"I'll see that it's taken care of. Is the new Technician acceptable?"

"Krahn? Quite acceptable, Commander. She'll be performing at less than peak efficiency, but that would be expected of any team member introduced at this late point in the mission."

He continued working without pause. I hesitated, casting about for a tactful manner in which to broach the next subject. Failing to find one, I simply took the approach that was most efficient.

"If I could have your undivided attention for a moment, Horc, there is a matter I would like to discuss with you."

"Certainly, Commander."

He set aside his instruments and met my gaze directly. Faced by this intent focus, I was suddenly ill-at-ease.

"Horc, you lost a team member today. Situations were such at the time I was unable to have private words with you on the matter. Though perhaps excusable, this was still negligence on my part as a Commander. To correct that situation, I have now set aside time to discuss the matter. Has the incident upset you or your team in any way? Should we make allowances for recovery time?"

"No, Commander. Aside from the extra time to brief the new team member which I have already noted to you, we require no special consideration."

"I am speaking here of your feelings in total, Horc. I wish to be informed if you harbor any resentment towards the Warriors' team for failing to provide sufficient protection, or——"

"Allow me to explain a little about the Technicians, Commander," interrupted Horc. "And perhaps it will clarify our position. Death is no more a stranger to the Technicians than it is to the Warriors, or, I suspect, the Scientists. Workshop accidents are a common occurrence, and they are frequently fatal. It is our job currently to find practical and safe applications for alien concepts and machinery, and in the process many are injured or killed. As an example, were you aware we lost over two hundred Technicians perfecting the design of the flyers?"

"No, I wasn't," I admitted.

"Few outside our caste are. Mind you, I'm not complaining. It's our duty, just as fighting the Enemy is yours. I am merely illustrating that this is not the first time we've lost a teammate. The main difference between your situation and ours is that we've never developed a combat zone comradery."

"A what?"

"A combat zone comradery. Unlike the Warriors, we are seldom in a position of working with teammates who have saved our lives. I would imagine that because of that, the Warriors feel a certain obligation to each other."

"The last Warrior who saved my life in battle was named Ssah. I killed her in a duel immediately after the mission was completed."

"I see," he said, apparently taken aback. "Perhaps I have overestimated my personal theories, and in doing so underestimated the Warriors."

"In the Warriors we react negatively to needless death, particularly if it was caused by carelessness or incompetence."

"In that, you are not unlike the Technicians. To reply to your original question, if there was any carelessness involved in Eehm's death, it was her own. As such, we neither mourn her passing, nor harbor any grudges against the Warriors."

"Very well. Then we will consider the subject closed. I apologize for distracting you from your work, but I wanted to deal with the matter as soon as possible."

"No damage done, Commander. We are well ahead of schedule on the View Screen. If you wish to pass the word to ready the flyers, the screen should be ready by the time they can take off."

"Excellent. The Scientists have been anxious to proceed with the mission."

"If I might comment, Commander?"

"Proceed."

"We Technicians have had more contact with the Scientists than the Warriors. They are a pushy lot given opportunity, and frequently short-sighted for all their wisdom. Though I expressed my feelings that I felt a Technician should lead this mission, I would add to that the observation that in lieu of a Technician, I feel much more confident of the success of the mission with a Warrior in command than I would with a Scientist in charge. In my opinion, you should trust your judgement over theirs."

"I had planned to, Horc, but I will keep your comments in mind."

I strapped one of the arm-units on, and, picking up two more, went looking for Zur. Discussion was fine, but it was time we got this mission underway.

Zur and I stood watching as the two flyers departed. Arm-units had now been issued to all team members, and as promised the View Screen was functional.

Mahz and Vahr were piloting the craft. I would have sent Kor instead of Vahr, but Vahr was a competent Warrior and a veteran of the Wasp campaign, and Kor was a valuable asset to fortification defenses.

"Shall we watch their progress at the View Screen, Commander?" suggested Zur.

Even though our arm-units could monitor all data fed to the View Screen, the larger screen would afford better monitoring. I signaled my agreement by starting for the fortification.

The flyers we had used in the Wasp campaign seemed crude when compared to the craft Mahz and Vahr were piloting. The new flyers had been modified to allow vertical takeoff and landing, a feature that would have negated the crash landing and jury-rig drop takeoff of our last mission. More important for the immediate assignment, the new flyers were each outfitted with three view-input units. These would scan the terrain the fliers passed over and feed the images directly back into the View Screen data banks for storage and/or immediate viewing. With proper cuing, the View Screen arm-units could then either display the entire area or give a close-up of a specific portion. This gave each member instant access to a three-dimensional pictoral map of our terrain once the data was input.

Horc and Tzu were already at the View Screen when Zur and I arrived. That was one of the effortless parts of being a Tzen Commander. If something really important was happening, you seldom had to call a meeting. The staff would gravitate to the key point on their own.

The four of us watched silently as the map formed on the View Screen. So far it was identical with our existing data, but it was good to have it confirmed.

"Horc!" I said, breaking the silence.

"Yes, Commander?"

"This ravine." I tapped the appropriate portion of the screen. "We're going to need some way of getting across it.

"An arc bridge?"

"A cable would be better. That and a jump ramp for skimmers. What we want is something we can cross, but the Leapers can't."

"Understood, Commander. We'll start on it as soon as we can get a Technician there for a firsthand look."

"Would additional close-ups help?"

"It would be advantageous."

I slipped on my booster band.

"Mahz!" I beamed.

"Yes, Commander!"

"The ravine you're approaching . . . after you've completed your preliminary sweep we would like some close-ups of the rim."

"Confirmed, Commander!"

As I started to remove the band, I noticed Tzu was checking something on her arm-unit.

"Something wrong, Tzu?"

"I'm not sure, Commander, but it is definitely interesting. Do you see those rock formations there . . . and there?"

"The large rocks with the small ones clustered about?"

"That's right. Do you notice anything strange about them?"

I studied them for a few moments.

"They seem to have a similar configuration. Each one is a large rock surrounded by brush and small rocks. Why? Are they some kind of marker?"

"I'm not sure, but look at this."

She extended her arm to share her arm-unit.

"This is the same area, but displaying data from the last campaign. The formations are there, but a different number of them, and in different locations."

I compared the display on her arm-unit with the display on the View Screen. She was right. The configuration of the formation had definitely changed.

"Do you have similar data from the other two campaigns?" I asked.

She cued an index list and studied it.

"No data from the campaign against the Aquatics . . . They were concentrating on the bodies of water then . . . but . . . yes, here it is."

She fed a cue into the arm-unit and extended again.

"This is the same area during the campaign against the Wasps."

Together we studied it. The rock formations on this display

were arrayed differently than on either of the others we had studied.

"Zur!"

"Yes, Commander."

"Take a look at this."

By the time he reached us, I had cued my arm-unit for the Leaper campaign display so we had all three examples in view.

"Look at these rock formations. They seem to be——"

"Commander!"

Mahz's voice beamed into my head, interrupting my discussion.

"Rahm here, Mahz."

"Coming onto your screen now! Request immediate instructions!"

"Commander!" Horc called.

"Coming! Tzu, Zur!"

We crowded around the View Screen. There, coming into view was a large anthill.

The Ants! The last members of the Coalition after the Leapers! We knew they would be present on this planet, but none of our data had indicated their activity in this area. This hill was a new installation, constructed since our last campaign. It was less than eight kilometers from our fortification!

CHAPTER
- 5 -

The discovery of the anthill understandably threw our team into a bit of a turmoil.

Word was passed to all team members as Alert status immediately went into effect. Mahz and Vahr, however, were ordered to finish their survey sweep as originally planned. Whatever our future plan would be, we would require information on the terrain around us.

Zur placed Kor in temporary command of the defense forces and joined the rest of the staff in our emergency planning session.

Tzu, speaking for the Scientists, had very strong opinions, not only on the subject at hand, but also on how it was to be discussed. I was beginning to expect this.

"But, Commander, the course of action we have to recommend is the only logical approach to this situation."

"Recommendations for courses of action and discussion of those recommendations will take place after we have had the necessary informational reports from the staff."

"If I might point out, Commander, time is of the utmost importance in this situation," she argued, her tail lashing impatiently.

"I agree. Far too important to waste arguing over meeting procedures."

"But——"

"And I will further point out that had we followed your initial

111

time-sensitive recommendations and pursued the Leapers, without a mapping sweep, we would have either missed the anthill completely or blundered into it unawares. Now I will again suggest you give your portion of the information report and save your valuable recommendations for later.''

"Very well, Commander. How detailed a report do you wish?''

"Summary only. As you have pointed out, time is of the essence. Address specifically those behavioral points pertinent to the immediate situation.''

She was silent for a few moments, organizing her thoughts; then she began.

"The Ants are the fourth species of the Coalition of Insects. According to the notes of the First Ones, confirmed by our own studies, they are the most intelligent members of the Coalition and hence the most dangerous. They were rated as being the most responsive to training in the operation of simple mechanical devices, and possess a definite-ordered society. In all probability, they were the masterminds behind the initial formation of the Coalition.''

"Question.''

"Yes, Horc.''

"Are they still operating machines, and if so, of what level complexity?''

"Unknown. They are credited with being able to pilot primitive starships after the First Ones modified the controls for them, and the continued spread of the Insects through the Universe indicates some machinery is still being utilized. However, whether these are the original ships or if improvements have been made is unknown. This is why the Scientists recommend that we—''

She broke off as I caught her eye and flattened my head. For a moment she held my gaze, then continued.

"Although they will forage for food on the surface of the land, they are primarily burrowing creatures. The bulk of their civilization is maintained in subterranean caves and caverns interconnected by a series of tunnels. These colony nests may extend over a radius of up to twenty kilometers with installations to a depth of two kilometers.''

"Physically, they are a bit larger than the Leapers, often reaching five meters in length. Even though it might be suspected they have poor eyesight from their underground existence, they seem to forage on the surface both day and night. Their primary natural weapon is a set of powerful mandibles, and they are reputed to be strong, vicious, and tenacious fighters.''

"You mentioned a civilization," I inserted. "What is known about that?"

"What little is known is unconfirmed. It is not unlike our own, having both Hunter and Constructor castes. The main difference would seem to be that they also have a Reproducer caste. However, this is all information from the First Ones."

"What are their vulnerabilities, physically?"

"Unknown, Zur; from their appearance we would postulate a similar physiology to the Wasps. But that is, at best, a guess."

"How fast do they dig their tunnels?" asked Horc.

"Unknown."

"How many Ants in a nest?" asked Zur.

"Unknown. It is believed to be in the thousands."

"Is the anthill we viewed a new nest, or a new outlet for an old colony?"

"Unknown, Commander."

There was a long moment of silence.

"If there are no further questions, . . ." I began.

"There is one more bit of information which could be important to our planning, Commander."

"Proceed, Tzu."

"They possess some method of passing information among themselves. Whether this is done by direct contact, by telepathy, or even genetically is unknown. This characteristic of the Ants defied even the First Ones' attempts to explain."

The silence was longer this time as we digested the information.

"Horc," I said finally, "what does the presence of the Ants mean to the effectiveness of our Defense Network?"

"The Network was designed to detect and destroy surface creatures such as the Leapers. While it will still be effective against surface hunters, it will be totally ineffective against burrowing," he replied.

"Will your team be able to devise an effective defense?"

"There are two possibilities we can explore. One would be a device to detect sounds of burrowing. The other would be a machine to locate subterranean hollow points. It is doubtful, however, that they would be effective to a depth of two kilometers. With the equipment we have on hand, we couldn't guarantee coverage much deeper than a quarter kilometer, half a kilometer maximum."

"How long until the devices could be in place?"

"We would have to design them before I could give you an

accurate appraisal of construction and installation time. I could have those estimates ready by this time tomorrow, however."

"Very well, Zur, what is your appraisal of our Warrior's defensive ability."

Zur did not hesitate, but plunged into his analysis.

"The campaign against the Wasps has given us undisputed air supremacy. The campaign against the Aquatics has guaranteed we will not have to fight for water. That leaves the Surface Packs, the Leapers, the Subterraneans and the Ants to present threats. As we are only required to fight a defensive holding campaign as opposed to a counterstroke, I am confident the Warriors will be able to hold the fortification against any surface or frontal attack up to and including a massed frontal assault. As to the possibility of a subterranean burrowing attack, we must rely on such devices as the Technicians are able to improvise for our defense. The Warriors will be unable to guarantee the safety of the fortification or the force in event of such an attack."

"I don't understand, Zur," commented Horc. "I was under the impression that part of the Warriors' duty was to be able to fight anything, any time, anywhere. In spite of this you are telling us that in event of a subterranean attack, the Warriors will be helpless and completely reliant upon the Technicians' devices?"

"You are correct in your observation of a Warrior's duty, Horc," answered Zur. "However, it is the duty of a Warrior Commander to give an accurate appraisal of his teams' abilities. We are not equipped physically or mechanically to enter into such combat, nor have any of the Tzen under my command received any training in subterranean battle. Though I can assure you that if such an attack occurs, the Warriors will fight in a manner befitting their caste, I would be lax in my duties as a Commander if I guaranteed their effectiveness. Unfounded assurance would only mislead the Commander and the other members of the staff, and could potentially prove disastrous should those assurances be relied upon."

"Question, Zur."

"Yes, Tzu?"

"You claim to be submitting a conservative appraisal of your team's abilities. Still you arrogantly guarantee a capacity to withstand an unknown force with unknown armaments. Is this not in itself a form of unfounded assurance?"

Zur looked at me, but I remained silent, thereby giving him unspoken authority to speak for the Warriors.

"The factors you refer to, Tzu, are, as you have said, unknown," he began. "Unlike the Scientists, the Warriors do not deal in unknown; we deal in realities. Were we to qualify our reports with provisions for the unknown, we would never enter into battle, for none can guarantee success against the unknown. The realities of the situation as set forth in your report are that we are faced with a force physically not unlike the Insects we have successfully battled in the past, capable of surface and subterranean movement, with no known weapons or machines modified for warfare. I must base my report on those facts, and by those facts my force will be able to provide security as long as the attack is made from the surface. Should the known facts be altered, I will have to reassess my evaluation. Until that time, my report stands unamended. In the past you have refused to accept my testimony as a Scientist. If you are expressing equal reluctance to accept my testimony as a Warrior——"

"Zur!" I interrupted. His head was sinking dangerously low. "Complete your report."

"Very well, Commander. There does seem to be a point of misunderstanding I would like to clarify. When I refer to the Warriors' ability to enter into subterranean battle, I am speaking of their ability to intercept and engage the Enemy in their tunnels. As the Tzen are themselves surface dwellers, the Enemy would be forced to surface to effect their actual attack. Once that happens, we are again referring to a surface attack, and our reservations concerning subterranean combat would no longer apply."

I surveyed the assemblage for several moments. They waited in silence. There were no additional questions.

"Very well. Having now heard the reports from the individual teams, I would be interested in hearing any recommendations from the staff regarding a course of action. Tzu, I believe you had some opinions in the matter?"

"I would apologize for my earlier impatience, Commander. You were quite right. Having heard the team reports, my recommendations are obvious and do not require formal verbalization."

"State them anyway, Tzu."

"Very well, Commander. All our plans are handicapped by a lack of confirmed information on the Ants. It is obvious from this that top priority must be given to a study of the Ants. This study would serve a double purpose: first, it would provide vital information for the Empire for its upcoming campaign against the Ants, and second, it would give us the necessary data upon which to base our decision as to whether or not to continue our current mission.''

"Thank you for your recommendations, Tzu. Now here are my orders.''

I shifted my gaze to include all three staff members.

"Our first concern is to secure the defense of the fortification. Horc, I want two of your team working on the design and installation of both types of subterranean detection devices you described. The third is to begin designing the requested method for crossing the ravine.

"Zur, I want your entire team on full alert until such time as the new defenses are in place. The only exception to this will be to establish an irregular observation flight over the area evidencing the unexplained rock movements. You are to avoid all contact with the Ants and particularly the anthill until our defenses are ready.

"Tzu, while the defenses are being prepared, I want your team to complete their study of the unidentified plants within the Defense Network. Also, I will expect a report from the Scientists as to their appraisal of the moving rock formations.''

I paused, then looked straight at Tzu as I continued.

"Once the defenses are in place, we will proceed with our original mission as planned.''

Tzu started to speak, then changed her mind and remained silent.

"In deference to the recommendations of the Scientists, the Technicians will construct two extra view-input units to be placed near the anthill, which will be fed into the memory banks for later review by the Scientists or the Empire. I will repeat, however, the current mission is to have top priority in our attention.

"I will remind the team that the next campaign is the next campaign. Our primary assignment is the current campaign . . . against the Leapers. The High Command was aware of the presence of the Ants on this planet when we were given our assignment; yet we were not assigned to gather data on them. We are assigned to find a natural Enemy to the Leapers, preferably with minimal loss of life; but safety of the team is not and has never been our primary concern. We are going to find that natural Enemy, and the Ants are merely another threat to that assignment.

"Those are my orders . . . those are the High Command's orders . . . and I trust I do not have to elaborate on the fate of any Tzen who knowingly disobeys them?''

CHAPTER
-6-

If the scientists took exception to my orders, they didn't show it.
Instead, they plunged into their assignments with enviable efficiency.

One by one the plants within the Defense Network were studied
and deemed harmless, with the obvious exception of the plant that
had killed our Technician shortly after our arrival. For a while I
allowed myself to hope that by a stroke of good fortune we might
find our natural enemy for the Leapers in that plant. This hope was
ended when the Scientists submitted their report. The plant was
deadly to Tzen, but not to the Leapers. As this was decidedly not
what we were seeking, we continued our search.

The moving boulders continued to defy explanation, a fact I
found increasingly irritating. This in itself surprised me, as I am
not a particularly curious Tzen. Upon examining my reaction, I
reached the conclusion that my increased curiosity was a result of
my prolonged contact with the Scientists. Even though my
discussions with them were largely attempts to quell their impatience, at the same time, I was being made aware of the vast
number of yet unanswered questions.

Having identified and analyzed the source of my unwelcome
emotions, I dismissed them. I am a Warrior, not a Scientist. I
concern myself with solving the problems at hand, not speculating
on the unknown. The moving boulders would have to wait until

additional data could be gathered, which in turn would have to wait until the defenses were secure.

Waiting! I was getting enough waiting this assignment to last a lifetime. While it was true my exposure to the Scientists was increasing my curiosity, another major factor was time, inactive time. Inactive time results in boredom, and boredom results in excessive thinking. I began wondering how widespread this problem was. With Deep Sleep being used only for space travel, the Tzen would be faced more and more with inactive time. Assuming others reacted as I did, filling the time with thinking, what affect would this have on the Empire?

I forced this line of thinking to a halt. I was doing it again. I am a Warrior, not a Scientist. Let the Scientists explore the implications and impacts of new patterns and discoveries. I would concern myself with immediate problems. Right now, the most pressing problem was . . . was how to deal with inactive time!

I suddenly realized that though the Scientists and Technicians were busy working on their respective assignments, the Warriors were currently in a state of forced inactivity. Realizing my own dubious reactions to that situation, this could present a significant problem.

I sought out Zur, who confirmed my suspicions.

"You are quite right, Commander. In fact, Mahz and I were discussing this point earlier, but were undecided as to whether or not to bring it to your attention."

"How is it showing itself?"

"In questions not pertinent to the subject at hand. That and overlong, wordy discussions. As a former—as a Warrior, Commander, I feel a concern for the effective performance of my team."

I cocked my head at him. It was quite unlike Zur to change thoughts in midsentence. Usually he was both concise and complete when he spoke.

"I am also concerned for the effective performance of my team, Zur. You started to say something about being a former Scientist. Why did you change your mind?"

He hesitated before answering, also quite unlike him.

"As you know, Commander, I have always been self-conscious about my non-Warrior background. Changing castes was not my desire or my decision, and I have always secretly regretted the move . . . until this assignment. Viewing the Scientists after a prolonged, forced separation, I find not only am I glad I was not accepted in their ranks, I wish that my name not be associated with them, even as a reference to the past."

I considered his statement with mixed emotions. On the one hand, I was pleased Zur now felt completely a part of the Warriors and not torn by divided loyalties. However, it boded ill for the mission for the head of the Warriors' team to harbor such strong and considered ill feelings toward the Scientists. Being at a loss for comment, I returned to the original subject.

"Have you considered a solution for the problem with the Warriors?"

He lapsed into thoughtful silence, but at least now his thoughts were diverted toward a constructive end.

"My analysis of the cause of the problem," he commenced finally, "is the marked difference between guard duty and active patrol. While both are necessary, guard duty is a prolonged, low-activity assignment. If guard duty is unbroken by an active pursuit, the mind tends to create its own activity, usually in an uncontrolled and therefore ineffective manner."

He was sounding like a Scientist again, but I felt it unwise to bring it to his attention.

"So you would propose . . . ?"

"Activity. Constructive activity. Perhaps some form of drill or practice."

"That could be potentially counterproductive, Zur. If the noise of target practice did not draw unwanted attention to us, the damage to the landscape would surely betray our position. Without the proper training equipment here, practice with the hand weapons could be potentially injurious to the Warriors, at a time we can ill afford casualties."

We pondered the problem in silence.

"What about the skimmers?" asked Zur finally.

I considered it.

"Possibly. Let me speak to Horc about it."

Horc was understandably annoyed at the request. His team was already overloaded with assignments with the defense and ravine-span designs. Still, he was a Tzen and followed orders without complaint. In an impressively short time span, the Technicians had checked out the skimmers and cleared them for use by the Warriors.

The skimmers were a modification of the water darts used in the campaign against the Aquatics. As four of us—myself, Zur, Mahz, and Kor—had missed that campaign, the extra practice in their handling was more than justified.

They were a two-seater craft with the seats mounted in tandem to conform to the vehicles' extreme streamlining. Even though there were dual controls, allowing the craft to be operated from either position, only one set of controls could be operated at a time. This was a necessary safety precaution, as the craft normally traveled at such high speeds that attempting to coordinate the efforts of two operators would inevitably result in a crash.

The reason for the skimmer's being a two-Tzen craft was the modified weapons system arming it. Our flyers had fixed weapon mounts that fired in one direction only, specifically, the direction in which you were flying. The skimmers, on the other hand, had swivel mount weapons that fired independent of the craft's movement. That is, you could move in one direction and fire in a different direction. This might sound like a remarkable and wonderful modification. It wasn't.

To understand this, one must first realize the reason the modification was necessary in the first place. The skimmers were originally designed for use on and under the water. The streamlining that made them so stable in that element, however, proved inadequate in open-air use. As such, they tended to rock or dip if you shifted your weight in them. This, of course, eliminated any hope of accuracy when firing a fixed-mount weapon. For a solution, instead of redesigning the ship, swivel-mount weapons were added. In theory, you could then keep your weapons trained on the target no matter what your craft was doing. In theory, I was actually looking forward to giving the Technicians firsthand experience of what it was like taking one of their brilliantly designed craft into an actual combat situation.

The reality of the situation was that instead of visually tracking a target and simply depressing a firing lug, you had to consciously aim the weapons. Of course, while you are doing this, you are supposed to be foot-piloting a high-speed craft. While it could be done, to accomplish it kept you busier than a lone nursery guard in the middle of a premature Hatching. Because of this, we used two Tzen per craft, one to handle the weapons and one to steer the craft. The only time we were called upon to do both would be in the unlikely event of one crew member's being killed or disabled. This situation was highly improbable. If one member is killed, usually both are destroyed, along with the craft.

There were other problems inherent in the swivel guns. With

fixed-mount guns, as long as you held formation, you were safe. Not so with the swivel guns. If you tracked a target too far, you would find yourself cutting the stabilizer off the skimmer next to you.

I have noted that more and more Warriors are abandoning the use of the swivel guns, preferring instead to close with the target and use a hand weapon from the open cockpit. Because the skimmers operate at such high speeds, even using a dueling stick like a club will result in a fatal wound.

The Warrior hierarchy did not discourage this practice. The Warriors were merely making the best of a bad situation. We had lodged formal protest over the design of the skimmers, and had been ordered to continue using them until a better craft could be designed. As such, we used the craft, though not always as the Technicians had intended. We practiced with them as often as situations would allow. We also, as a caste, waited for the opportunity to send a Technician into battle in one.

As Zur had predicted, the skimmer practice provided much-needed activity for the Warriors. We practiced maneuvering the craft at both high and low speeds, we practiced patrol formations, we practiced maneuvering two formations in a confined area. Zur suggested we devise a drill on the use of hand weapons from a skimmer, but I refused. While we did not discourage the practice, I did not want to encourage it by ordering them to practice the maneuver. Instead, we gave them a specific time period each day for "unstructured drill" during which time they could practice handling the skimmers in any manner they wished. I suspect they used the time to drill with the hand weapons, but I have suspicions only, as Zur, Mahz, and I took great pains to be occupied elsewhere when such practice was taking place.

Finally, when we had exhausted our imagination finding new drills, we jury-rigged nets on our own without the assistance of the Technicians and set the Warriors to work running down warm-bloods with their skimmers to supplement the food stores. The Technicians' team was openly scornful of our net design, but it worked.

However, despite all our efforts, the Warriors had an unaccustomed surplus of inactive time at their disposal. Much of this was spent in idle conversation, a pastime hitherto unheard of in the Warriors. The Warriors from the New Hatching seemed particularly susceptible to this. I chanced to overhear such a conversation one day.

"The more I think about it," Hif was saying, "the more it occurs to me that all our training as Warriors, the skimmers, the hand weapons, everything, is futile if not needless. What do you think, Kor?"

Kor was still held in awe by many of the New Hatching, and justifiably so. Not only was she a noted veteran, she still possessed one of the most spectacular sets of combat reflexes in the Empire, despite several generations of selective breeding and genetic experimentation.

"I am a Warrior," she replied abruptly. "I wasn't trained to think; I was trained to fight."

"But Kor," Sirk persisted, "we're talking about fighting; or not fighting, to be specific. Surely there are better ways to handle the Insects than direct combat. Chemical or Bacteriological warfare would be so much more effective. The Warriors' decision to——"

"If you want decisions, talk to one of the Commanders. I'm not trained to make decisions; I'm trained to fight."

"But——"

"I have no time for such talk. I'm going to check my weapons. I'd advise you to do the same."

"Again? We just wanted to . . ."

But she was gone.

"There goes a Warrior's Warrior," came Vahr's voice. "She's right, you know. There's a reason for everything in the Empire. Asking about it is only a waste of time. If there wasn't a reason, the situation wouldn't exist. The fact the High Command issues an order is all the proof you need that a reason exists."

"But don't you ever ask questions?"

There was a moment of silence before Vahr replied.

"I did once, just after the campaign against the Wasps. The casualty rates on the planet we hit exceeded even the Empire's calculations. When I saw so many Tzen die, I asked questions not unlike the ones you asked Kor. Wasn't there a better way? Why risk lives unnecessarily? In fact, I got permission to take time out from training to try to find the answers."

"What happened?"

"Two things. First, I found the answer to my questions. In short, we don't use chemicals or bacteria for the same reason you don't cut off your arm to get rid of scale mites. We don't want to destroy what we're trying to save. We're in this war because the First Ones upset the ecological balance of the Universe. They allowed the Insects to spread off-planet, away from natural enemies or control. Unchecked, they'll spread through the Universe, denuding every habitable planet they find. That is the imbalance we're trying to correct . . . for our own sakes. We won't do it by unbalancing things further. Chemicals kill indiscriminately. Bacteria, once started, may be impossible to stop. If we want to preserve the Universe, not destroy it ourselves, the war must be fought on the simplest level possible.''

"But, by that logic, aren't we the same as the Insects? I mean, aren't we spreading beyond our planet and therefore disrupting the balance?''

"Possibly. But unlike the Insects, we respect the balance and try to upset it as little as possible. If we destroyed planets to dispose of the Insects, we'd be as bad as they are. We don't. So the gamble is the possibility of our disrupting the Universe against the certainty of the Insects' doing it if left unchecked.''

"You mentioned two things happened as a result of your research. What was the other?''

There was a long pause before he replied.

"I lost two teammates in the campaign against the Aquatics,'' he said softly. "Ridiculous situations. With a little more practice, I might have saved them. But I hadn't been practicing. I had been looking for answers to questions I had no business asking.''

"Warriors die in combat.''

"I know that, Hatchling, better than you ever will!''

"But there's no guarantee you could have——''

"No guarantee, but a possibility. That possibility is worth my full concentration. Kor knows that, and so should I. I'm going to check my weapons.''

"But we wanted to . . .''

I missed the rest of the conversation. I had just been beamed by Horc. The defenses were in place. We could begin the mission.

CHAPTER
-7-

"We're in position, Commander."

"Does Hif observe anything unusual about the boulders?"

"No. She claims they are identical in color to the rocks which abound throughout the area."

I studied the boulders in the View Screen. The Technicians had established a bank of View Screens in the fortification, allowing us to monitor the images relayed by the view-input units mounted on either the flyers or the skimmers. By this method we were able to indirectly observe whatever transpired on a patrol or assignment.

The boulder stood alone in a small field of knee-high grass. It was three meters high and roughly spherical in shape. There was nothing particularly noteworthy about it except for two things. First, it was identical to several other boulders we had observed in this area. Second, it hadn't been here two days before. However innocent it looked, this was one of our mysterious "moving boulders."

"Any reaction from the Scientist?" I beamed.

"Zome? No, he seems quite content to follow our orders."

"I meant does he have any comments on the boulder?"

"No. He is as much at a loss to explain the phenomena now as the entire Scientist's team was from studying the View Screens."

Beside me in the fortification, Tzu shifted her weight impatiently. Unable to hear the telepathic communication between Zur and me, she was doubtless wondering what the delay was. However, this time, for a change, she remained silent.

"Bracket the boulder with your skimmers and use far-focus for closer examination."

The scene in the View Screens changed as the two Skimmers moved to take positions on opposite sides of the boulder.

Now it was my turn to wait as they studied the target and telepathically discussed their observations. During the interim, I considered the scout team. I had been in conference with Horc when they departed, and this was my first opportunity to check Zur's choice and deployment of the troops.

The team included three Warriors and, reluctantly, a Scientist. We were trying to keep the Scientists inside the fortification as much as possible, minimizing the chances of losing them to an attack. Of the three teams, they were the hardest to replace and therefore the most valuable. This tactic, however, was easier to order than to enforce. The natural curiosity of the Scientists led them outside whenever the opportunity presented itself or was manufactured. In this specific situation, however, I had to admit their logic was justified. Firsthand observations of a Scientist in this puzzle could be invaluable, even though so far he had not made a significant contribution.

I studied the pairings, now visible in the screens as the skimmers faced each other.

The Scientist, Zome, and Kor shared one skimmer. Because the Scientist was inexperienced, Kor would probably be controlling both the steering and the weapons. Well, if any Tzen could do it, Kor could.

Zur and Hif were teamed in the second skimmer. I supposed Hif's color-sighted ability made her a logical choice over the more experienced Vahr. Also, if they weren't included on assignments, how would the new Warriors gain experience?

"The team reports nothing unusual in the appearance of the boulder, Commander," came Zur's message. "It seems to be a rock; nothing more."

It occurred to me that if indeed our target turned out to be a rock and nothing more, we might be indulging in one of the most massive overkills in the records of the Warriors. If it wasn't, however . . .

"Proceed with the investigation, Zur."

"Acknowledged, Commander."

The skimmers were moving now. The craft with Zome and Kor

moved to a position forty meters from the boulder and settled facing it. Good! They would act as a fixed position covering the other craft. Not having to control its movements, Kor could devote her full attention to handling the weapons. When Kor concentrated on weapons, I was confident she could handle two boulders, unknown or not.

Zur's craft, probably with Hif piloting, moved off to a distance of some hundred meters. It waited until Kor was in position, then darted forward. Taking care not to pass between the boulder and Kor's guns, it swept past the target at top speed, almost brushing it as it passed. Carrying by, they turned the skimmer and swept the target again.

There was no apparent change in the boulder. . . . Or was there? My eyes darted from screen to screen. Had it quivered? Or was the movement I detected due to the shifting of the view-input units?

Zur's skimmer was approaching again, slower this time. I could see them in the View Screens relaying Kor's input units. Zur had his flex-mace out. Apparently he had joined the ranks of Warriors who shunned the swivel-mount guns.

Suddenly it happened, with such speed that only later review enabled us to sort the action out. The boulder exploded into life, pouncing on Zur's craft with a leap that defied description. A spider.

A monstrously huge Spider.

The screens showing Zur's display flashed a sight of the ground, then blanked out. My eyes jumped to Kor's screen, just in time to see the spider turn and start in that direction. It was incredibly fast, swelling swiftly in the screens to blot out all view of anything else. Quick as it was, though, Kor was quicker. We could see the cold-beams lance out, striking the spider repeatedly as it moved, but with no apparent effect. The view started to shift, and at first I thought Kor was attempting to maneuver the craft. Then it jarred to a halt, displaying a bush and an expanse of grass, and I realized what had happened. Two skimmers down, visual contact lost.

"By the Black Swamps!" Horc exploded, echoing my thoughts. "Whoever designed those skimmers should be killed, if I have to challenge them myself."

"What's wrong with those cold-beams, Technician?" Tzu interrupted. "Can't your team even maintain existing equipment?"

"Nothing's wrong with them," Horc retorted. "The beast's natural defenses stopped them."

"Ridiculous. Those beams will cut through——"

"See for yourself. We'll recall the sequence from the memory——"

"Use another screen," I said.

"But Commander, another screen would——"

"Anyone who interferes with the current monitor display answers to me. I want to see this as it happens, not out of a memory recall."

"Forgive my asking, Commander," Horc inserted with quiet politeness, "but see what?"

I realized he was right. Staring at a picture of a bush was not going to give me any additional information. I also realized that despite our height differential, I was staring up at him.

Slowly I forced my head up to its normal level.

"Leave it," I said, but more calmly.

"Zur here, Commander."

I held up a hand to the other two as I replied to Zur's beamed message.

"Report, Zur."

"Situation is in hand, Commander. Our assailant has been eliminated."

"What is the condition of your team?"

"Hif's arm is broken. . . . No casualties beyond that."

As I received the message, the view of the bush changed as the downed skimmer was pivoted to point back at the scene of the recent action. Zur was apparently beaming as he turned the skimmer; we could see the other three team members in the screen. Kor was working to right the other skimmer. Hif was assisting despite her broken arm. Zome was apparently examining the body of the dead spider.

"Both skimmers seem to be operational," Zur's report continued, "though my own flyer seems to have sustained some surface damage in the nose area."

"Confirmed, Zur," I replied. "The view-input units on your skimmer are inoperational."

I noticed Tzu was trying to get my attention.

"What is it, Tzu?"

"With your permission, Commander, I'd like to communicate some instructions to Zome."

"Certainly."

I had no hesitation in yielding on this point. Zur had given me his assurances the situation was in hand. Details could wait until their return. For the time being, it was more important to let the Scientists proceed with their work.

"Zur," I beamed, "pass your booster band to Zome."

"Acknowledged, Commander."

"Horc," I said as I passed my booster band to Tzu, "a word with you?"

"Certainly, Commander."

We retired to the far side of the dome to avoid distracting Tzu at her work.

"You made a comment just now I would like to have clarified."

"About the cold-beams?"

"No, about the skimmers."

"Oh, that. My apologies, Commander. It was an unforgiveable outburst. I would ask that you recall we technicians are unused to viewing combat firsthand."

"Actually I was interested in your implied criticism of the design of the skimmers. I was under the impression the Technicians considered it a masterpiece."

"You are confusing the Technicians as a caste with the individuals who compose it."

I waited, but he did not continue. I fought a brief battle with myself over conduct befitting a Warrior, but this time curiosity won.

"Explain, Horc."

"Commander?"

"The differences you referenced. I would like them clarified . . . for my information as Commander of this mission," I added hastily.

"I am unsure as to the necessity of an explanation. Surely there are differences of opinion within the Warriors' caste? Why should you expect the Technicians to be any different? Regardless of caste, we're all still Tzen."

I considered his answer. It was logical, so logical in fact I was surprised it had never occurred to me before. "I had never considered it in that light before, Horc. The Technicians always seemed a very united, stubborn caste to me, both in attitude and opinion."

"That is not unusual, Commander. Do you recall my question

about the duty of the Warriors' caste at the conference on the Ants?''

''Yes.''

''Well, until then I had considered the Warriors to have a caste identity: effective, but swaggering and arrogant. Zur's admission of the limitations of his team forced me to view the Warriors differently than I had previously. Perhaps our difficulty is that prior to this mission, we only dealt with the lower echelon of each other's caste. I have observed that the lower individuals stand in their caste, the more fiercely they will defend it.''

I suddenly realized I was being drawn into a much more thoughtful discussion than I cared to partake in.

''Returning to my original question, Horc, what is your opinion of the design of the skimmers?''

He hesitated before answering.

''Normally I would not criticize a project I was not working on, just as you would not criticize a campaign you had not fought in. However, as in my moment of weakness I let my feelings be known, I might as well clarify my position.

''The skimmers were modified from the water darts. That in itself indicates the High Command was concentrating on other priorities. When you modify a design instead of devising a new one, inadequacies and shortcomings are inevitable. Then you modify the modifications. The result is the kind of sloppy performance you just witnessed. In short, you invest a lot of time and effort to produce a device of dubious value. I personally would rather see the work put in on something specifically designed for the situation it will be used in.''

''Then you agree the skimmers are poorly designed?'' I asked.

''To a point I was surprised the Warriors accepted them.''

''We didn't. Our formal protest was turned down by the High Command.''

''Really?'' He sounded surprised. ''My respect for the Warriors is strengthened knowing that.''

I decided to seize the opportunity while it presented itself.

''Realizing we are in agreement on this point, is there a chance your team could design further modifications to the skimmers?''

He thought for several moments.

''Possibly,'' he said at last. ''Though after watching the actual performance of the craft, I would be more inclined to discontinue it completely. We could disassemble them and perhaps use the parts in another design completely.''

"How long would it take for such a project?"

"I obviously can't commit to a specific time span, but with the team I have here——"

"Commander."

Tzu was beckoning from the View Screens.

"Zur wants to confer with you."

Something was wrong. Zur wouldn't need my counsel unless there was a major change in the situation.

Breaking off the conversation, I strode hurriedly to the screens, accepting the booster band as I went.

"Rahm here."

"Commander, I'd like to have your advice on this."

I hurriedly scanned the operational screens. They displayed a view of ridge and brush, but nothing noticeably unusual.

"Explain, Zur."

"The clump of brush by the dead tree. Examine it closely."

I did. At first I saw nothing, but as I used far-focus I saw it. An Ant.

"Kor just noticed it, Commander. It seems to be observing us."

"How long has it been there?"

"Unknown. It may have been there through our entire skirmish with the spider."

I studied the Ant, but my mind was elsewhere. Mentally, I was reviewing the briefing we had received from Tzu; intelligent . . . capable of understanding machinery . . . able to communicate with the nest.

CHAPTER
-8-

Surprisingly enough, the Scientists did not seize upon the incident to renew their arguments for a closer study of the Ants. If anything, their efforts in that direction slackened. They even abandoned their covert monitoring of the view-input units by the anthill, leaving the View Screens unwatched for unprecedented periods of time. Instead, they pursued the mission with renewed, almost frantic energy. Not that there wasn't enough to occupy their time: there were countless specimens to collect and observe. Also, there was the Spider.

After they had realized they were being observed by the Ants, the team had cut short their field studies. Instead, they had transported the spider's carcass back to the fortification, intact. This was accomplished with no small difficulty by draping this spider across one of the skimmers and piloting it back. This involved actually crawling under the body and peering from between its legs to steer. I was quite proud of the nerves of the Warriors who performed this task. It is not pleasant to spend a prolonged period of time in such close proximity with the body of an Enemy, particularly one that has come close to killing you. Still, they carried out the assignment without falter or complaint. It did cause quite a stir when they hit the defense network, though.

Zur had beamed ahead that they were coming in. He neglected to mention the spider. The Warriors on guard had not taken cover and were caught in the open when the team burst into view. When you are expecting to see a teammate, the sight of a huge spider coming out of the brush at you can be unsettling, particularly if it is skimming the ground at unnatural speed.

Only the fact that the second skimmer, unadorned, was clearly accompanying the spider averted disaster. If a Warrior is startled, he tends to react with his weapons.

I was disappointed when I learned the Scientists had almost immediately dismissed the spiders as being unsuitable as a natural enemy for the Leapers.

"Rahk, Zome, and myself all concur, Commander," stated Tzu, as if it were both a unique and final statement.

"While it will be interesting to study the exoskeleton which was impervious to our cold-beams, and its poison will give us a definite advantage, the spiders cannot be considered a serious candidate for the desired natural enemy."

"Explain."

"First is their hunting pattern. They appear to be primarily ambush hunters, remaining in one place until a victim wanders in range before striking. This method is far too random and slow for a species we want to exterminate the Leapers.

"The size of their digestive tract also indicates a light hunter. It gives every indication of a creature which feeds only occasionally, taking long rest periods to allow the food intake to digest. Again this is unsuitable for our needs. What we are looking for is a creature or plant with a high metabolic rate, one which is driven to feed constantly and gluttonously.

"With the displayed hunting and feeding pattern, it would require capturing and transporting them in vast numbers if the tactic were to be at all successful."

"What about egg masses?" I interrupted.

"Also out of the question."

She stooped and picked up a fist-sized rock at random from the ground.

"Is this a spider egg mass?" she asked.

"No," I responded immediately.

"We Scientists are not so sure. The clusters of rocks we first observed around the spiders are actually egg masses, camouflaged like the spider itself. They are produced in a variety of sizes, apparently depending upon the feeding habits of the adult, and adhere to the sides of the female before dropping off. As I have said, they are extremely well camouflaged, to the point where we are unable to differentiate egg mass from rock until we attempt to break it.''

To demonstrate her point, she picked up a second rock and smashed it against the first. The rock split open at the impact, and she examined it out of habit.

"It seems you were right, Commander," she said letting the pieces fall. "It was just a rock. However, had it been an egg mass, we would have destroyed it performing that test."

"Couldn't you devise some other test?"

"Possibly, but there is no point in designing one."

"Why?"

"Because whether transported as adult specimens or as egg masses, the number of spiders necessary for the campaign would exceed safety limits."

"Safety limits?"

"As you recall, Commander, we encountered some difficulty in securing the specimens we have. While it is unlikely we would fall within the Spider's natural diet, it is obvious they will attack Tzen if provoked. We would therefore not only be spreading an Enemy for the Leapers, but one for ourselves as well. What is more, to effectively deal with the Leapers, we would also constitute a threat to the empire. The last thing we want to do is replace one Enemy with another, and particularly not an Enemy who is immune to our cold-beams."

"Speaking of that immunity, Tzu, what is the possibility that the Ants may have a similar exoskeleton?"

She considered for a few moments before answering.

"Unknown, Commander. The Scientist team is currently praying to the Black Swamps we never have occasion to find out."

This surprised me, as it seemed contradictory to the curious nature of the Scientists.

"Explain, Tzu."

"The time to investigate the Ants would have been before they knew about our presence. Now that they know we are here, it is only a matter of time before they act on that knowledge. As such, the Scientists feel it is in the best interest of safety to complete our mission in the shortest time possible and depart. Our position here is tenuous at best, and it becomes more so with the passage of time."

With that, she turned and strode away.

While she had given me much to think on, I postponed such

activity until later. There were other, more pressing matters demanding my time currently. To that end, I sought out Zur.

"How is Hif's arm?" I inquired.

"Fine, Commander. The Scientists injected her with a compound to speed the bone mending. She should be ready for light duty in time for the next guard shift, and for full duty by tomorrow."

"Good. Has Horc spoken to you about the skimmer design?"

"Yes, Commander."

"What is your opinion?"

"While it was enlightening to learn a Technician shares the Warriors' opinion of the skimmers, I declined his offer."

The answer was unexpected.

"Explain, Zur."

"Although obviously unstable, the skimmers are still the fastest means of ground transport available to us. As the mission progresses, we will be forced to canvas farther and farther afield seeking specimens for the Scientists. To accomplish this efficiently, we will have to cover great quantities of ground as fast as possible. While the flyers can serve to a certain degree as spotters, actual observations and capture can only be affected at ground level."

"It has been observed on numerous occasions, Zur, that the instability of their design all but negates the use of weapons. Do you not agree that the skimmers are apt to place you in potentially dangerous situations, while at the same time stripping your team of their ability to deal with those situations?"

"It is our plan, Commander, to utilize them as transports only, dismounting and proceeding on foot when the desired area is reached. As you well know, a Tzen Warrior is a formidable opponent, even when afoot."

"I still do not understand your position, Zur. While what you say is logical, it is a solution to a problem which could just as easily be circumvented. What is your objection to allowing the Technicians to redesign the vehicle to fit our needs?"

"Time, Commander. While I will not dispute the efficiency of the Technicians, such work would take time, time we can ill afford. In the time it would take them to redesign the skimmer, we might be able to find the object of our mission and depart."

"Am I to take it, then, that you share the Scientists' position that——"

Suddenly, he held up a hand to silence me.

He stood motionless, head cocked to one side, and I realized he was receiving a telepathic communication. I waited, but as time stretched on, I grew impatient, and curious. He was obviously either receiving a report or engaged in a lengthy exchange. I knew of no current activity of the Warriors' requiring such a communication.

Finally he turned to me once again.

"Commander, a situation has developed you should be appraised of."

"What is it?"

"One of our Warriors, Sirk to be specific, has disappeared."

"Explain."

"He was on guard, fully armed and wearing a booster band for communication. He failed to report in, and has been unresponsive to attempts to contact him."

"Was he within the Defense Network?"

"Unknown, Commander. As you know, the detectors have been set to ignore the movements of a Tzen. As such, we have no knowledge as to whether he was lured outside the Network or if our defenses have been breached."

"Very well. Institute a search at once."

"It has been done, Commander. Mahz led the search party. That was him reporting in just now. There was no trace of Sirk, nor any signs of a struggle."

"A search has already been conducted? Why wasn't I informed?"

Zur hesitated before answering.

"The Warrior team has been dissatisfied with our conduct in the battle against the spider, particularly as it was witnessed by the other castes. As such, we were reluctant to sound the alarm until we were certain a crisis existed. We had no wish to look foolish in addition to being ineffective."

"You haven't answered my question, Zur. I am of the Warrior caste and would have held the information in confidence. Why wasn't I informed?"

The pause was longer this time.

"Whether you are aware of it or not, Rahm, you have been becoming increasingly distant from the average Warrior. My team has not been insensitive to this, and tends to view you as something apart from the team. They were as reluctant to appear foolish in front of you as they were to avoid embarrassment before the Technicians or Scientists."

I also took time before answering, but in my case it was a struggle for control rather than thought.

"Zur," I said finally, "in the future I would ask that you remember two things, and that you pass them on to your team. First, I am the Commander of this mission and as such, am entitled to be appraised of each new development regardless of who it embarrasses.

"Secondly," I dropped my voice to a low hiss, "I am a Warrior, and the next team member who deliberately withholds information from me, regardless of caste, will answer to me on the dueling ground, either here or upon completion of the mission."

CHAPTER
-9-

We never found Sirk's body. Even though a disappearance such as this is not an unusual occurrence of the Warrior's caste, it was annoying. Without the body, we had no additional information. We did not know what killed him or how, or even if our defenses had been breached. It was an ineffective way to die.

Still, the mission progressed at a satisfactory speed. An astounding number of specimens were observed, analyzed, and discarded by the Scientists. After several uncomfortable attempts to serve as moderator, I approved a plan allowing the Scientists to make their requests for additional equipment directly to the Technicians. This plan proved workable, and the Technicians were kept busy in their labs designing and building the desired items.

The Warriors were not idle either. When not standing guard or collecting specimens, they were escorting observation expeditions into the field.

My own time was occupied trying to absorb and coordinate the reports and plans fed me by my staff. My insistence to be included on any new developments had been relayed through the entire team, and now every incident was being passed on to me, no matter how small or insignificant. I might have regretted the order, were I not so grateful for something to do to keep me from being inactive.

As you may gather from this, the problem of inactive time continued to plague our mission. Despite the frequency and intensity of assignments, individual members still found themselves with long periods of inactive time at their disposal. Idle conversation was now considered commonplace, almost unworthy of notice. The latest development was idle conversations between members of different castes. While this should have been predictable, it still took me a while to get used to.

I recall one conversation in particular that surprised me, as it transcended not only caste lines, but chain of command as well.

"A word with you, Commander, if you have a moment?"

"Certainly, Rahk."

Rahk was the junior of the three Scientists, and I had had little contact with him since his outburst when the fortification first landed.

"I have a theory I would like you to consider, Commander. One which I think has not been previously brought to your attention."

"Have you discussed it with Tzu?"

"Yes, but she has been reluctant to forward it to you."

"Did she explain why?"

"Yes, she gave two reasons. First, she pointed out we are adequately equipped to test the theory. It is her wish that we present proven theories only to you."

"Do you disagree with the policy?"

"In most cases, no, but in this instance I must take exception. Even though my theory is unproven, if correct it could have direct bearing on the success of the mission."

"Very well, I can understand your position. However, you mentioned Tzu had two reasons for withholding the information. What was the other?"

"Actually, her second reason was merely an extension of the first."

"Clarify."

"The Scientists have frequently voiced suggestions or opinions in the past which you have countermanded. Not that we are critical of this. You were within your rights as Commander, and the progress of the mission has proven your judgment to be sound. However, it has caused Tzu to feel, perhaps unjustifiably so, that you will have a tendency to reject out-of-hand recommendations of the Scientists on future plans. In an effort to reestablish the credibility of our caste in your eyes, she is screening our reports to be sure that only firm, proven facts and recommendations are passed to you."

I considered this.

"I acknowledge the logic of her beliefs, Rahk, though I do not agree that they are accurate. For this reason, I will listen to your theory.

"I will ask, however," I continued before he could speak, "that you pause first and reconsider its importance. Bypassing the chain of command, particularly in the field, can have long-lasting and undesirable aftereffects and should not be taken lightly. Are you sure your theory's impact justifies such a risk?"

Rahk thought for several moments before responding. I waited patiently.

"I am, Commander," he said at last.

"Proceed."

"It has to do with our sleep patterns."

"Sleep?"

"Yes, that and our eating habits."

"Continue."

"Historically, Tzen of all castes have gone into Deep Sleep between periods of activity. This was necessary to ensure minimal consumption of food and other resources.

"This has changed with the advent of the new technology. Food and space are plentiful on the colony ships, and space travel has placed an ever-increasing number of planets at our disposal. As a result, the necessity of Deep Sleep has become obsolete. In fact, with the exception of the sick or injured, the only time a Tzen is required to undergo Deep Sleep is when traveling in a transport ship to attack a new planet."

"I am aware of all this, Rahk," I interrupted. "Proceed with your theory."

"It is my contention that Deep Sleep performed a function beyond simple conservation of resources. There is a replenishment of body cells which takes place during sleep which is necessary for a Tzen to function efficiently."

"A replenishment of what?" I asked.

"Allow me to rephrase that, Commander. The body and mind of a Tzen experience fatigue in prolonged use, similar to a weapon which is fired at full force for an extended period."

"I assume you are referring to the blasters as opposed to our traditional hand weapons."

"Yes, I am. Now just as a blaster must be allowed to rest to function normally, a Tzen must sleep to rejuvenate mind and body."

"I am not sure I understand your analogy, Rahk," I communicated. "Every blaster has two specific rates of use; the maximum rate, and the maximum sustained rate. The maximum rate is that rate a weapon is capable of firing at any given moment at full force. Firing a weapon at that rate will give a great amount of energy for a short time, but after that time the weapon will malfunction. There is also, however, the maximum sustained rate. This rate is lower than the maximum rate, but if used at that rate, the weapon can function indefinitely, at least theoretically. If your analogy is correct, then it should be possible for a Tzen to function at a maximum sustained rate forever without sleep."

"That is correct, Commander. However, there is some question as to what that maximum sustained rate is. It is my contention that we normally function at a level well above our maximum sustained rate. As such, unless a schedule of regular periods of sleep is established and enforced, I fear we will find that we are functioning at less than peak efficiency."

I pondered this.

"How does our feeding pattern enter into this?"

"The cells require certain—" he lapsed into thoughtful silence for a moment. "I'm sorry, Commander. I am unable to think of a simple way to explain it. I am unaccustomed to speaking to Tzen not of the Scientist caste. I will have to ask that you simply believe me when I say that, like sleep, a certain regular intake of food is necessary."

"And you say you are unable to prove this theory?"

"Not to Tzu's satisfaction. It would require extensive testing of Tzen from all castes both before and after sleep to determine their relative effectiveness. For at least cursory proof, however, I would like to point to the performance of our current team."

"What about the performance of our team?"

"Few if any of the team have slept since our arrival on this planet. I feel this is beginning to show in our performance, specifically in the Warriors' difficulty in dealing with the Spider. I feel a continued decline in our effectiveness could be disastrous, particularly as the insects will undoubtedly become more efficient as our stay here grows longer.

"You are convinced the Insects will give increased resistance?" I asked. I was not eager to comment on the performance of the Warrior caste.

"I have been examining the reports of your first expedition, Commander. As a result, I am of the opinion the Empire is underestimating the intelligence of the Insects."

"Explain. . . ."

"When you first were forced to crash land, the Leapers would not venture under the trees, yet your account of Aahk's death specifically references the Leapers' attacking while under cover of the forest. This in itself indicates an alarming adaptive ability. Later, however, you describe in great detail how the Leapers laid an ambush for you and your two companions. This cannot be ignored. In an amazingly short time, the Leapers had not only recognized the Tzen as an enemy, they were actively mounting countermeasures. They were not merely pursuing you on chance encounters, they were actively hunting you. Also, remember we are speaking of the Leapers, a species rated as being less intelligent than the Ants."

He stopped, suddenly aware he was being carried away with his emotions. Composing himself, he continued.

"Based on these observations. I feel it is not a possibility, but a certainty, that as the mission progresses, we can expect increased difficulties with the Insects. For this reason, I recommend that the team be encouraged, if not required, to get as much sleep as possible . . . now, while they are able. We will need every Tzen operating at peak efficiency soon."

Despite my skepticism, I was impressed by his arguments.

"I will take your recommendations under consideration, Rahk," I said.

I was sincere in my promise, and planned to implement his plan as soon as I had consulted with my staff. Before I could, however, something occurred that forced me to change my priorities.

I was in conference with Horc concerning the priority of the Technicians' assignments when I noticed something.

"Horc," I said, interrupting his speech, "all the skimmers are here."

"Yes, Commander."

"But isn't there a patrol out?"

"Yes, Commander. They declined the use of a skimmer."

"Why?"

"I was not consulted in the decision."

Breaking off the conference, I sought out Zur.

"It was the team's decision, Commander," he informed me. "As the destination for their patrol was less than two kilometers beyond the Defense Network, they decided to walk the distance rather than utilize the faster but less stable means of transport afforded by the skimmers."

"Who is on the patrol?"

"Kor and Vahr, escorting Tzu."

I approved of the use of veteran Warriors on such a mission, but still felt uneasy.

"Without a skimmer, we do not have visual contact."

"That is correct, Commander. I pointed this out to them, but they stood by their decision. They have, however, been keeping regular contact by booster band."

"Contact them and confirm their status."

"But they aren't due to contact us for——"

"Contact them. If they complain, tell them it was on my orders."

"Very well, Commander."

He slipped on his booster band. I waited impatiently. I wondered if I was misusing my authority as Commander to quiet my own fears, but discarded the thought. I had learned as a Warrior not to ignore my instincts, and seldom had I experienced misgivings as strong as I experienced when I learned the patrol was out without a skimmer.

"They are not responding, Commander."

"Contact Horc and have him get two flyers ready. You and I are going to——"

"Commander!"

It was Zome's voice beaming into my head.

"Rahm here," I responded.

"Set your arm-unit for the input unit by the anthill, immediately!"

Zome did not have the authority to give me orders, but something in his voice made me respond. Reflexively, I extended my arm to allow Zur to share the view as the scene swam into focus.

There was a frenzy of activity at the anthill. A party of Ants was returning, bearing aloft a prize. They were triumphantly carrying our three missing teammates. Judging from their lack of movement, they were either dead or unconscious as they were dragged out of sight down the hole.

CHAPTER
- 10 -

The loss of three teammates had a definite impact on the remaining members. Of particular note was Tzu, sorely missed as a Scientist, and irreplaceable as the head of the Scientists' team. Of no less loss, though some might dispute it, were Kor and Vahr. The loss of two veteran Warriors, particularly one of Kor's abilities, could only lessen our chances of success or even survival. Although still nine strong, the team was disproportionately weakened.

The situation was serious enough to require my calling a staff meeting. I was loath to do this, as I felt our meetings were becoming needlessly frequent, but we could ill afford uncoordinated action or thought at this time. Lack of information, and therefore lack of unity, has doomed many a campaign in a crisis that could have been salvaged.

"An appraisal of the Warrior situation, Zur?" I asked to begin the meeting.

"The Warriors should be able to perform with the existing force, Commander. It cannot be discounted, however, that with the loss of four teammates, three of them Warriors, we may be pitted against a force we are incapable of dealing with. Of particular concern is the potential ineffectiveness of our cold-beams. Both Warriors lost on the last assignment were armed with cold-beam hand blasters, and Kor's reflexes were well known to all. Still, they were unable to secure sufficient time to beam a distress call or even a warning to the fortification. From this we must assume increased probability that such weapons are as ineffective against the Ants as they were against the Spiders. I would therefore recommend we give serious consideration to widespread use of hot-beams for the duration of the mission.''

I considered this. Zome, now representing the Scientists, remained silent, a fact for which I was grateful. It was obviously the Scientists' role to raise protest at the danger to the local ecology that use of the hot-beams would involve. The danger was obvious enough to go without saying, and he didn't say a thing. Lost in concentration though I was, I appreciated it.

''Horc,'' I said finally, ''would it be possible for the Technicians to devise some method for containing any incidental fires started by the use of the hot-beams within the Defense Network?''

''We could do it either by establishing a firebreak around the network, or by a similar circular array of heat-triggered fire extinguishers. Of course, neither of these solutions are acceptable.''

''Why not?''

''Either method would be difficult if not impossible to camouflage, and would therefore effectively pinpoint our position to the enemy.''

''If I might point out, Horc, we have already lost three, possibly four, teammates to the Enemy. This indicates that they are fully aware of our presence, and if our exact location is not currently known, it very probably soon will be. I will therefore instruct you to install the necessary devices for fire containment. It is better that we begin to plan our defenses for such a confrontation than merely hope it will not occur.''

''Very well, Commander.''

''Zome, I realize the difficulty of your position, and would normally allow you a certain grace period to reacclimate yourself to the duties of command. Unfortunately, circumstances do not permit this. Do you have even an estimate for us as to how much additional time will be required to find an acceptable natural enemy to the Leapers?''

''I do, Commander. It is my belief we have already found it.''

''Explain.''

''For some time now the Scientists have been investigating a species of warmbloods indigenous to this planet. They are small, only about a half meter in length, and are completely harmless to the Tzen. Their specific food is the eggs of the Leapers, which they sniff out and burrow after, each one consuming ten to fifty a day. It is our belief that seeding the Leaper-held plants with large quantities of these warmbloods, coupled with a concentrated ground and air strike against the adult Leapers, could effectively eliminate that species of the Insect Coalition.'' His voice was uncharacteristically enthusiastic.

"Warmbloods are notoriously short-lived,'' interrupted Horc. "How will they survive the flight back to the colony ship?"

"This particular species is highly prolific,'' answered Zome. "They should be able to produce new generations while on board the transport ship to replace those that die.''

"If they are so potentially effective,'' interjected Zur, "why have they been unable to eliminate the Leapers on this planet?"

"The natural enemy for this species, a carnivorous plant, also abounds on this planet. It claims such a high percentage of the species' population that only its high reproductive rate has allowed the species to survive at all. For this particular planet, we would raise a high population in the colony ships to offset the normal mortality rate. Then, including the carnivorous plants on the target list along with the adult Leapers, we would dump them back here to deal with the eggs. By the time the plants reestablished themselves from seeds, the warmbloods' work should be done.''

"What do they eat besides Leaper eggs?'' asked Horc. "What would we feed them in transit, or on the colony ships for that matter?"

"We have induced them to accept a chemical substitute in the lab, one which we can easily produce, even on board ship. I should note that we were careful to test one thing. They will not eat Tzen eggs.''

"How hard are they to catch?'' Zur inquired. "What will be involved in obtaining a breeding stock to take back with us?"

"There is a particular chirp they emit when ready to breed, a chirp they use to attract a mate. It is possible to reproduce this sound mechanically, and properly amplified by the Technicians, it should be easy to draw them to our fortification for capture and transport.

"This trait is particularly advantageous, since if they begin to overpopulate the target planets, we will be able to attract them to a central point for disposal or dispersal.''

"I have a question, Zome.''

"Yes, Commander?"

"The species you describe seems to be the perfect solution to our problem. In fact, it is so perfect, I must inquire as to why it was not brought to our attention before?"

For the first time in his presentation, Zome hesitated before replying.

"Tzu does . . . did not like warmbloods. She was at best reluctant to recommend spreading this species or any warmblood through the universe. As such, she delayed reporting our findings while she searched for another alternative. She was investigating another predatory species of Insect, one outside the Coalition, when she had her encounter with the Ants."

"What was her objection to warmbloods?" asked Zur.

"She expressed what I believe to be a personal theory. It maintains that considering the brain-size-to-body-mass ratio, that the warmbloods are potentially intelligent, even more intelligent than the Insects or even the Tzen. If properly directed, that intelligence could be a potential threat to the Empire."

"Warmbloods?" interrupted Horc. "A threat to the Empire?"

"Having insufficient data to calculate the relative intelligence of warmblood species, much less the probability of such an occurrence, she was prone to treat all warmbloods with equal suspicion."

"I'm no Scientist, Zome," Horc commented, "but I find that theory hard to accept. To challenge the Empire would require not only intelligence, but technology. To the best of my knowledge, warmbloods are not physically *able* to operate machines, much less develop them."

"As you have said, Horc, you are not a Scientist. Species of warmbloods have been discovered with grasping forepaws not unlike our own hands, and therefore capable of operating machinery. What is more, until we discovered the notes of the First Ones, we would have insisted it was physically impossible for an Insect to operate a machine. Intelligent beings will develop devices which can be operated by their own physical configuration."

"Zome—" Zur began, but the Scientist raised a restraining hand.

"Before we pursue the subject further, I would like to clarify my own position. I personally disagree with Tzu's theory. If nothing else, I feel the narrow temperature range warmbloods can tolerate negates their effective danger to the Empire. However, as a Scientist, I must acknowledge the possibility just as Tzu did. I merely discount the probability."

"Tzu's apprehensions are noted, Zome," I said. "However, I believe we are in agreement. Any species we find will have potential dangers inherent, and searching for a probably nonexist-ent perfect species is both time-consuming and dangerous. The one benefit I can see to the species under examination is that if we have made a mistake, it can be recalled by the chirp machines. If there are no objections, then, I will accept the designated warm-blood species as our target, and we will proceed with collection.''

Once our target was agreed upon, the mission proceeded smoothly. The chirp machine devised by the Technicians drew the warm-bloods in at such a high rate that for a while we were hard-pressed to construct cages fast enough to hold them.

A booster beam call to the transport ship brought the crew back to full active status, and the cage problem was soon solved. The Technicians on board began constructing large holding pens, and daily runs from the shuttle craft began filling them, leaving us with empty cages to fill.

The ground team was not lulled just because the end of the mission was in sight, however. Horc and Rahk had taken assign-ment on board the ship looking after the warmbloods as they were ferried up, leaving us with only seven team members on the ground. To counterbalance our weakness, Zome and Ihr armed themselves from the arsenal and accepted temporary assignment with the Warriors as guards, leaving only Krahn to collect the warmbloods and load the cages.

It was interesting that these two, Zome from the Scientists and Ihr from the Technicians, would volunteer for this duty. I had detected in Zome's eagerness to accept field assignments a hunger for action and admiration for the Warriors. In his case, it was a chance to try another role without changing castes.

Ihr was a different story entirely. From the onset of the mission, she had been openly disdainful of the Warriors, to a point where Horc had found it necessary to reprimand her several times. Her willingness to stand guard could only be interpreted in one way—she was out to prove that she could do a Warrior's job as well as or better than any Warrior.

Two non-Warriors, one friendly, one hostile—I did not care what their motives were. They were Tzen, and I was glad to have them armed and watching the perimeter.

Despite the smoothness of the mission, I was uneasy. My Warrior's instinct told me no plan, including our current one, would transpire as predicted.

I was right.

I was in conference with Zome when it happened. We were discussing the necessary quantities of warmbloods to transport and had reached agreement. The load currently waiting to be picked up and one more should provide breeding stock of sufficient quantity for the proposed project. It was then the call came.

"Attack Alert! Weapons ready!"

I reacted instantly to the message beamed into my head, as did every other team member in sight. We waited for clarification, but none came. The message had been in a strained tone, negating identification.

"Who sounded the Alert?" I beamed at last.

There was no answer.

"Mahz!" I beamed. He was currently covering the gun turret.

"Yes, Commander!"

"Anything on the Network?"

"No, Commander."

I pondered the problem, weapon in hand.

"Commander!"

It was Hif's voice beamed into my head.

"Report, Hif!"

"I have visual contact. Something moving toward the fortification from the Southeast . . . fifty meters out."

"Identify!"

"Unknown. I can see brush moving, but that's all."

"All members pull back to the fortification!" I beamed. "Mahz!"

"Here, Commander."

"Anything on the network to the Southeast?"

"No, Commander."

The team was assembling now, Zur hastily assigning them positions with gestures and telepathy.

"I can see it now, Commander," came Mahz's voice. "It's Kor!"

"Kor?" I echoed.

It was Kor. We watched her final painful approach, Zur moving to help her. She was badly mangled and missing one arm.

"Hold your position," I beamed to the rest of the team.

CHAPTER
-11-

Zur assisted Kor to a position behind our defensive line and eased her to the ground near the base of the fortification.

"Permission to leave formation, Commander?" called Zome softly.

"Reason?"

"To bring medical supplies and administer——"

"No!" Kor's voice interrupted, firm, and surprisingly calm.

"Kor!" Zur admonished.

"I must report first . . . important."

"Commander, she'll die if I don't——"

"They are going to attack . . . the Ants. . . . They'll try to stop the information from reaching the Empire. . . ."

"Commander!" Zome was insistent.

I made my decision.

"We'll hear her report. Zur, I want you to rearrange the defenses. I want you, Zome, and the ranking Technician . . . Ihr, stationed near enough to hear this report, but I want you all facing outward to watch for attack."

"Yes, Commander," and he was moving, acting instantly to carry out the order.

"Thank you, Commander," whispered Kor weakly.

I ignored her.

"Mahz!" I beamed.

"Yes, Commander!"

"Put on a booster band and contact the transport immediately. Tell them we need that shuttlecraft down here as soon as they can manage it."

"Yes, Commander."

"Ready, Commander." Zur was back.

"Very well, Kor, proceed with your report."

"They have machines. . . . They . . . they're studying us . . . using data to plan tactics——"

"What kind of machines?" interrupted Ihr.

"How are they studying us?" asked Zome.

"Ihr, Zome, I will say this once. We will not tolerate interruptions to this report. Kor! You are of the Warrior caste. You therefore know how to report in a concise orderly fashion. Cease this undisciplined babbling and report properly!"

The rebuff seemed to calm her.

"Yes, Commander. We were captured . . . all three of us. . . ."

She paused as if trying to organize her thoughts. I waited patiently, wondering about the fate of the other two captives.

"Some sort of stun ray . . . carry it slung under their bodies. . . . Maximum range unknown . . . trigger mechanism unknown. We were hit at about fifty meters. . . . They struck Vahr and me first, possibly because of our weapons, then took Tzu. . . . Only saw two weapons. So they can be fired at least twice without recharge or reloading. . . . Effect is immediate . . . full loss of motor nerve control and partial loss of mental faculties. . . ."

She was weakening. I noticed the wound from her missing arm was still bleeding. Using my hand, I tried to pinch off the arteries. I was not wholly successful, but at least now she was losing blood at a slower rate.

"The Ants were both swift and organized in their movements. . . . We were stripped completely, weapons, harness, even booster bands before we could think clearly enough to try to send a message."

"We were then carried back to the anthill and inside. . . . We could see and think, but couldn't move . . . dim lighting . . . dumped on floor . . ."

She stopped and stretched her head back. I realized she was suffering from the pain of her wounds. I waited.

"Dumped on floor in room with dim lighting. . . . We were examined . . . probed by their antennae . . . checked for sex. . . . knew what they were looking for . . . then piled together. . . . Examining Ants withdrew . . . replaced by six guards . . . larger, heavier mandibles. . . .

"Finally gained control of motor nerves. . . . Effects of stun beam wear off eventually. . . . Examined chamber. . . . Tzu said it was specifically a chamber for captives . . . one entrance, water supply. . . . Particularly noted lighting . . . came from luminous rocks . . . not a natural formation . . . brought in . . . changed occasionally by guards. . . . Light not necessary for Ants; must be for prisoners. . . .

"Examining Ants returned once we were conscious. . . . Crowded first Tzu, then me toward Vahr. . . . Tzu deduced they wanted us to breed . . . Vahr and I complied, Tzu would not. . . . Warmbloods brought and given to Vahr and me. . . . Tzu prevented from eating. . . .

"Pattern continued. . . . Laid eggs, but would not let Ants near them. . . . They did not insist. . . . Suggested Tzu also comply . . . refused. . . . Would not help Enemy learn about Tzen. . . .

"Began planning escape. . . . Could approach entrance, but guards would not let us leave chamber. . . . From entrance we could see another chamber across the tunnel . . . machines . . ."

"Commander!" came Mahz's voice into my mind.

"Rahm here."

"I have a report on the shuttlecraft."

"Delay report."

I focused my attention on Kor as she continued.

"Could not see entire other chamber. . . . There was a kind of View Screen . . . not full image like ours . . . stick figures on glowing screen. . . . Display showed our fortification and the anthill . . . stick figures of Tzen around fortification. . . . Number of Tzen changed from time to time . . . assumed showing defenses and patrols. . . . Could not see controls or operators.

"Planned escape. . . . Had noted speed of Ants while being carried on surface . . . used estimated speed and memorized turns taken carried in dark. . . . Thought we could find our way out. . . . Decided not to carry glow rocks . . . would pinpoint position. . . . Vahr and I would provide fighting cover for Tzu's escape . . . get Scientist out. . . ."

"Commander," came Mahz's voice again.

"Rahm here."

"Intruders in the Network, Southeast."

"Identify."

"Leapers. Twenty of them."

"Movement?"

"Holding position at seventy-five meters."

"Attack Alert," I called to the team. "Leapers massing. Seventy-five meters, Southeast."

I turned back to Kor.

"Continue your report."

"We made our escape attempt. . . . Vahr began to act erratically . . . running back and forth . . . falling on floor. . . . Finally ran to eggs and began smashing them with his feet.

"Three guards moved to subdue him. . . . He fought. . . . They seemed unwilling to hurt him. . . . Killed one . . . Tzu and I made no move to escape. . . . two of the remaining guards moved to assist . . . only one guard left on entrance . . .

"There were several rocks in chamber . . . same size as my steel balls. . . . Used one to kill entrance guard. . . . We ran. . . . Vahr broke loose and took position at entrance to slow pursuit. . . .

"Running blind in dark. . . . Hit walls. . . . Tunnels not patrolled. . . . Ran into an Ant from behind . . . killed it. . . . Ran into one head-on . . . caught me by arm. . . . Tzu continued alone. . . . Killed the Ant but lost the arm . . . kept running. . . .

"Message beamed from Tzu. . . . Encountered large number of Ants . . . blocking tunnel to surface. . . . She ran down another tunnel . . . led them off. . . .

"I got to the surface without encountering another Ant . . . headed for fortification. . . . Several Ants emerged and started after me, then turned back. . . ."

"Commander!" came Mahz's voice. "More Leapers north, accompanied by several Ants!"

"Confirmed," I beamed.

"That concludes my report." Kor's voice was suddenly coherent again. "Special commendation recommended for Tzu. She died like a—"

Her body spasmed, and was still.

"Mahz," I beamed, "status report."

"No visual contact, but instruments still show the two groups. No activity since the last report. They seem to be waiting for something."

"Estimated arrival of shuttlecraft?"

"The transport is in a bad orbital position. If they send it out, it won't have enough power to lift off again. Earliest possible arrival is just after sunset."

"Update status as conditions change, but report directly to Zur."

"Confirmed, Commander."

"Zome!" I called softly.

"Here, Commander."

"Examine Kor and stand by to report."

"Confirmed."

He moved to Kor's body.

"Ihr! Analysis of Kor's report."

There was no response.

"Ihr!"

"Yes, Commander. I . . . in a moment."

I started to press her, then realized she was taking Kor's death badly.

"Ignore it." I beamed to her. "Make your report. You are acting head of the Technicians."

"But Commander," she beamed back, "the last thing I said to Kor . . . before she was captured . . . I said I thought the Warriors——"

"Warrior or Technician, she was a Tzen. So are you. Now report."

"But——"

"She's dead . . . and the rest of us could be the same unless we learn from her report. Now give your analysis!"

"The Ants' technology is apparently inferior to our own. The View Screen described indicates two things. First, they have not yet mastered direct input methods. Stick figures as opposed to full visuals indicate a display of manually input statistics. It is possible that there are several input stations, and also the possibility of several viewing screens displaying common data. It seems unlikely, however, that they would content themselves with representative figures if full visuals were possible.

"Secondly, they are apparently unable to modify equipment." Her voice was strengthening as she continued. "The fact that our teammates could observe the screen from a distance would imply it was a light display. This feature is probably unnecessary to the dark-dwelling Ants. The fact they have not modified this to their own use, despite the fact they have had access to the First Ones' technology longer than we have, indicates a low technical ability.''

''Could it be,'' I interrupted, ''that they did not anticipate another species' penetrating that far into their nests? That would make a modification for an unlighted display an unnecessary expenditure of time.''

''Being familiar with the design of View Screens, I can definitely state that visual light displays are more difficult to build and operate. To a being with technical knowledge, an unlit display would be a simple modification, and one which would ease both construction and operation. As they have not made that modification, I feel it indicates they do not fully understand the principle of the machinery they are operating, and are simply imitating what has been done before.''

''Understood. Proceed.''

''The stun rays are another example of faulty technology. There are far more effective methods for an Insect to employ a weapon than slinging it under its body. Used in the current manner, it would be extremely difficult to aim on uneven terrain. What is more, to use it when firing from cover would mean the Ant would have to expose itself completely to the Enemy before its weapon could be brought into play.''

''How would you explain the fact that they have a weapon not currently in our arsenal?''

''You would have to ask the Scientists, Commander. To the best of my knowledge, however, the Technicians have never been asked to construct one.''

''Zome! Your comments and analyses?''

''Kor is dead, Commander.''

''Yes, I assumed as much. Now your analysis.''

''None of her injuries seem to be caused by any mechanical weapon. From this we can assume that unless specifically prepared for combat, the Ants rely upon their natural weapons.

''As to the stun ray, while the Scientists are not currently aware of such a weapon, it is logically a device such as would have been employed by the First Ones. It could have been passed over in their notes as being unsuitable to our purposes. Tzen will usually either kill an organism or leave it alone.''

''It would be useful on missions such as this, when we are assigned to capture live specimens,'' I commented.

''That is true, Commander, but investigative expeditions such as this are a relatively new venture. Stun rays could have been discarded and forgotten before the need for these missions was known."

"Possibly. Proceed with your report."

"The examination described by Kor indicates prior knowledge of Tzen anatomy. This means the Ants have either obtained data from our earlier campaigns here, or that we have finally discovered what happened to Sirk. In either case, it shows the Ants are also capable of investigative study. They are both aware of the Tzen, and eager for additional data. This last is demonstrated by the fact they were willing to risk attempting to capture live and armed Tzen to obtain subjects for study. We will have to assume if they are intelligent enough to do that, they are intelligent enough to use what they learn."

I waited for a moment to be sure he had completed his report.

"Mahz!" I beamed.

"Here, Commander."

"Resume reporting updates directly to me."

"Confirmed, Commander."

"Zur, report and analyze."

"There are currently three groups of Insects in the immediate vicinity. From their position and actions, they are all aware of our presence, and preparing for attack. There are two groups of Leapers, apparently under the command of Ants, located Southeast and north of the fortification. There is another group, composed entirely of Ants, directly west of us. All groups are currently stationary, apparently waiting for some signal or occurrence before they begin their attack.

"The shuttlecraft will not arrive until after sundown. It would be optimistic to assume they will not attack until then, so we must plan our defense.

"We will assume all three groups will attack simultaneously, though possibly the group of Ants to the west will delay their attack, hoping the other two groups will cause us to shift our positions. If there are weapons used in this attack, they will probably be with that group.

"There are several points in our favor in the upcoming battle. First, the Enemy is apparently still unaware of our Defense Net which is currently pinpointing their positions and movements. Second, as we killed the Spider with hand weapons only, they are not aware of our hot-beams or their effect.

"It is doubtful the stun beams described by Kor are effective beyond fifty meters. If nothing else, it would be next to impossible to use them accurately at a greater range. The range of our hand blasters and particularly the turret gun greatly exceed that.

"Unfortunately, the turret gun can only fire in one direction at a time.

"Our strategy will be to deal with the Enemy at maximum distance. The turret gun will concentrate its fire on the group of Ants to the west, as that is the most potentially dangerous. The rest of us must deal with the groups to the north and Southeast."

"Zur!" I interrupted. "Is it not true that the swivel guns on the skimmers have a greater range than our hand blasters?"

"That is correct, Commander."

"Then if we array the skimmers . . ."

"Commander!" Mahz's voice came to me.

"Rahm here."

"Instruments indicate digging. There is a tunnel in progress to the Southwest."

CHAPTER
- 12 -

"Request, Commander."

"Yes, Zur?" I beamed back.

"If opportunity presents itself, I would like your permission to dispose of Kor's body personally."

"What method would you propose?"

"I would use my hand blaster to obliterate her body."

"Explain."

"She was an exceptional Warrior. She deserves a better end than serving as Ant food."

"Permission granted . . . providing opportunity presents itself. We do not want to prematurely display the power of our weapons."

"Of course, Commander."

Trust Zur to think of details like that under the most adverse situations. Then again, Kor's body was on his side of the fortification. He and Krah would have little to do but stare at it as we waited for the attack.

Our position was tenuous as best. The tunneling from the Southwest had stopped about thirty meters out. The other three groups of Insects had not moved, though another pack of Leapers had joined the group to the Southeast.

We had opened the top of the base disc of the fortification, giving us a circular trench from which to operate. Our force was split into three two-Tzen teams; Zur and Krahn covering the group to the Southeast, Hif an Zome covering the north, and Ihr and I covering the all-Ant group to the west. Mahz at turret gun was assigned to watch for the tunnel opening when it appeared, and cover anything that emerged with his superior firepower.

I scanned the terrain to the west of our position, but could see nothing, even using far-focus. A thick stand of trees fifty meters distant obscured my view. If it were not for our Defense Network, I would be unaware of the Enemy lurking there.

I wondered what the Insects were waiting for. It was almost sunset. Perhaps they were planning a night attack. I discarded the idea. That would be too much to hope for. Besides, the Leapers were not that effective as night fighters.

"Commander." It was Mahz's voice.

"Rahm here," I beamed back.

"More Ants arriving to the west. They're moving slowly, apparently dragging something."

"Identify."

"Unknown, Commander. Large and bulky, possibly mechanical."

I didn't like the implications of that. I shot a glance at the cages of warmbloods, still stacked in place beside the fortification. They alone seemed unmoved by the situation.

"Shuttlecraft status report?" I beamed.

"Still has not departed. . . . Attack Alert, groups from north and Southeast closing."

"Attack Alert!" I relayed, but it was unnecessary.

The sounds of the hot-beams were deadly soft as the other two teams opened fire on the advancing Enemy. The sound was soon lost in the shriek of dying Leapers.

"Zur," I beamed, "the hot-beams are effective against the Ants?"

"Most satisfactory, Commander," came the reply.

"West group is closing, Commander," Mahz beamed. "Moving slowly."

"Confirmed," I replied.

"Enemy incoming," I said to Ihr softly.

"Ready, Commander." Ihr's voice was tight.

I reminded myself she was a Technician and as such unused to combat.

"West status report?" I beamed to Mahz.

"I can't see anything," Ihr complained, glaring through the gathering twilight shadows.

I ignored her.

"Still closing, Commander," came Mahz's report.

"They're out there," I informed Ihr.

"Then let's see them."

Before I realized what she was doing, she rose and fired blindly to the west. Her hot-beam immediately touched off a small brushfire. In its light, I could see a small group of Ants gathered behind a large piece of machinery.

"Ihr . . ." I began, but too late.

A ray lanced out from the Ant's machine, cutting her in half at the torso. So much for the self-styled Warrior-Technician. The beam shot out again, opening a gash in the fortification dome behind me.

"Cold-beam!" I broadcast to the other teams, kicking Ihr's body to one side.

"Shall I try for it, Commander?" came Mahz's hail.

"No! Continue watching for the tunnel."

I did not want to disclose the turret gun's presence until absolutely necessary, particularly not with cold-beams around.

I moved along the trench to my left, then cautiously raised my head for a look.

"It seems to be a large, bulky mechanism," I beamed to the force at the fortification. "Any indication of similar devices in the area?"

"Nothing on the Network," reported Mahz.

"No visual contact to the Southeast," Zur beamed.

"Nothing to the north," came Hif's voice.

The Ants were close now. I raised my hand blaster, aimed carefully, and fired. I was rewarded by seeing the machine collapse and smoke as the attending Ants abandoned it. Then the advancing Ants were on me.

I burned two to my right, then spun and got another as it tumbled into the trench behind me. I backpedaled, burning another, not realizing until later that it had some mechanism attached to its underside, presumably a stun ray.

Such weapons might be effective to ambush patrols, but not in open combat against a Tzen of the Warrior caste. I was constantly moving, presenting an ever-shifting target to the Enemy. Twice I abandoned the trench, clearing a space in the swarm with my blaster before rolling back to relative safety.

My wedge-sword was out now, and I used it freely on living and dead foes alike as the trench became more congested with bodies. I crawled sometimes over, sometimes under the smoldering corpses of Ants in my frantic evade-and-attack pattern.

Suddenly, the flow ebbed. I realized it was dark; the scene was lit by scattered fires touched off by our hot-beams. A beam hissed out from above me, scoring heavily in the ranks of the Ants. It was Mahz, giving me cover fire from the turret gun.

"Mahz! I order you to cover the tunnel!"

"I stopped that thrust, Commander. They broke off the attack after I burned the first ten as they emerged."

I burned another Ant.

"Cover it anyway."

The ants had spent a lot of time building that tunnel. I couldn't believe they would abandon it so easily. Too many battles had been lost by assuming a retreat.

"Incoming from your right, Commander," came Hif's voice, and a moment later she appeared.

"The north group?" I queried, blasting at a group of Ants by the burning tree stand.

"Eliminated. Apparently it was only a feint."

"Zome?"

"Helping Zur and Krahn," she replied.

"Change places with Krahn," I ordered.

"But, Commander . . ."

"I need a Technician over here." I gestured at the tree stand. "Their extinguishers are putting out the fires we need for light."

"Understood, Commander."

She moved off. I glared at the fires as they flickered out. We'd just have to rely on the firebreak to prevent widespread ecological damage. Right now we needed that light.

"Status report on the shuttlecraft?" I beamed to Mahz.

"On the way, Commander."

"Incoming from your right, Commander!" and Krahn appeared. She was wobbly, but apparently taking to combat better than Ihr had.

"Do you know the exact location of the extinguishers you planted to the west?" I asked, sweep-burning three Ants that were attempting to flank us.

"Yes, Commander."

"Start burning them out with your blaster. We need those fires."

"Commander!" came Mahz's voice.

"Rahm here."

"Strange readings on the tunnel. The hollow indicator shows it's lengthening, heading for the fortification, but there are no digging sounds."

"Cold-beam! Cold-beam in the tunnel!" I broadcast.

"I'll handle it, Commander," came Hif's voice.

"Shuttlecraft is down, Commander. Twenty meters due south."

"Evacuate at once!"

The shuttlecraft was unarmed, and I did not want it overrun.

As one, Krahn and I left the trench and begin sprinting for the shuttlecraft, burning Ants as we ran.

I saw Hif by the tunnel opening. She dropped a minigrenade down the opening, stepped back to avoid the explosion, then jumped in herself, blaster at ready. She knew as well as we did there would be no returning from the tunnel, but now our withdrawal was covered from that direction.

Zur and Zome were waiting by the shuttlecraft, pouring fire into a group of Ants pressing them hard from the Southeast. Apparently the Ants had taken up the bulk of the battle after the Leapers had been eliminated.

"Where's Mahz?" I asked, turning to train my weapons on the Ants pushing us from the West.

"Still in the gun turret, providing cover fire as ordered," replied Zur.

That had not been my intention.

"Mahz!" I beamed.

"Here, Commander."

"Set the destruct mechanism on the fortification, then put the turret gun on auto-target and withdraw."

"Confirmed, Commander."

"Shuttle pilot!" I beamed.

"Here, Commander." I was surprised to hear Horc's voice.

"Stand by for immediate takeoff when our last member reaches us."

There was a hesitation before he replied.

"Confirmed, Commander."

I realized he had been expecting to pick up a larger force than was currently in evidence.

"Concentrate cover fire for Mahz's withdrawal," I called to the rest of the team.

We could tell when the turret gun went on auto-target: it began swiveling randomly back and forth, choosing its targets by Network-triggered priority.

Mahz appeared a moment later. He had to blast his way through several Ants who apparently realized a lone Tzen was an easier target than our group by the shuttlecraft.

We concentrated our fire on the other Ants moving to block his retreat, but as so often happens with uncoordinated group fire, we missed one.

The Network was set to ignore Tzen, and it did. The turret gun swiveled and fired on the remaining Ant, coldly unheeding of the fact that Mahz was in its line of fire as it triggered the beam.

BOOK THREE

BOOK THREE

CHAPTER
-1-

I paced restlessly around the confines of my private quarters. Though theoretically solitude was supposed to aid the thought process, I found it disquieting.

I was not accustomed to solitude. In my entire career, from early training into my combat experiences, I had been surrounded by other Tzen. Even in deep sleep I had shared a rack or a bay with other Warriors. Any moment alone had been both fleeting and coincidental.

Now I and all the other Candidates on the colony ship had been assigned private quarters until we had completed our analysis. Although it was a direct order from the High Command and doubtless for the best, it made me feel uncomfortable.

My tail thumped against the wall, and I realized it was beginning to lash uncontrollably. This would not do. Mental agitation was acceptable only if it did not adversely affect my performance. It was time to curb my wandering thoughts.

I considered eating, but rejected the thought. I was not really hungry, and an intake of food at this time would only make me sluggish.

Sleep was another possibility. We were now required to devote a certain percentage of our time to sleep, whether in regular small allotments or in periodic long slumbers. I also rejected this thought. I had not progressed sufficiently with the analysis for my satisfaction. The sooner I completed my task, the sooner I could leave the isolation of private quarters. I would sleep while my analysis was being reviewed.

Clearly, the best plan of action was to return to my work. I turned once more to my work station, viewing it with mild distaste. There were several racks of data tapes as well as a multi-screen viewer, which crowded the small confines of the room.

The tapes were sorted into five groups. The first group was the accumulated data on the Ants, both confirmed and speculative, though carefully labeled to distinguish between the two. The second group contained the Technicians' report on the equipment that would be available for this campaign. The last three groups dealt with specific data on three different Ant-held planets.

The task confronting me and the other Candidates was to devise battle plans for assaulting each of the planets. The High Command's review of these plans would determine which of us would be assigned as Planetary Commanders in the upcoming campaign. There are no guaranteed assignments in the Warriors. Many of my fellow Candidates in this exercise had been Planetary Commanders in the last campaign. They would have to once again prove their analytic abilities if they were to retain their rank for this campaign. Also, it was common knowledge that there were many Warriors who had previously been Planetary Commanders who were not included in the current list of Candidates.

There was a rasp of claws on the door. I positioned myself in the doorway and triggered its opening. Zur was standing outside in the corridor holding a small box in his hand. I stood aside to show my willingness to accept his company, and he entered.

"I saw your name on the list of Candidates, Rahm," he stated without ceremony.

"That is correct," I confirmed, "though by the Black Swamps I don't know why. My progress with the assignment thus far verifies my original impression that I am not qualified for this type of work."

He cocked his head at me in question.

"I should have thought that a Warrior of your experience would be quite adept at this analysis," he commented.

"Perhaps in theory," I replied. "In actuality I find little in my prior experience to assist me in this."

"Explain?" he requested.

"Even though I have held certain lower-level authoritative positions, they have always been of an execution nature. I have been a tactician, not a strategist. I have always been presented with a plan, and my task was to modify it according to existing conditions and put it into action."

I gestured to the racks of data tapes.

"Now, instead of adapting an existing plan, I am required to devise a plan and state its requirements. Instead of being given a plan, an objective, ten Warriors, and three skimmers, and told to deploy them, I am given an objective, and asked how many Warriors and what equipment would be required to achieve that objective. It involves an entirely different logic process, one that I am not sure I possess."

Zur thought about this for several moments.

"I see your difficulty," he said at last, "but I may have a possible solution for you, if I might suggest it."

"Accepted," I said.

"You are being overwhelmed with possibilities. There are so many variables you are unable to focus on any one course of action. My suggestion is this: choose an arbitrary force, a specific number of Warriors, and a random selection of equipment. Then go ahead and devise a battle plan as if that was all you had to work with. Organize your assault and estimate your casualties. Then halve the force and devise a new plan. Then double the original force and plan it again. If I am correct, you will rapidly discover that in one situation you are handicapped by a shortage of Warriors, in another there are excess Warriors. Perhaps in one situation you will find yourself realizing that two or more pieces of equipment would take the place of ten Warriors. In any case, by establishing some of your variables as constants, you should be able to better analyze the problem."

I considered this. It seemed a logical approach.

"I will attempt to implement this method, Zur," I said. "It seems an efficient approach to problem solving."

"It is one of the primary systems employed by the Scientists caste," Zur commented. "I see no reason why it should not work equally well for a Warrior."

Somehow, this made me uncomfortable, but I withheld comment.

"This is actually the reason for my intrusion," Zur said, placing the box he was carrying in the corner. "It may aid you in your efforts."

I examined the device from a distance. My exposure to the

Technicians on my last assignment had reinforced my normal instincts to not touch any machinery I was not familiar with.

"Explain?" I requested.

"The Scientists have found that many of the older Tzen are unused to the silence inherent in privacy. To assist those individuals in their adaptation to the new systems, they instructed the Technicians to construct sound boxes such as this."

He paused, and flipped a switch on the side of the box.

Immediately, faint sounds began to issue from the device. There were sounds of feet moving back and forth, tails rasping along the floor, the low murmur of voices. Intermittently, I could make out the clank and rasp of weapons being tended to.

"It is designed to emulate the sound of other Tzen," Zur continued. "I have specifically set the sound mix to resemble a group of Warriors. Hopefully it will create a more familiar atmosphere for you to work in."

I listened for a few moments. It did indeed sound like I was in the middle of a bay of Warriors pursuing their normal activities.

I realized that as I was listening, much of the uneasiness I had been experiencing of late was slipping away. My muscles were relaxing from unrealized tensions, and my mind was focusing better.

As my thoughts became more settled and orderly, a question occurred to me.

"Why are you doing this, Zur?"

"Although I am no longer a Scientist, I have maintained my habit of scanning the listings of theories and discoveries of the Scientists' caste as they are made public. This particular innovation was given such a low-priority rating I was almost certain that with the pressures of your new assignment, it had escaped your notice. I therefore took it upon myself to bring it to your attention, as it could potentially ease your task."

"That is specifically what I am inquiring after, Zur. Why are you concerning yourself with my well-being? What bearing does my success or failure have on you?"

"My plan is for the good of the Empire, Rahm," he stated, "though I will acknowledge it is selfish in that it favors my interpretation of what is best for the Empire."

"Might I inquire as to the nature of your plan, as I seem to be an integral part of it?"

"Certainly. First, I should inform you that I refused assignment as a candidate."

This was a double surprise to me. I had not noticed that Zur's name was not on the list of Candidates. Had I given it any thought, I would have assumed if my name was there, his would be also. But more than this, I was surprised he had refused assignment.

"I have spent much time studying the structure of the Warriors' caste since I transferred," he continued. "As a result of those studies, I am of the opinion I could best serve the Empire in a specific position, but that position is not as a Planetary Commander. My logic is that I will stand a better chance of being appointed to my chosen position if a Commander I have worked with, specifically you, attains the rank of Planetary Commander and requests me for his force. To that end, I am being individually supportive of your efforts."

"What is the position you desire, Zur?"

"Second-in-command and Commander of the reserve force," he answered promptly.

I considered this.

"Might I inquire," I asked, "why you prefer that position over assignment as a Planetary Commander?"

"My reasons are two, Rahm. First, my experience in the Warriors' caste thus far has been of a supportive nature as opposed to a direct leadership role. I am confident of my abilities in that capacity, and would prefer to continue in the role I feel most efficient in."

"You were in command of the Warrior contingent in our last assignment," I pointed out.

"Reporting directly to you. That is entirely different from being the final authority in the field."

"Acknowledged," I said.

"Secondly, though I still lack the eagerness for combat that marks one raised in the Warrior caste, I find that once I enter into battle I am as effective as any Warrior, and often more so. I feel my original training as a Scientist enables me to more rapidly observe, summarize, and appraise the factors weighing on any specific situation. This ability would be best utilized in directing the efforts of a reserve force, where the situation they would be facing would be significantly different from that in the original battle plan."

His answers were, as always, well thought out and logical.

"I will take your thoughts under consideration, Zur, if I receive assignment as Planetary Commander. It occurs to me, however, there may be a reluctance on the part of the High Command to assign two Warriors with our firsthand experience at dealing with the Ants to the same strike force.''

''That is a factor beyond our control, Rahm. For the moment, I am content in the knowledge you would find my proposal worthy of serious consideration.''

''My opinions will have little importance if I do not receive a Command assignment,'' I reminded him.

''Of that I have every confidence,'' Zur answered. ''Perhaps I did not make myself clear, Rahm. I offer assistance only to make your analysis easier, not because I feel you would not be assigned if I did not contribute. I am sure that in your case this exercise is merely a formality. The High Command would have to be foolish to pass you over for a Command assignment, and although I have not always agreed with their decisions, I have never known them to be foolish.''

He turned and left without further comment.

I pondered his last statement. Zur was seldom, if ever, wrong in his analysis. He had correctly anticipated my first appointment as flight leader even before he joined the Warriors' caste. His thoughts were not to be taken lightly.

Grudgingly, I turned my attentions once more to my analysis. Even if Zur was correct, even if this analysis was merely a formality, it still had to be done.

The familiar noises issuing from the sound box aided my concentration as I readdressed myself to my proposed battle plans.

CHAPTER
-2-

I studied my four strike team Commanders as they familiarized themselves with the data packs they had just been issued.

I assumed that Zur was engaged in the same study, though neither of us spoke. It was a natural enough reaction, as this was the first time we had met these Warriors.

This was not to imply, however, that they were unknown to us or that we had never discussed them. On the contrary, they had been carefully selected by Zur and myself after several long wake-spans of reviewing individual records of available Warriors.

This selection process had proved to be far more difficult than I would ever have imagined. There were numerous qualified Warriors with little among their records to distinguish them. They were so similar, in fact, that it was a momentary temptation to simply state "no preference" and allow the High Command to assign the necessary Warriors to us. In the end, however, we took the time to examine the records and select our strike team leaders. If there was a slight edge to be gained by selecting certain qualifications over others, it was well worth the time spent.

There were no specific qualifications, such as seniority, breeding, or test records, that decided our choices. Rather, we looked for specific individuals whom we felt would be best able to fill our needs.

Heem's last assignment had been as a Warrior advisor to the Scientists' caste. He had served in this capacity, sometimes observing, sometimes taking weapons in hand to demonstrate a point, during the period when the Scientists were performing the tests and experiments that constituted the main data base on the Ants currently used for reference. I had been advised by Zur that not all the test results known to the Scientists were published. Mostly this was to insure concision of reporting, but occasionally data was omitted because no satisfactory explanation had been found. Scientists were loath to state speculation or opinion as fact. As a Warrior, I was more concerned with reliable observation than with explanation. If an organism I'm fighting breathes fire, I want to know about it even if no one has figured out exactly how it is accomplished. It was hoped that Heem would be able to provide such firsthand data.

Tur-Kam was selected for different reasons. Her prior experience had been as a trainer. Her extensive knowledge of current training techniques and the comparative merits of available facilities and trainers would provide valuable counsel as to how to get maximum effectiveness out of the available preparation time. Her own combat and leadership potential ratings were impressively high, and the frequency with which she had been bred bore mute testimony to the High Command's respect for her abilities.

Zah-Rah I anticipated would be one of our strongest strike team leaders. She would have to be, for the target anthill for her force was exceptionally complex and difficult. She was one of the candidates who had not been assigned to a Planetary Commander position. I had requested and received copies of her attack proposals, and upon receiving them found her methods and philosophies meritorious and compatible with my own. I felt we were extremely fortunate to have acquired her for our strike force.

Kah-Tu had the least experience of any of the strike team leaders. However, his combat and leadership potential ratings were phenomenal. It was noted in his records that only his lack of combat experience had kept him from being assigned as a Candidate, and therefore a potential Planetary Commander. Selecting him as a strike team leader might have been considered risky by some, but not by me. Others would not attach any significance to another entry in his record; the one stating he was the result of a breeding between Kor, who had served with me in two earlier assignments, and Zur, my current second-in-command.

The group's attention was drawn to the door as one final Warrior entered the squad bay we were using for a headquarters. She walked with the slight unsteadiness that marked one who had only recently boarded a colony ship and was still adjusting to the centrifugal force gravity.

This was Raht, the last of our five strike team leaders. Her tardiness was acceptable, as there was valid reason for its occurrence. She has just returned from assignment, leading a flight of scout flyers on a mission over one of the Ant-held Planets. She had accepted her current position in our force while en route back to the colony ship.

"Are you capable of participating in our briefing, Raht?" I asked.

"In a moment, Commander," she replied unhesitatingly. "As soon as I refresh myself with a drink of water."

We waited as she stepped to the water dispenser and drank deeply. It was not uncommon for a Tzen to experience a dehydration from space travel.

Raht was another valuable member of our team. Her work as a scout meant she was familiar with all the latest equipment available and had firsthand knowledge of the inevitable difficulties and idiosyncrasies inherent therein. What was more, she doubtless had additional knowledge of the Ants that was even now being studied by the Scientists and High Command prior to general release.

"Ready, Commander," Raht stated, taking her data pack from Zur. I was impressed by her perseverance. Most Warriors would have requested reorientation time between combat assignments. I wondered if her attitude could be at all traced to her longevity. For the last three Hatchings, the policy of assigning two-syllable names had been in effect. Thus her name, like those of Zur, Heem, and myself marked her as a survivor of an earlier era of the Empire.

"Before we begin," I said, "there is one point of clarification which should be communicated to you. It has now been confirmed that due to transportation timing, any Warrior accepting assignment on this Force will be exempt from the final mission against the Leapers. By the time that strike force has completed its mission and returned to the colony ship, our own force will have finished its preparations for the upcoming campaign and be well on its way to its Target Planet. If any of you wish to withdraw your acceptance of position in this strike force so that you might be included in the final Leaper assault, you should do so at this time. Even though your participation in that assault would negate your rejoining our specific strike force, there would be positions

available in the Planetary strike forces which would be forming
and training after our departure.''

I paused to give them opportunity to speak.

The five team leaders waited impassively for me to continue.
Zur was right again. I had been sure we would lose at least one to
the final Leaper assault.

''Very well,'' I said at last. ''I, Rahm, as Planetary Commander
duly confirmed and authorized by the High Command, formally
confirm the acceptance of appointment to the position of strike
team Commander of Heem, Tur-Kam, Zah-Rah, Kah-Tu, and
Raht.''

As I spoke, the team leaders looked at each other in mild
appraisal. This was the first time they had heard the names of their
fellow staff members.

''Zur has accepted appointment as my second-in-command and
Commander of the reserve force,'' I continued. ''In event of my
absence or incapacitation, he will assume full command of the
force until the High Command appoints a successor.''

The formalities over, I nodded to Zur, who turned on the row of
view tables. Immediately, Tri-D projections of the five anthills
appeared, one over each table.

''These are our targets,'' I said. ''As you can see, we have been
assigned one of the more formidable planets, one having five
rather than the average two or three anthills. The mission of this
campaign is to destroy the queens and the egg beds of the Ants.''

I turned from the tables to address them directly.

''Each of you will command a team assaulting one of those
anthills. The specific data and plans pertaining to your anthill are
contained in the data pack you have been issued. You are to
review that data immediately and inform Zur or myself of any
proposed changes in the battle plan or support requirements. You
will also prepare and present for the entire staff a summary of the
battle plan for your specific anthill.''

I paused and reviewed my words thus far for ommissions before
turning to the next subject.

''As we are one of the first wave of Planetary strike forces, you
will have a wide choice of Warriors to build your specific teams
from. I would caution you, however, not to take an excessive
amount of time in submitting requests for specific team members.
The longer it takes to form your team, the less time they will have
to train. If I feel you are taking too long to name your preferences,

I will give you one time warning. If after that you are still unable to make a decision, your force will simply be assigned to you.

''The quartering assignments for your teams and the tentative training schedules are included in your data packs. If you would propose any changes to that schedule, discuss them with either Zur or me immediately. I would anticipate one question, and point out that if the training period seems both long and intense, remember the nature of our mission will require that much of the combat be done in the tunnels of the anthills. As the Warriors are unaccustomed to fighting in complete darkness, maximum time must be allowed for familiarization with the new equipment if they are to perform at peak efficiency.''

I faced them squarely for my closing comments.

''You will all be quartered here with Zur and me. Once your teams are formed, you will be on call to me at all times. If I call a staff meeting, I will expect to see you, not your second-in-commands. Serious illness or injury will be the only excuse for nonattendance, and if your impairment is serious, we will not expect you to recover and will seek a replacement. I mention this so you will not overextend yourselves between sleep periods. Do not allow yourself to become fatigued to the brink of exhaustion, for your planned sleep may be interrupted.

''As we are one of the first strike forces to be sent out, we will have to adapt to any new developments or equipment in minimum time, or not at all. Are there questions?''

The team leaders were silent for several moments as they digested the briefing.

I waited.

''Question, Commander!''

''Yes, Tur-Kam?''

''Would you clarify the necessity for destroying the egg beds as well as the queens?''

I turned to Zur and nodded for him to reply.

''It has been discovered,'' he began, ''that in event of a queen's death, the Ants are able to inject additives to certain eggs to produce a new queen. Therefore, if we are to succeed in exterminating the Ants as a continuing species, we must destroy the eggs as well as the queens.''

''Commander?''

''Yes, Raht?''

''In our selection of specific Warriors, particularly our second-in-commands, are there any Warriors you would deem unaccept-able?"

"While you will be expected to review your choices with Zur or myself prior to acting on them, we currently have no prejudices against any individual, Hatching, or ability group which would result in an immediate veto."

"Question, Commander."

"Yes, Kah-Tu?"

"What are your anticipated casualties on this mission?"

"If the assault proceeds according to plan without unanticipated resistance, we expect to survive the mission with no more than seventy percent casualties."

No one said anything else.

CHAPTER
-3-

Zur accompanied me as I rode the shuttle flyer to the Technicians' portion of the colony ship. Actually, I realized, the term "colony ship" was a misnomer. The reality of the situation was that the colony was actually a collection of smaller ships traveling in close alignment without any physical connection between them. Although they theoretically could be joined together to form one massive unit, and each new module was designed with that purpose in mind, the fact of the matter was that they had not been so arranged since shortly after the Empire relocated its population into them. Each massive module was a self-contained, stand-alone unit. When it was necessary to form a new colony ship, orders were simply issued for certain modules to set a new course, and there would be two colony ships where before there had been only one. How many such colony ships there were currently in the Empire I neither knew nor cared.

The modules that composed the Technicians' portion of the ship were easily distinguished from the others on the screen. They were the ones that were solid discs as opposed to the rings that were the Scientists' and Warriors' modules. I had never known the reason for this until the first time an occasion arose necessitating a visit to the Technicians' section. Once there, it became obvious. Unlike the Scientists and Warriors, who worked and trained in the centrifugal-force-simulated gravity of rim-module, the Technicians did much of their work in the near-zero gravity that existed at the center of the module. In fact, certain subcastes of Technicians, such as the pilot of our shuttle craft, the transport pilots, and the heavy construction workers, were specifically bred for zero-gravity work and spent the majority if not all of their lives in that condition.

The docking process interrupted my thoughts. We departed the shuttlecraft without exchanging words with the pilot. As I have noted before, exchanges between members of different castes are rare except at certain rank-levels.

A Technician was waiting to receive us as we disembarked.

"I am Or-Sah," he introduced himself. "I have been assigned to answer your questions."

"This is Rahm," Zur responded, "a Planetary Commander of the Warriors, here to inspect the progress on various pieces of equipment being prepared for the Ant campaign."

I did not question why Zur did not introduce himself. Part of the reason I had him accompany me on these trips was that he was far more familiar with intercaste protocol than I.

"First," I stated, "I would wish to inspect the new Borer units."

"Certainly, Commander," replied Or-sah without hesitation. "This way."

The Borer units were an improvement on the fortification we had used in our last mission. Instead of simply burning their way into a ground-level position, the new units were fitted with telescoping walls that extended downward as a tunnel was burned to accommodate them. Although all the units were of the same general design, they had to be individually modified. As each anthill was unique, the Borers designated to each anthill had to be built to penetrate to different depths. In cases where the chosen path for the Borer intersected existing Ant tunnels, ledges and firing slots had to be added to enable the Warriors to defend the tunnel from assault.

"Here is the prototype of the Borer unit, Commander," Or-sah said, leading us into a large chamber.

High above us, work crews were laboring, furiously constructing additional units. We ignored them and studied the unit at our level.

One feature that was immediately apparent to the eye was the additional armament. The weapons at the top of the dome were heavier and more numerous, and there were additional weapons mounted along the perimeter of the unit.

"Have the lock-out mechanisms of the auto weapons been modified?" I asked.

"They have," Or-sah confirmed. "They will now recognize and bypass a Tzen in their field of fire, though I personally have never understood the need for such a requirement."

I kept my silence, but involuntarily my head lowered.

"On our last mission," Zur commented conversationally, "the Commander lost a team member because one of the auto mounts opened fire while he was in line with the target."

"But the specifics of this campaign state that no Warriors will be on the ground outside the Borer units," the Technician argued. "Why should the Technicians have to waste valuable time designing——"

"Are the walls of this tube in their finished state?" I interrupted.

"Yes they are, Commander."

"Why haven't they been treated for cold-beam immunity?"

"Because it isn't necessary, Commander," Or-sah replied. "The Energy-Drain units should render the Ants' weapons ineffectual."

I found the patronizing tone of his voice irritating.

"And if they do not, every Warrior in the tube will be vulnerable to having his escape route cut off," I commented.

"The Technicians have every confidence in the Energy-Drain units."

"Have they been live-tested?" I asked.

"The Warriors' caste vetoed any live testing," Or-Sah retorted. "The reasoning given was that if the units were successful, it would give the Ants forewarning and provide them with time to develop a countermeasure."

I noticed that now it was Or-sah who was lowering his head. I considered his position, and found his anger justified. It would be irritating to be forbidden to test a piece of equipment, then have to answer complaints that it was untested . . . particularly when both the veto and the challenge came from members of the same caste.

"Perhaps," I suggested, "you could provide me additional information as to the nature of the Energy-Drain units. My lack of understanding of the official releases on them is doubtless contributing to my reluctance in accepting their effectiveness."

He seemed surprised at the request, but responded nonetheless.

"Certainly, Commander," he began. "The xylomorphic interface utilized by the Ants——"

"Excuse me, Or-sah," I interrupted, "but are you familiar with a Technician named Horc?"

"Yes I am, Commander," he replied. "I served under him on my last assignment."

"Would you happen to know if he is available for consultation at this time?"

Or-sah hesitated before answering.

"Horc is dead," he said finally. "Killed in a duel with a Warrior."

That surprised me.

"That does not seem logical," I commented. "Warriors are currently forbidden to challenge outside their caste."

"Horc was the challenger," Or-sah explained.

"Then are there any other Technicians available who are used to dealing with members of other castes?" I asked. "Although your explanations may be clear to another Technician, as a Warrior I find them beyond my comprehension and vocabulary."

He maintained a thoughtful silence for a few moments.

"Perhaps I can try again, Commander," he suggested finally. "I feel there is a growing need for communication between the castes, and I will not develop that ability in myself if I delegate the job to others."

"Proceed," I acknowledged.

"Both the Ants and the Empire utilize the same power-source, specifically that developed by the First Ones. Even though we have succeeded in applying it to a higher level of technology, it is still the same energy-source. It is as if the Ants and the Empire each maintained a cave with a circular opening to let the sunlight in; even though the caves are different, the openings and the sunlight are the same. Because of this, the Ants can run their machines from our power sources and we can run our machines from theirs."

He paused. When I did not interrupt, he continued.

"In preparation for the Ant campaign, we have made two major developments. First, we modified our power-source and changed the configuration of our machines to accept it. In the analogy, we have effectively created a new sun, one which will shine through the hole in our cave, but not through the hole in the Ants' cave."

"How is that done?" I asked.

"I would be unable to explain it without becoming extremely

technical, Commander," Or-sah replied. "Simply accept that we have done it."

"Very well," I said. "Continue."

"Now. The situation exists where we can run our machines from our power-source or theirs. The Ants, on the other hand, can only utilize their own power. When that is used up, their machines become nonfunctional. Our second major development is a machine, one which runs on the Ants' power-source. It consumes their power at an unbelievable rate, and converts it to power which replenishes our own new power-source. These are the Energy-Drainers. In simple terms, they make us stronger by diverting the Ants' energy away from them and to us."

I considered his explanation.

"Is this power drain instantaneous?" I asked.

"No," he admitted, "but the battle plans call for the units to be dropped in advance of the actual assault. The Ants' power should be drained prior to the strike teams' landing."

"What if the Ants have power sources they do not activate until the assault begins?"

"Then they would have power for a short time before the Energy-Drain units could fully deplete them."

"In that case," I concluded, "I will formally submit a request to the High Command that all Borer units be treated for cold-beam immunity."

"That is your prerogative, Commander," the Technician replied.

"I would examine the progress in arming the shuttlecraft next," I stated.

"Certainly, Commander. This way."

Zur broke off his inspection of the Borer prototype and fell in step as we left.

"Might I ask a personal question, Commander?" Or-sah said as we went.

"Proceed."

"Do you or your aide find the current designs for individual blasters ineffective?"

That question surprised me, though I could see where, as a Technician, he would be eager to know the answer. I glanced at Zur, who indicated no desire to respond.

"No," I said for the two of us, "we don't."

"I had simply noted that both of you wear only the old hand weapons," Or-sah explained.

He lapsed into silence, apparently unable to bring himself to ask why.

He had given me food for thought, however. In hindsight, I realized that all five strike team leaders . . . in fact all the Warriors I had recently encountered, wore blasters either in addition to or to the exclusion of the old hand weapons. I made a mental note to add a blaster to my personal armament again. It would not do to have it appear a Planetary Commander was not staying abreast of new developments.

CHAPTER
-4-

I was performing one of my scheduled reviews of the force in training. Although these were normally one of my less distasteful duties as Commander, I was finding more and more that I had to schedule these reviews or they would be overlooked in my numerous other tasks in preparing for the upcoming campaign.

As prescribed by the High Command, the Warriors were all training in the new echo helmets. Unfortunately, this made it impossible to distinguish among individuals. During training, the echo helmets had extra face plates to obscure the vision, simulating total darkness and forcing the Warrior to rely solely on the data provided by the helmets' sensors. The difficulty was that the face plate also obscured the individual's features, making casual identification difficult if not impossible, save in cases where radical physical differences such as height or an amputated tail marked the Warrior.

Zur and the five strike team leaders accompanied me as I made my review. Aside from that, training progressed normally . . . at least theoretically. I say theoretically, because there were numerous subtle points of difference between what I was observing and what I knew from experience to be a typical day's training.

For one thing, it was rare that a trainer would actively take part in the training. They, like myself, were usually overburdened with administrative details of scheduling and training design and therefore had to delegate the actual training process to their staff.

It was not uncommon for a Warrior to cycle through an entire training phase without once directly encountering the trainer responsible. Today, however, the trainers were very much in evidence. Whether directly supervising the training or simply overseeing, their presence was extremely noticeable.

Then there was the appearance of the training bays themselves. Though orderliness is necessary when working with or around live weapons, there is usually a certain amount of clutter and disorder associated with training. When the primary focus is on training, Warriors tend to let things fall where they fall. They would police the area afterward, but for the time being their main concern was experimenting with new possibilities and combinations to perfect their skill as the fighting arm of the Empire. The training bays I was seeing were so orderly I had the definite impression that I was viewing an exhibition rather than a fighting force at practice.

I was not so sure of my observations as to raise comment at this time, however. Rather, I determined that my next review would be unscheduled and unannounced, even to my staff. I would compare my observations of that review with my current impressions before deciding if there was cause for alarm.

Something caught my eye as I scanned the training Warriors. I halted my progress, causing my staff to press closer to me and stand in a waiting semicircle around me.

We were on one of the elevated walkways overlooking a maze. The Warriors below were maneuvering the corridors utilizing the echo helmets, and pausing sporadically to fire at pseudo-Ant targets that appeared singly or in groups to block their path. The transparent walls of the maze gave clear view of the exercise, but what caught my attention was elsewhere.

"Zur!" I beamed to my second-in-command.

Because of the sensitivity of the echo helmets, we did not speak aloud in the training bays.

"Yes, Commander!"

"Summon that Warrior to me. . . . The one who is waiting in line . . . third from the front."

"Certainly, Commander."

I waited as my request was relayed.

One of the specific things I was studying in this review was the weapons rigs of the individual Warriors. As I have mentioned, audible sound can have a confusing effect on the echo helmets, and individual weapons carried in the traditional battle rigs had a tendency to make noise . . . slight, but noise nonetheless. As many developments in the Warriors' caste have come from solutions individuals have devised in the field in response to specific problems, I was eager to see what modifications were developing.

That is what I had been looking for. It was not what caught my eye.

The indicated Warrior was approaching our group now. I was pleased to note he had not removed his echo helmet. The force were rapidly approaching the point where they would be as natural maneuvering from the echo helmet data as with their normal vision.

"I am Rahm," I beamed to him, stepping forward. "May I examine your wedge-sword?"

"Yes, Commander," responded the Warrior, smoothly snatching the weapon from his harness and extending it to me handle first.

I took the sword and examined it closely. It was identical to my own weapon in size, heft, and balance, except for the pommel weight at the butt of the weapon. It was this that had caught my eye. Rather than being smoothly tooled like my own, it was fashioned as an irregular lump.

"I am puzzled by the design of your pommel, Warrior," I beamed. "What improvement does this deviation from the normal pattern signify?"

There was a moment's hesitation before the Warrior replied.

"None, Commander."

"Then why use this design over the standard?"

"It's fashioned to resemble the head of an Ant, Commander."

I examined the pommel again. He was right. Now that I was looking for that specific feature, the pommel did roughly approximate the head of an Ant.

"But why would you want a pommel that looks like the head of an Ant?"

"It . . . it gives me pleasure to look at it, Commander."

I was beginning to think there was something significant indicated here. Perhaps a recurrence of the inactive time problem I had experienced on my last mission.

"Where did you obtain this weapon, Warrior?"

"From the Technicians, Commander, like any other weapon. I'm sure if the Commander is interested, one would be available for him, too. I notice several of his staff already have them."

Startled by this statement, I shot a glance at my waiting staff.

The Warrior was right! Zah-Rah and Raht were wearing weapons similar to the one I was holding, I had simply not noticed before.

"Very well, Warrior," I beamed, returning his sword. "That will be all. You may resume your training again."

The Warrior turned and strode away.

I resumed my tour of review.

"One moment, Commander!"

It was Tur-Kam's voice beamed into my head. I halted and turned to face her. The ex-Trainer was intently watching the retreating figure of the Warrior.

"What is it, Tur-Kam?" I beamed.

"With your permission, Commander, I would like to investigate something."

"Proceed."

The Warrior I had conversed with suddenly halted, turned, and retraced his steps back to our group. I realized he must be responding to Tur-Kam's hail.

She stepped forward to meet him, and there was a silent exchange for a few moments. Then the Warrior removed his echo helmet and handed it to Tur-Kam. She examined it closely.

"Commander! This warrants your attention."

I joined them, and she passed me the helmet.

"I thought this Warrior's movements were too sure for one just learning the intricacies of an echo helmet," she beamed. "If you examine this unit, you will see it has been modified to allow his normal vision to bypass the face plate."

She was right. Though undetectable while the helmet was on, the modification was readily apparent when viewed from this vantage.

"Zur!" I beamed.

"Yes, Commander."

"Spread this order. All training in this bay is to cease. All Warriors are to remove their echo helmets. Immediately."

I passed the helmet to my staff and waited for the Warriors below to comply with my orders. Within moments, they were all standing with faces upturned toward our position. I stepped to the edge of the walkway.

"The trainer of this Warrior will present himself to me immediately," I announced.

"Commander," Tur-Kam said, quietly stepping to my side, "If there is to be a duel, I would request permission to represent the

Empire. This incident is a reflection on all trainers and therefore on me. I would therefore ask preference of challenge.''

"I disagree, Commander," said Zah-Rah stepping to my other side. "This Warrior is in my strike team. If preference of challenge is to be awarded, it should be mine."

"Your opinions are noted," I replied. "Return to your places."

The trainer was approaching as they complied with my order. I took the echo helmet from Raht and passed it to her.

"Examine this helmet," I ordered.

She took the helmet and examined it closely.

"With your permission, Commander?" she asked.

She stepped to the edge of the walkway and beckoned to one of the Warriors below, presumably her second-in-command.

We waited as the Warrior hastened to join us. The entire episode was potentially quite serious. The trainers are a privileged subgroup of the Warriors, but there is a price for their status. They are responsible for everything that takes place during training.

The new Warrior joined us, and the trainer passed the helmet to him without a word. The brevity of his inspection was not lost on me or the trainer.

"Your comments?" I asked.

"None, Commander," the trainer replied.

Her assistant started to step forward, but she held up a hand to restrain him.

"I am responsible for this portion of the training," she continued, "and therefore stand ready to answer for any transgression which may have transpired."

"Face the Warriors," I said.

She hesitated, then turned and stepped to the edge of the walkway.

I raised my voice to address the entire bay.

"It has been brought to my attention that the progress in training I have viewed today has been falsified. If this had not been discovered, had I been allowed to think you were more prepared than you are, I might have committed you to battle before you were actually ready. If that situation would have occurred, you would have been soundly defeated. The Empire's campaign against the Ants would have failed, and we would have been too depleted in numbers to mount another attack."

I pointed to the trainer.

"This Warrior was responsible for your current . phase of training. Her neglect of duty does not constitute a difference of opinion or an affront of any individual, group, or caste. It is a direct threat to the Empire.''

I signaled to Zur. His alter-mace came off his harness and struck in one smooth blur of motion. The trainer's body hurtled off the walkway and crashed limply on the floor below.

''She dies not as a Tzen and a Warrior in a duel or in service to the Empire, but as an Enemy and a threat to our existence.''

I turned and continued my review, my staff accompanying me.

As we entered the next training bay, we could hear behind us the cautious sounds of the Warriors resuming their training.

CHAPTER
-5-

". . . The earlier possibilities of the Ants' utilizing either poison gas or an acid spray have been discarded. While these devices are within the grasp of their technology, there have been no indications to date of their use or development."

Of all my duties, I found these briefings with representatives of the Scientists' caste the most distasteful. The briefing was particularly uncomfortable as I was without Zur's counsel. He was justifiably preoccupied working with his reserve force. Unfortunately, this left me to deal with the Scientists alone.

"We are still working on a means of disrupting the Ants' communications, but at this time it seems unlikely an adequate counter will be perfected prior to your departure. Effective countermeasures have been developed, however, to deal with the stun rays."

She indicated a small flat mechanism on the table at the side of the room.

"They are worn strapped to the chest, and field tests have proved they will nullify the effect of a stun ray. The Technicians are currently producing them for issue in the near future."

"Has the exact range of a stun ray been defined yet?" I interrupted.

"No," the Scientist answered. "It seems to vary according to the amount of energy fed into the projector."

I made a mental note to require all transport crew members to wear these units. Having the Planet-side Warriors immune to the stun rays would be of limited merit if the Ants could succeed in using them against the orbiting transports.

"We have continued monitoring the indirect surveillance of the spacecraft housed in the anthills," the Scientist continued. "There have been no sounds or other indications of work or modifications being performed. Therefore, it is assumed the Ants are still utilizing the primitive craft originally given them by the First Ones. The armed shuttlecraft should be sufficient to insure no Ants will escape once the final assault begins."

"Do the Ants' spacecraft utilize the same power source as their weapons?" I asked.

"That is correct."

"Then won't the Energy-Drain units perfected by the Technicians negate the use of the spacecraft?"

"The Energy-Drain units were developed independently by the Technicians," the Scientist pointed out. "Until the principle has been tested and confirmed by the Scientists' caste, I would be hesitant to comment as to its reliability."

"Will those confirmation tests be performed prior to my force's departure?"

"I am not familiar with that project's priority rating, Commander. I will investigate and inform you immediately."

"Very well. What is the next item for review?"

"That completes the agenda for this briefing, Commander. Do you have any questions?"

I thought carefully for several minutes before replying.

"Would it be permissible to ask a question not related to this mission? One of a nonmilitary nature?"

"Certainly, Commander. I have been assigned to supply you with information. There have been no instructions limiting the scope of that information."

I considered my question carefully before verbalizing it.

"Could you comment as to whether or not the nonactive time now available to the individual is having an adverse affect on the Empire?"

The Scientist cocked her head, her tail twitched minutely.

"Could you clarify your question, Commander?"

I began to pace restlessly. I was unaccustomed to expressing my thoughts to Scientists.

"Since returning from my last mission, I have become increasingly aware of certain changes in the Empire. For the most part, I ignored them, as they had no direct bearing on me or the performance of my duties. Recently, however, an incident occurred which I could not ignore for its potential implications."

"What incident was that?" she asked.

"The details are unimportant. It involved a deliberate deception."

"A deception? That doesn't seem logical."

"My staff discovered it in my presence," I reiterated. "A premeditated falsification of training progress. My question is, is this a widespread problem throughout the Empire or was it an isolated case?"

I waited as the Scientist pondered my question.

"No other such incidents have been reported to the Scientists, Commander," she said at last, "though I cannot say whether this is because no similar incidents have occurred or if they were simply deemed unimportant."

"Unimportant?" Despite my self-pledged control, I felt my head begin to lower. "Such a falsification can only be interpreted as a direct threat to the Empire."

"I find your logic unclear, Commander."

"If I had believed the deception, I might have committed my force prematurely."

"But would you have?"

My tail began to lash slightly.

"Clarify your question?" I requested.

"Your exact words were that you might have committed your force," the Scientist replied. "I was inquiring as to whether or not you actually would have. If the deception had gone undetected, if you had believed everything you saw, would you have immediately reported to the High Command that your force was ready for combat?"

"Certainly not," I responded. "The force's training is far from complete. There is considerable time remaining before our scheduled departure, and it is my duty and that of my staff to be sure that time is utilized to best advantage."

"Then by your own admission, the incident was of no importance."

"You have missed the point entirely," I said.

"Perhaps, Commander. Could you clarify your position?"

I paused to organize my thoughts.

"As a Commander of the Warriors' caste, I must be sensitive to the implications of an event beyond the immediate. I must concern myself with potentials, not just confirmed realities.''

"Commander, are you attempting to explain the necessity of considering potentials to a member of the Scientists' caste?''

I lapsed into silence realizing both the truth of her observation and the futility of my efforts. The break in the conversation lengthened as I cast about for a new way to phrase my question.

"Commander," the Scientist said at last, "might I ask a question?''

"Certainly," I replied.

"How many Hatchings have you survived?''

I cocked my head.

"Clarify?'' I requested.

"How many Hatchings have there been since your own?''

"I have no accurate knowledge of that," I admitted. "My career began when the Empire was still in the Black Swamps. During those times the number and frequency of the Hatchings were kept secret, particularly from line Warriors such as I.''

"Do you know why that was necessary?''

"Yes. There was a period, three campaigns before the current war, when the Enemy we were fighting, the Day Swimmers, were not only intelligent, they were also able to decipher our speech. Information on the Hatchings was withheld so that a captured Warrior could not be forced into yielding it to the Enemy. It has been an axiom among our caste that the only way to be sure a Warrior will not talk when tortured is to give him nothing to talk about.''

"But," the Scientist persisted, "since that time Hatching information has been available for the asking. How many Hatchings do you recall?''

"I have never concerned myself with such matters," I said. "I learned originally to function in the absence of such information, and have never encountered evidence since to convince me of its necessity.''

"Commander, my own career began here on the colony ship, after the campaign against the Wasps. Though I have never kept close note, I personally know of over thirty Hatchings since my own. Perhaps you could estimate from that——''

"I fail to see the point of this line of questioning," I interrupted. "What is it you are attempting to discover?''

Now it was the Scientist who paused before answering.

"Commander," she began at last, "among my fellow caste

members, I am considered old and knowledgeable. Yet I have only vague knowledge of life in the Black Swamps, and would have to go to the data tapes to obtain information of the War against the Day Swimmers you reference so easily.''

''There is no doubt my veteran's status played a major role in my candidacy, if that is your point,'' I prompted impatiently.

''More than that, Commander. It means your attitudes were shaped and set in a period completely alien to today's Warrior's.''

''Scientist,'' I said, ''are you questioning my qualifications as a Commander of the Warriors' caste?''

''Not at all,'' she said hastily. ''Hear me out, Commander. If my information is correct, the current battle plans allow for sixty-three to ninety-two percent casualties. In the early campaigns of the Empire, victory itself was uncertain. This could account for your difficulty in understanding the logic processes of the newer Hatchings.''

''Clarify?'' I requested.

I was growing increasingly aware of the time being consumed in this interview. What I had hoped would be answered with a brief statement was developing into a lengthy conversation.

''The newer Hatchings enjoy a security you never had, Commander. Whereas you were taught that the Empire hung in the balance in every battle, the younger Warriors have a strong conviction the Empire will survive. As such, they are more concerned with their standing in the Empire than you ever were. This is not to say they are not aware of the importance of the upcoming campaign against the Ants. They are still Tzen and Warriors and would never knowingly participate in any activity they believed would weaken the force. However, they also have an interest in their roles after the battle, and as such are not above trying to create the best possible impression on their superiors, in this case you.''

I decided it was time to bring this discussion to a close.

''Your comments and observations have been most beneficial,'' I said formally. ''I shall be on my guard to insure this new feeling of security does not endanger the force's preparations for battle.''

''But Commander—'' the Scientist began.

''My duties require my presence elsewhere,'' I interrupted. ''As always, the Scientists have proved their undeniable value in support of the Warriors' caste and the Empire.''

I turned and strode away before she would resume her oration. As I went, I chided myself briefly for having attempted to pose a

nonspecific question to a Scientist. As expected, the answer had
been cryptic and had not directly addressed the question posed.

I resolved not to enter into another briefing session without
Zur's accompanying me. Perhaps I would even delegate that
portion of the preparations completely to him. My duty was to
prepare my force for battle, not play word games with a Scientist.

CHAPTER
-6-

The Tri-D Projection maps of the anthills were a minor marvel. They were possible through a modification of the jury-rigged device the Technicians had developed on our last mission. The original device simply indicated the presence of a subterranean hollow such as a cave or a tunnel. This had proved to be an invaluable aid in setting our defenses, giving us forewarning of the Ants' attempts to tunnel toward our fortification.

The new modification, however, made the device a powerful addition to our offensive effort as well. Instead of simply indicating the existence of a tunnel, the new devices could also determine its size and depth from the surface. A scout flyer armed with one of these devices crisscrossing the air over an anthill could now bring back a map of the tunnels and caverns composing that network.

My staff was currently assembled in front of one of those maps, the map of the second anthill, Raht's assignment.

"The difficulties in assaulting this particular anthill are obvious," I stated in opening. "As you can see, one of the major egg chambers lies here, under this lake."

I indicated the specific location on the map.

"I have called this meeting to seek your counsel on a problem which has arisen, or more specifically has failed to be corrected. The latest progress report from the Technicians indicates they have been unable to perfect a watertight Borer unit. What is more, their current projections for a completion time on that task fall well beyond our anticipated departure date. That means our original plan to bore directly to that chamber is no longer valid. We will have to formulate and implement a new plan if the assault is to be successful.''

I waited as they pondered the problem. Raht bent over to examine the map more closely, a gesture I realized was merely a formality to help her think, as she had long since committed the map to memory.

''Commander,'' began Zah-Rah, ''am I correct in assuming a force will have to traverse the tunnels from one of the other bore points? If so, it seems logical that they would have to come from this point, as it is the nearest to their objective.''

''With your permission, Commander?'' Raht requested.

''Certainly, Raht.''

''That is not a viable possibility, Zah-Rah,'' she began. ''They would have to travel one of these two tunnels. Our current plans call for both those tunnels to be collapsed by Surface Thumpers. Failure to do that would allow the Ants to bring support units into position to protect the queen's chamber, here.''

''Have you considered the possibility of creating our own tunnels?'' suggested Heem.

''Clarify?'' I requested.

''It is a known fact that Ants utilize cold-beams in the construction of their tunnels. As we also have cold-beams, it occurs to me we could employ them in a similar fashion. If we sank a Bore shaft, say here, we could then use the cold-beams to tunnel horizontally to reach the egg chamber.''

I considered the proposal. It seemed to be an effective and ingenious solution to the problem. I was about to comment to that effect, when I noticed Zur was consulting the data tapes.

''Do you have something to add to the discussion, Zur?'' I asked.

''One moment, Commander. I seem to recall . . . yes, here it is.''

He studied the data tape before continuing.

''I regret to say horizontal tunneling will not be possible in this situation.''

''Explain?'' requested Heem.

''Although it is true the Ants employ cold-beams to bore their tunnels, it is merely to supplement their own abilities. Constructing a tunnel requires more than boring a horizontal hole. It also involves some type of bracing to prevent its collapse. The Ants accomplish this with a form of cement they make with their own saliva. We have no such ability, and to attempt to construct a tunnel without support could only be disastrous.''

"What if the tunnel is through solid rock? Wouldn't that negate the necessity for additional bracing?'' Heem asked.

"That is what I was checking on the data tapes,'' Zur replied. "The region of the second anthill is characterized by loose, sandy soil, not solid rock.''

"Perhaps the Technicians could devise a spray cement for us to use,'' Heem persisted.

"I will inquire as to that possibility,'' I intervened. "However, realizing we are in this predicament due to the Technicians' inability to comply with a simple request, and considering the lack of time before our departure, I do not feel it would be wise to rely completely on a new discovery as a solution to our problem. Another answer will have to be devised.''

"Commander?''

"Yes, Zur.''

"Perhaps we are treating the lake as an obstacle instead of utilizing it.''

"Explain?'' I requested.

"We know the eggs are vulnerable to water. Couldn't we simply drop one of the water darts we used against the Aquatics into the lake with instructions to direct its cold-beams against the lake floor at this point? Such an attack would flood the chamber, effectively destroying the eggs with minimal loss of personnel.''

"What would prevent the Ants from evacuating the eggs through one of the tunnels?'' asked Kah-Tu.

"We could collapse the connecting tunnels with Surface Thumpers,'' replied Zur.

"How could the water dart determine the precise spot to apply its rays?'' commented Tur-Kam.

"The chamber is of sufficient size, the precise spot would not be important,'' Zur countered.

"I have to disagree,'' Heem injected. "In the campaign against the Aquatics, we discovered the cold-beam's effectiveness is severely restricted by water. In fact, it is doubtful that even with a precise target the beam would be able to break the chamber.''

"Commander?''

"Yes, Raht?"

"I think I have the answer. Instead of collapsing both of these tunnels with Surface Thumpers, we could only collapse this one. That would leave this route to the egg chambers available for our use from the near bore hole."

"As you pointed out earlier, Raht, that would jeopardize the attack on the Queen's chamber."

"I am aware of that, Commander. What I would suggest is that when we reach this point in the tunnel, we use our coldbeams and minigrenades to collapse the portion behind us, thus barring its use to the Ants."

I did not bother to point out that this action would effectively seal the force's route of retreat as well. Raht was doubtless aware of that factor when she suggested the plan.

"Do you feel you could traverse the tunnel with a sufficient number of your force intact to destroy the egg chamber?" I asked.

"That is my plan, Commander. If I find our casualties have depleted our force too severely to be effective, I will order the weapons be brought to bear on the ceiling of the chamber. As Zur pointed out, flooding the chamber will complete our mission, and it should be easier to accomplish from inside the chamber than from the lake."

If there was any doubt that what Raht was proposing was a suicide mission, this last amendment dispelled it.

"Very well," I said. "You are aware that this could very well be the key to deciding whether our assault of this Planet is a success or a failure. I expect, therefore, that you will give careful thought as to which Warriors you assign to this mission, particularly the leader."

"I plan to lead that team myself, Commander," she replied.

"As you wish," I replied. "Feel free to draw personnel from the other strike teams as you deem necessary. Any disputes as to the availability of individuals for this mission I will deal with personally."

I swept the assemblage with my gaze. There were no lowered heads or other indications of any exception being taken to my order. That was good. Raht was an exceptional Warrior, and her loss would be noted. I did not want her sacrifice to be in vain. If that particular attack failed, it would not be because another strike team leader was unwilling to release the necessary key Warriors for reassignment.

"That concludes our meeting," I said. "Return to your teams in training now, remembering time is short before our departure. Zur, I would have a word with you."

"Certainly, Commander."

We waited until the others had filed out of the room.

"Zur," I said finally, "I require your clarification of something I noticed reviewing the equipment lists being prepared for loading onto the transports. Why is it that we require two different types of shuttlecraft?"

"One is the ground-to-space shuttle such as was used to pick us up from our last mission, Commander," Zur stated. "The other is of the type currently used between modules of the colony ship; only the ones we will be carrying will be armed as pursuit ships should the Ants attempt to escape via their spacecraft."

"Can't we use one kind of Shuttlecraft to fulfill both needs?" I asked.

"Not possible, Commander. The heavy armor of the ground shuttles is not compatible with the maneuverability necessary for a space shuttle pursuit ship. Besides, it has been ordered that the Technicians will pilot the ground shuttles, while the Warriors will pilot the pursuit ships."

"I remember now," I said. "The order seemed illogical to me at the time. The Technicians are far more accustomed to piloting the space shuttles than the Warriors are. It would seem natural that the assignment would fall to them, not us."

"In this instance, piloting the space shuttles involves direct combat with the Enemy," Zur pointed out. "As such, it is within the duties of the Warriors' caste."

"Very well, that completed my questions, Zur."

"While we have a moment, Commander, there is something I should report to you."

"What is it?"

"I was asked to oversee a duel in your absence."

"A duel? Who was involved?"

"Two of the trainers . . . actually they were only staff members, not full trainers. One of them you might recall, the second-in-command of the trainer you had executed."

"What was the duel over?" I asked.

"They didn't inform me, and I did not ask. The second-in-command I referenced emerged the victor and seemed satisfied that the incident was closed."

"Do you see any difficulties arising from this episode, Zur?" I queried.

"No, Commander. I merely felt you should be informed of what had transpired."

"I will make note of it," I said. "You may return to your duties now.

As he left, I tried to recall what else I had intended to ask him, but whatever it was eluded my memory.

CHAPTER
- 7 -

I was reduced to waiting again. Perhaps the hectic pace of my duties on board the colony ship had reduced my tolerance for inactive time or increased my metabolic rate. Whatever the case, I found I liked waiting even less than I had on previous assignments.

I was in one of three transports currently in orbit over the target planet. Zah-Rah and Kah-Tu's teams shared one ship, Tur-Kam's and Heem's another. Raht's team and Zur's reserve force were quartered aboard my designated control ship.

The mission thus far had progressed smoothly. The reports and data from the advance scout ships showed no significant additions to the anthills. The team leaders had received their final briefing, which they were currently relaying to their respective forces. The power-sources and Energy-Drainers had been successfully dropped and were performing perfectly. I should have been pleased and contented. I wasn't. I was impatient.

Zur seemed unmoved by the delay as he waited with me in the control compartment. Rather than burden his force with the final briefings, we had decided they need only be given final data if the need for their involvement arose, and then only that data that applied to their specific assignment.

In the meantime, Zur stood as motionless as a statue in front of the bank of View Screens, apparently oblivious to the passage of time. I wondered if he had discovered some modified form of sleep to drop into at times like this. I almost asked him, but decided against it at the last moment. If he had, it would be improper for me to interrupt his trance before it was absolutely necessary.

I decided to review the late dispatches from the High Command once again, more from wanting something to do than from necessity.

The Technicians had finally perfected a watertight Borer unit. Similarly the cement spray we had requested was now ready. Unfortunately neither of these had been available prior to our departure from the colony ship.

While it was a mystery to me why the High Command bothered to send dispatches such as these, it did set me to thinking. Before attaining my current level of command and therefore having access to such dispatches, I had not been aware of the time lapse involved in traversing space. It seemed mildly incredible to me that two, perhaps three, flights of Warriors had been trained and dispatched since our departure from the colony ship.

It made me realize that the complexities of coordination involved in my own position were dwarfed by the task of the High Command in bringing the resources of the entire Empire to bear in one massive assault against the Ants.

It also brought to mind an unresolved problem I had previously ignored pending inactive time to fully study the matter.

"Zur?"

"Yes, Commander."

"How many Hatchings have you survived?"

There was a pause before he answered.

"I am not sure I understand your question, Commander."

"How many Hatchings have there been since you began your career?" I clarified.

I had the vague feeling I had had this conversation before.

"I do not know," Zur replied. "Why is this information important?

"While on the colony ship, I asked a Scientist to comment on the changes in the Empire. She seemed to feel the answer to that question played a large part in her reply. I was unable to decipher what she said, and I was hoping you might be able to clarify her analysis."

Zur pondered the subject for several moments.

"Do you feel outdated, Commander?" he asked finally.

"Explain?" I requested.

"Are you finding it increasingly difficult to communicate with other Warriors, to comprehend their motivations?"

"The Scientist asked similar questions at the time," I countered. "Yet when I asked if she was questioning my qualifications as a Commander, her reply was negative."

"She probably wasn't," Zur explained. "She was pointing out that you were different—not incompetent, merely different."

"Clarify?" I requested.

"The Empire has changed since you and I began our careers. I am aware of it, and apparently so are you, although you cannot identify the specifics. Warriors today think differently, react differently than you or I do. You notice I do not say better, merely different."

Both our hands turned as one of the ready lights came on on the control panel. That was for our ship. Raht was ready.

"I do not resent this change," Zur continued, "nor do I attempt to change myself. I am what I am, and I simply trust in the Empire to find an assignment where a Warrior of my attitudes and skills are necessary. While it is possible that a time will come when my usefulness will fade, I am confident that at some future date the need will arise again and I will be awakened from Deep Sleep."

"Could you elaborate on your views of the future?" I prompted.

"As you know, Tzen do not kill or destroy out of inconvenience," he said. "Even assuming the assault on the Ants is successful and the last of the Coalition is destroyed, the High Command will not abandon its Warriors. Whether from a yet undiscovered species which bars the path of our colonization or if Tzu's mythical race of intelligent warmbloods develops, there will arise a threat to the Empire. Such is the Law of Nature. Just as the Coalition encountered a natural Enemy in us, we in turn will eventually encounter a natural Enemy whose power rivals our own. On that day, the Warriors will be awakened. As such, we need not worry about outliving our usefulness."

I thought about this for some time.

"I must admit," I said at last, "I had never given serious consideration to outliving my usefulness."

"I would not concern myself with the problem," replied Zur, "were I you, Commander. In many ways, you have changed much more readily than I."

"Explain?" I requested.

"The change has been obvious, Commander," Zur asserted. "Whether your rise in rank has been because of your change, or you have changed to fit the rank is irrelevant. The change is there.''

"I am not aware of a change,'' I stated.

"Only because you are not prone to self-analysis. There was a time when you knew each Warrior under your command intimately. You deemed it vital to the performance of your duties. Now, I doubt if you even know the names of your strike team leaders' second-in-commands. I would hasten to point out this is not intended as criticism. A certain amount of detachment is necessary in a Commander. But it is a definite deviation from your earlier patterns.''

The second ready light came on. This time from Tur-Kam and Heem's ship. The period of waiting was nearly over.

Zur started to continue, but I held up my hand for silence. While his points were interesting to ponder in inactive time, I did not want any distractions when we finally entered into battle.

The third light remained unlit.

It occurred to me it would be ironic if the final assault against the Coalition failed because of a malfunctioning ready light.

The light still remained dark.

I considered summoning a Technician to check the device. I was about to ask Zur's opinion, when the third and final light came on, completing the pattern.

The entire force was ready.

With forced calm, I signaled the attack, and the final assault began.

CHAPTER
-8-

There was a delay before the View Screens were activated. The first move of our assault was dropping the flyers, both the old single-Warrior and the new, larger, three-Warrior variety.

The view-input units were mounted on the undersides of the flyers, and did not begin sending images until the flyers leveled off to start their attack. I could have had a visual report via the View Screens beginning the moment they were dropped from the transports, but decided the additional wait was preferable to having multiple displays of their free-fall to the planet.

The View Screens were grouped by anthill to avoid confusion in interpreting their displays. Zur and I watched in silence as one at a time they winked to life.

"Heem, Commander," came a message. "Report view-input unit malfunction on flyer four."

"Acknowledged," I replied.

The report was audible because of a late development by the Scientists. To ease strain on Planetary Commanders, they had devised a unit that could convert booster-band-relayed telepathic messages into actual sound, and reversed the process to send messages. Even though messages to the Planetary Commander were sent by strike team leaders only, in an assault such as this messages were numerous and complex enough to make this new device a major aid.

We ignored the single blank View Screen and watched the

others. The first assignment of the flyers was to seal the anthills, using explosives to collapse the tunnels at and around their surface accesses. Simultaneous with this action, they were to drop the Communication Disrupters. I personally placed little faith in these units, not because I disbelieved in their efficiency, but because we had no means of verifying if they were functioning properly or not. The blank View Screen gave mute testimony that not all devices were foolproof, regardless of the reassurances supplied by the Technicians. We still used the Disrupter units, however, since in a combat situation communications are vital, and any possibility of sabotaging the Enemy's efforts to pool and coordinate information was to be pursued. I simply didn't rely on their success in my planning.

"Tur-Kam, Commander. Borer units landed and functioning."

"Acknowledged."

That would be the fourth anthill. I checked the View Screens to confirm the operation. The fourth anthill had only three accesses to seal, so it was logical they would be the first to begin the actual attack.

"Heem, Commander. Borer units landed and functioning."

"Acknowledged."

Fifth Anthill. I hastened to obtain visual confirmation from the View Screens. This was a relatively difficult task. As I have noted, the view-input units were mounted on the Flyers, and the flyers were far from inactive at this point.

As the Borer units were landing, the flyers were drop-placing the Surface Thumpers, a job calling for precision handling of the machines. More often than not, the View Screens afforded only a close-up view of the ground flashing by at high speed as the flyers raced to complete their mission.

There had been some debate as to whether the Surface Thumpers should be dropped prior to or simultaneous with the landing of the Borer units. If we had dropped them earlier, it would have given the flyers more time to perform the maneuver. Our utilizing the simultaneous drop gave the Ants less time to counter the move.

"Zah-Rah, Commander. Borer units landed and functioning."

"Acknowledged."

First anthill. Hopefully, by now the Ants would be in utter turmoil. Even if they had anticipated our attack, they should have had no forewarning as to its format. Without advance knowledge of the Borer units, they would have had to expect a direct assault on the tunnels. Our move of sealing the surface tunnels and collapsing others should have introduced an unexpected element into their defense plans.

"Raht, Commander. Borer units landed and functioning."

"Acknowledged."

Second anthill! Something was wrong. The third anthill should have reported in before the second.

"Kah-Tu!" I beamed.

"Yes, Commander."

"Report status immediately."

"Encountering unexpected surface resistance, Commander. The Ants are digging new holes to the surface as fast as we can seal them."

The kaleidoscope display on the View Screens confirmed this. Despite the frenzied efforts of the flyers, Ants were boiling to the surface and dashing angrily about.

"There are loose soil conditions in that area, Commander," Zur informed me. "It is doubtful we will be able to successfully stop that countermove."

"Proceed with Borer unit drop," I ordered.

"Acknowledged, Commander."

We had fought the Wasps to gain air supremacy. Now was when it should prove its worth.

"Zur!"

"Yes, Commander."

"Alert your reserves to stand by and report back to me."

"At once, Commander."

If we were encountering difficulties this early in the assault, it could be taken as guaranteed we would need the reserves before it was over.

One of the View Screens went blank.

First anthill! I waited.

"Zah-Rah, Commander," came the report. "Flyer down."

"Report," I ordered.

"Reason unknown, Commander. Flyer was dropping Surface Thumpers and failed to pull out of run. Assumed mechanical failure."

"Acknowledged."

I had hoped for more firm information. Mechanical failure in a flyer is rare.

"Kah-Tu, Commander. Borer units landed and functioning."

"Acknowledged."

Third anthill. The battle was now joined on all fronts. I checked the screens. The Ants were gathering in clumps and rushing the Borer units.

"Kah-Tu."

"Yes, Commander."

"Split your flyers. Half are to abandon their efforts to seal the tunnels and instead provide cover fire for the Borer units. The other half are to coordinate their efforts and using Surface Thumpers attempt to seal the surface access tunnels at a lower point in the Network."

"Acknowledged, Commander."

This would be a true test of the force's training and effectiveness under fire. It was one thing to drill and prepare to drop the Thumpers on a specific, preplanned target. It was another matter entirely to select a target from the Tri-D maps, translate it to the actual field situation, set the Surface Thumpers, and successfully execute the maneuver, all while in the middle of a combat situation.

"Reserves standing by, Commander."

I had not observed Zur's entrance, but he was at my side again.

"Acknowledged."

"Another view-input malfunction?" he asked, noticing the second blank View Screen.

"Flyer down," I said. "Unconfirmed mechanical failure."

As I spoke, another View Screen went blank.

"Zah-Rah, Commander. Flyer down."

"Report!"

"Reason unknown, Commander. Situation similar to first incident."

Two flyers down at the same anthill!

"There is something wrong, Commander," Zur interrupted. "It is illogical that two flyers would suffer mechanical failure in the same area."

Something in his assertion prompted a question in my mind.

"Zah-Rah. Was the second flyer downed in the same area as the first?"

There was a pause before the response came. Zah-Rah was with one of the Borer units, so the question and reply had to be relayed to the remaining flyers.

"Affirmative, Commander. Second flyer went down after attempting a drop run over the same area as the first."

"Instruct flyers to avoid that area. Order a high-altitude sound scan of that area and report results to me immediately."

"Acknowledged, Commander."

I stared suspiciously at the View Screens for the other anthills, but no similar crashes occurred.

"Raht, Commander. My section is in the tunnels and has collapsed the designated portion behind us. We are continuing toward the egg chamber. Forty-three percent casualties so far."

"Acknowledged."

"Kah-Tu, Commander. Surface access has been collapsed as ordered. Surface resistance weakening."

"Acknowledged."

I started for the View Screens to confirm the claim.

"Zah-Rah, Commander. Sound scan reports evidence of machinery in designated area. No visual confirmation."

"Acknowledged."

My worst fears were realized.

"Rahm to all strike teams," I beamed. "Suspected cold-beam activity from Enemy. Possible firing on flyers. All units report full current status on my command. Zah-Rah!"

"First anthill. Borer units extended or extending. One egg chamber breached. Fifty-seven percent casualties so far. Possible ground fire on flyers."

"Raht!"

There was no reply.

"Kah-Tu!"

"Third anthill. Borer units extended. Two egg chambers and queen's chamber breached. Cold-beam attacks reported on tubes, but they have ceased with no damage inflicted. Seventy-seven percent casualties so far."

"Tur-Kam!"

There was no reply.

"Heem!"

"Fifth anthill. Borer units extended or extending. Queen's chamber breached. Sixty-seven percent casualties so far."

"Raht, second call."

"Second anthill. Borer units extended. Queen's chamber and one egg chamber breached. Fifty-four percent casualties so far."

"Tur-Kam, second call!"

There was no reply.

"Rahm to fourth anthill flyer leader."

"Here, Commander."

"Status report on your strike force."

There was a pause before the reply came.

"Unknown, Commander. We have not been contacted by our leader since the Borer units landed and are currently unable to establish communication."

"Acknowledged."

I turned to Zur.

"Your target is the fourth anthill. Brief your team as they drop."

"In what force shall we attack, Commander?"

"Full force. Anticipated resistance is unknown."

"At once, Commander."

I returned to the View Screens without watching him depart.

CHAPTER
-9-

"Kah-Tu, Commander. Rain commencing at third anthill."

"Acknowledged."

We had known of the potential bad weather conditions when we commenced the assaults, but we were required to proceed to insure coordination with the other Planetary assaults. If anything, we were fortunate to only experience adverse weather at one of the five anthills. Rain would severely limit the effectiveness of the flyer support and could made the eventual withdrawal and pickup more hazardous.

"Mir-Zat, Commander. Assuming command at first anthill."

"Acknowledged."

First anthill! Zah-Rah was dead. The first . . . no, possibly the second casualty among the strike team leaders.

"Zur!"

"Yes, Commander."

"Status report!"

"Fourth anthill, Commander. Ordered flyers to drop all Surface Thumpers in an effort to maximize disruption of defenses."

"Evidence of original strike force?"

"Negative, Commander. We will be in the Borer units shortly. Will report findings at that time."

"Acknowledged."

"Raht, Commander. Target egg chamber for our section defended by cold-beams. Suffering heavy casualties."

"Will you be able to carry the objective?"

"Affirmative, Commander."

"Acknowledged."

Cold-beams again! There was a pattern forming here, but I wasn't allowed time to analyze it.

"Heem, Commander. Have received reports of Ants moving eggs from one of the egg chambers as it was destroyed."

"Order immediate pursuit. Find the new egg catch and destroy it."

"Acknowledged, Commander."

The collapsed tunnels were supposed to keep the Ants from moving the eggs. Apparently it wasn't working at the fifth anthill. If the Ants succeeded in their gambit, if they saved some eggs from our attack, the species would survive and the campaign would have failed.

"Zur, Commander. We are in the Borer units and proceeding with the assignment against minimal resistance. Have discovered original strike force."

"Report."

"Strike force rendered helpless by stun rays. Borer units breached manually by Ants. No survivors of the original strike force. We have cleared the Borer units of Ants. The units are still functional, and we are proceeding with the mission."

"Were the members of the original strike force wearing the antistun plates?"

"Affirmative, Commander. Apparently the Ants have either modified their stun ray, or have in their possession a weapon we are yet unfamiliar with. Our reserve force, however, has encountered no difficulties such as those apparently encountered by the original strike force. Perhaps the Energy-Drain units have successfully stopped the weapon's functioning."

"Acknowledged," I replied.

That was it! I had the answer to the vague pattern I had been sensing. The Energy-Drainers had been effective, but each anthill had a reserve energy unit. Apparently the Communication Distrupters had prevented coordinated effort between the anthills, so each anthill had utilized the reserve unit in their own way before it too was drained of energy.

The first anthill had used their energy to attack the flyers, while the second anthill had used cold-beams in an effort to defend one egg chamber. Cold-beams had been used, too, at the third anthill, whereas the fourth anthill had successfully employed a modified stun ray to wipe out that strike force. That left . . .

"Heem, Commander! Urgent! Fifth anthill is launching space-craft!"

"Acknowledged."

Now we knew what the fifth anthill was using their energy for.

"Rahm to space-shuttle pilots! Launch your craft immediately! Take position over fifth anthill."

I waited impatiently through their ripple of acknowledgments.

"Heem!"

"Yes, Commander!"

"Report."

"We investigated the tunnel through which the Ants had been evacuating eggs. This is a new tunnel, apparently constructed since we began our attack. The tunnel led to a chamber housing spacecraft. It was heavily defended, and we were unable to prevent launching."

"How many spacecraft were launched?"

"Only one, Commander."

"Proceed with your withdrawal."

"Acknowledged, Commander."

"Rahm to space-shuttle Leader. Your target is one, repeat one spacecraft. Stop it at all costs!"

"Acknowledged, Commander."

If that ship escaped with a cargo of eggs, we would have failed and the Empire would be in grave jeopardy.

"Ar-Tac, Commander. Assuming command of second anthill."

I forced my mind away from the escaping spacecraft. Raht was dead.

"Can you confirm completion of Raht's mission?"

"Affirmative, Commander. Flyers report water level in lake dropping rapidly, indicating egg chamber successfully destroyed. Are commencing our withdrawal."

"Casualty report."

"Seventy-two percent so far, Commander."

"Acknowledged."

"Kah-Tu, Commander. All targets in third anthill have been destroyed. Eighty-seven percent casualties so far. We are encountering strong resistance on our withdrawal attempts. Remaining force is insufficient to regain the surface. Request reinforcements."

I was afraid of this. The weather conditions were having their expected effect on the retreat.

"Reserve force has been totally committed. No reinforcements are available."

There was a pause before the reply came.

"I understand. Commander. Request permission to release our flyers to rendevous with transport."

"Permission granted."

"Acknowledged, Commander."

Kah-Tu was dead. She acknowledged this and was attempting to salvage part of her strike force.

"Space-shuttle Leader, Commander. We have encountered the Ant spacecraft and destroyed it."

"Report."

"Spacecraft was apparently unprepared for combat. By going into low orbit, we were able to intercept it before it had an opportunity to change course from launch pattern. Cold-beams were effective in completely destroying the craft."

"Return to transports."

"Acknowledged, Commander."

It was reassuring to know some phase of this assault had been executed without difficulty.

"Mir-Zat, Commander. All targets in the first anthill have been destroyed. We are commencing our withdrawal. Sixty-eight percent casualties so far."

"Acknowledged."

"Flyer leader from third anthill to Commander. Request permission to land flyers and assist in strike team's withdrawal."

That gave me pause. Apparently the flyers from Kah-Tu's force were refusing her order to rendevous with the transports, asking instead to try to rescue the stranded ground force.

"Permission granted. Land your flyers out of range of the auto-weapon scanners."

"Acknowledged. Our gratitude, Commander."

If there was a chance to save the stranded force, it should be pursued. While I would not have ordered Warriors into such a precarious position, I would not deny them their request for such action.

"Second transport pilot to Commander. Urgent! We are going down."

"Report!"

"Apparent maneuvering malfunction of space shuttle when

attempting to dock with our transport. Damage severe and irreparable. We are losing orbital pattern and anticipate burn entry to planet's atmosphere.''

''Acknowledged!''

One transport! Gone! This possibility had never entered into my plans.

''Rahm to space shuttle. Do not, repeat, do not attempt to dock with transports. Undetermined malfunction of your vehicles has caused destruction of Transport Two. Attempt to land in vicinity of anthills and regroup with strike teams for pickup.''

I ignored their acknowledgments. The shuttle pilots knew as well as I that their vehicles were not designed to survive a planet landing. My order was only an acceptable alternative to waiting in space until their air supply ran out.

''Zur, Commander. All targets in the fourth anthill have been destroyed, commencing withdrawal. Fifty-nine percent casualties so far.''

''Acknowledged.''

All anthills were accounted for now, except one.

''Rahm to Kah-Tu. What is your status?''

There was no reply.

''Rahm to third anthill flyer leader. Report your status.''

There was no reply.

''Rahm to any Warrior in the third anthill strike force. What is your status?''

There was no reply.

The attempt to rescue the stranded force in the third anthill had failed.

CHAPTER
- 10 -

The loss of a transport severely changed our pickup calculations. Instead of 30 percent of our original force, we could now only transport 20 percent back to the colony ship. Even with the loss of two full strike teams, we would doubtless have to leave some Warriors behind.

I gave my last order of the attack.

"Rahm to all strike team Leaders and acting Leaders. Our attack has been successfully completed. Coordinate your pickup requirements directly with the transport pilots. Transports One and Three only are available."

As soon as I received their acknowledgments, I left the control compartment and headed for my sleeping quarters.

I understood now both why Planetary Commanders were required to eat prior to an assault, and why they were not required to report to High Command prior to their return to the colony ship.

Although I had not physically lifted a weapon against the Enemy in this last campaign, I felt more fatigued than I had after any previous assignment. I began to believe the claims of the Technicians and Scientists that they could be just as fatigued as the Warriors even though they never were involved in direct combat.

Still, I did not go to sleep immediately. Instead, I found myself idly pondering several questions.

Under what circumstances would I be awakened again? Would the High Command require a detailed report from me? Would I be involved in the colonization of new planets, assuming the War against the Coalition was truly over? Or would it be as Zur postulated, that I would only be awakened again if a major species challenged the Empire?

Zur! It suddenly occurred to me that his force was the last to complete their mission. Logically, this meant they would be the last survivors to be picked up, and therefore it was highly probable that all or some of them would be left behind. Would Zur be one of the survivors? Or would he be stranded, included among the casualties?

I realized suddenly that these questions bore no more importance to me than . . . than whether or not a species of intelligent warmbloods evolved. I was a Tzen and a Warrior, and I had been efficient in the performance of my duty to the Empire.

I went to sleep.